"Writers like Flannery O'Connor or William Faulkner would welcome Gay as their peer for getting characters so entangled in the roots of a family tree."

—*Star Tribune* (Minneapolis)

"[A]s charming as it is wise. Hellfire—in all the right ways."

—*Kirkus Reviews*

"[Gay] brings to these stories the same astounding talent that earned his two novels . . . devoted following."

—*Booklist*

"Supple and beautifully told tales . . . saturated with an intense sense of place, their vividness and authenticity are impossible to fake."

—*The San Diego Union-Tribune*

"Gay writes about old folks marvelously. . . . [His] words ring like crystal. . . . "

—*Washington Post Book World*

"As always, Gay's description and dialogue are amazing. . . . Writing like this keeps you reading."

—*The Orlando Sentinel*

"After two stunning novels that combined the esoteric language of Cormac McCarthy with the subtle humor of Larry Brown, Gay delivers a concise craft work in his first short-story collection. . . . Much in the same way that Erskine Caldwell created slice-of-life Southern stories that were full of humor, conflict, and even forbidden sensuality many years ago, so now does William Gay."

—*The Oregonian* (Portland, Oregon)

"[Gay's] strong words never fail to paint a precise picture. . . . Fans of his novels will find lots of meaty reading here."

—*Chattanooga Times*

"William Gay writes like a man possessed."

—*The Montgomery Advertiser*

"Gay's characters come right up and bite you. . . . [His] well-chosen words propel the reader straight through his 13 stories."

—*The Denver Post*

"Even Faulkner would have been proud to call these words his own."

—*The Atlanta Journal Constitution*

"Gay captivates with bristling tales of old men, bootleggers, and wife-beaters in rural Tennessee . . . his prose is as natural and pure as it comes."

—*Newsweek*

"This book will have you laughing, fearful, and utterly filled with suspense—often all within the same well-crafted story."

—*Southern Living*

"A literary country music song. . . . With deft and lyrical prose, he captures the poignancy of loss, isolation and double-fisted grief, of disappointment, rage, jealousy, violence and heartbreak."

—GoMemphis.com

Also by William Gay

The Long Home
Provinces of Night

I
Hate
to
See
That
Evening
Sun
Go
Down

Collected Stories
William Gay

FREE PRESS

NEW YORK   LONDON   TORONTO   SYDNEY   SINGAPORE

This book is for my friends Beth Ann Fennelly
and Tom Franklin, and for their daughter,
Claire Elizabeth.

FREE PRESS
A Division of Simon & Schuster, Inc.
1230 Avenue of the Americas
New York, NY 10020

First Free Press trade paperback edition 2003

FREE PRESS and colophon are trademarks of Simon & Schuster, Inc.

For information about special discounts for bulk purchases,
please contact Simon & Schuster Special Sales at
1-800-456-6798 or business@simonandschuster.com.

DESIGNED BY PAUL DIPPOLITO

Manufactured in the United States of America

10 9 8 7 6 5 4 3 2 1

The Library of Congress has cataloged the hardcover edition as follows:

Gay, William.
I hate to see that evening sun go down : collected stories / William Gay.
p. cm.
1. Southern States—Social life and customs—Fiction. I. Title.

PS3557.A985 I15 2002
813'.54—dc21

2002073945

"I Hate to See That Evening Sun Go Down" first appeared in *The Georgia
Review*, Fall 1998; "A Death in the Woods" first appeared in *GQ*, May 2000;
(*continued on page 306*)

ISBN 0-7432-4088-X
      0-7432-4292-0 (Pbk)

Contents

I
Hate
to
See
That
Evening
Sun
Go
Down

I Hate to See That Evening Sun Go Down

WHEN THE TAXICAB let old man Meecham out in the dusty roadbed by his mailbox the first thing he noticed was that someone was living in his house. There was a woman hanging out wash on the clothesline and a young girl sunning herself in a rickety lawn chair and an old dust-colored Plymouth with a flat tire parked in Meecham's driveway. All this so disoriented the old man that he dropped the cardboard suitcase he was holding and forgot about paying the cab driver. He thought for a dizzy moment that he had directed the driver to the wrong place: but there was the fading clapboard house and the warm umber roof of the barn bisected by the slope of ridge and on top of that the name ABNER MEECHAM on the mailbox in his own halting brushstrokes.

Looks like you got company, the cab driver said.

Beyond the white corner of the house the woman stood holding a bedsheet up to the line and she was studying him transfixed with a clothespin in her mouth. She seemed frozen to the ground, motionless as statuary a sculptor in a whimsical mood might have wrought of a sharecropper's wife.

How much was it I owed you? Meecham asked, finally remembering. He fumbled out a wallet with a chain affixed to it and a clasp hooked to a belt and turned slightly to the side as an old man does when studying a wallet's contents.

Well. Twenty dollars. That seems like a lot but it's a right smart way from Linden.

And worth ever nickel of it, the old man said, selecting at length a bill and proffering it through the window. Twenty dollars' worth of distance from Linden, Tennessee, is fine with me. If I was a wealthy man I would of bought more of it.

Glad to of brought you, the driver said. You be careful in all this heat. Meecham raised a hand in farewell, dismissal. He was already forgetting the driver and was at picking up his luggage and preparing to investigate these folks making free with his property.

As he passed the lawn chair the girl casually tucked a pale breast into her halter top. Hidy. Do I know you? She removed a pair of plastic-framed sunglasses as if she might study him more closely.

You will here in a minute. He was a fierce-looking old man slightly stooped wearing dungarees and a blue chambray workshirt. The shirt was faded a pale blue from repeated laundering and he had the top button fastened against his Adam's apple. On his head he wore a canvas porkpie hat cocked over one bristling eyebrow and the hat and his washed-out blue eyes were almost the exact hue of his shirt. Who are you people and what are you doing here?

I'm Pamela Choat and I'm sunbathin, the girl said, misunderstanding or in the old man's view pretending to. I'm gettin me a tan. Mama's hangin out clothes and Daddy's around here somewhere.

I mean what are you even doin here? Why are you here?

The girl put her sunglasses back on and turned her oiled face to the weight of the sun. We live here, she said.

That can't be. I live here, this is my place.

You better talk to Mama, the girl said. Behind the opaque lenses of the sunglasses perhaps her eyes were closed. Meecham turned. The woman was crossing the yard toward him. He noticed with a proprietary air that the grass needed cutting. He'd been gone less than two months and already the place was going to seed.

Ain't you Mr. Meecham?

I certainly am, the old man said. He leaned on his walking stick. The stick was made to represent a snake and the curve he clasped was an asp's head. I don't believe I've made your acquaintance.

I'm Mrs. Choat, she said. Ludie Choat, Lonzo's wife. You remember Lonzo Choat.

Lord God, the old man said.

We rented this place from your boy.

The hell you say.

Why yes. We got a paper and everything. We thought you was in the old folk's home in Perry County.

I was. I ain't no more. I need to use the telephone.

We ain't got no telephone.

Of course there's a telephone. We always had a telephone.

The woman regarded him with a bland bovine patience, as if she were explaining something to a somewhat backward child. There was a curiously blank look about her, the look of the innocent or the deranged. There's one but it don't work. You can't talk on it. It ain't hooked up or somethin. You need to talk to Lonzo. He'll be up here directly.

I'm an old man, Meecham said. I may die directly. Where is he and I'll just go to him.

He's down there in the barn fixin a tire.

Choat was in the hall of the barn and he seemed locked in mortal combat with the flat tire. He was stripped to the waist and he was wringing wet with sweat. His belly looped slackly over the waistband of his trousers but his shoulders and back were knotted with muscle. He had a crowbar jammed between the tire and rim and was trying to pry it free. Then he held the crowbar in position with a foot and tried to break the tire loose from the rim with a splitting hammer. Meecham noticed with satisfaction that it showed no sign of giving.

When the old man's shadow fell across the chaff and straw and dried manure of the hall Choat looked up. Some dark emotion, dislike or hostility or simply annoyance, flickered across his face like summer lightning and was gone. Choat laid the splitting hammer aside and squatted in the earth. He wiped sweat out of his eyes and left a streak of greasy dirt in the wake of his hand. Meecham suddenly saw how like a hog Choat looked, his red porcine jowls and piggy little eyes, as if as time passed he had taken on the characteristics of his namesake.

You not got a spare?

This is the spare. I believe I know you. You're lawyer Meecham's daddy. We heard you was in a nursin home. What are you doin here?

I didn't take to nursin, Meecham said. Is it true that Paul rented you folks this place?

He damn sure did. A ninety-day lease with a option to buy.

The old man felt dizzy. He was almost apoplectic with rage. He felt he was going to have a seizure, a stroke, some kind of attack. The idea of Choat eating at his table, sleeping in his bed was bad enough; the idea that he might own it, call it his, was not to be borne.

Buy? You wasn't ever nothin but a loafer. You never owned so much as a pair of pliers. That's my wreckin bar and splittin hammer right there. And if you think you can buy a farm this size with food stamps you're badly mistaken.

Choat just shook his head. He grinned. A drop of sweat beaded on the end of his nose, fell. Blackheads thick as freckles fanned out from his eyes and there were black crescents of dirt beneath his fingernails.

You still as contrary as you ever was. You remember the time I tried to rent that lit old tenant shack from you?

No.

You wouldn't rent it to me. Ain't life funny?

I never rented that house to anybody. It was built too close to the main house to begin with and there wouldn't have been any privacy for either place. That must have been twenty-five years ago.

Ever how long it was I needed it and I didn't get it. And life is funny. We aim to buy this place. I got a boy in Memphis, he's a plumbin contractor. Does these big commercial jobs. He's aimin to buy and we're fixin to tend it. And you can forget about the food stamps. He makes plenty of money. He buys and sells lawyers like they was Kmart specials.

Well I ain't seen none of this famous money. And the fact of the matter is this place ain't Paul's to sell. It's my place and will be till I die. It may be Paul's then and he can do what he wants to with it. But after this I doubt it. In fact I'm pretty sure Paul's shot at this place just went up in smoke.

They fixed it up legal.

If I was you I'd be packin up my stuff.

We'll see.

We goddamn sure will. Where's that paper?

Choat got up. It's up to the house. We'll have to go up there.

Then let's be for goin, the old man said.

THE OLD MAN SAT ON THE DOORSTEP of the tenant house in the shade for a while and thought about things. It was almost twelve miles back to Ackerman's Field, the nearest town and the one in which Paul did his lawyering. He had no telephone. He had no car; in actuality he owned a two-year-old Oldsmobile and a four-wheel-drive cream-colored Toyota pickup, but Paul had taken them to town for storage and he expected that by now they were somewhere in Mexico with the serial numbers eradicated. He had money, but nowhere to spend it. He had a neighbor across the ridge but he was too weary to walk over there now. Choat's car had a flat tire, but he had not even factored that into the equation. Folks in hell would be eating Eskimo Pies before Lonzo Choat hauled him anywhere.

Anyway he was home, and it was good to be here. He opened the suitcase and examined its contents. A change of clothing. A razor and a can of shaving cream. A bar of soap. A toothbrush and the sort of miniature tube of toothpaste you see in motel and hospital rooms. A tin of Vienna sausages and a cellophane-wrapped package of crackers he'd brought in case he got hungry on the cab ride. It occurred to him now that he hadn't eaten since breakfast at the nursing home.

He glanced toward the house. The woman was standing in the door watching him as if she'd learn his intentions, some quality of apprehension in her posture. He looked away and he heard the screen door fall to.

The day was waning. Beyond the frame farmhouse light was

fleeing westward and bullbats came sheer and plumb out of the tops of the darkling trees as if they'd harry the dusk on. A whippoorwill called and some old nigh-lost emotion somewhere between exaltation and pain rose in him and twisted sharp as a knife. As if all his days had honed down to this lone whippoorwill calling out of the twilight.

The old man sat for a time just taking all this in. Whippoorwills had been in short supply in the nursing home and it was a blessing not to smell Lysol. He breathed in deeply and he could smell the trees still holding the day's heat and the evocative odor of honeysuckle and the cool citrusy smell of pine needles.

Well, I never held myself above tenant farmin, he said to himself.

At least the lights worked and he guessed Paul was still paying the light bill. He figured the first one to come due in Choat's name would be the last. The house was jammed with the accumulation of the years. He had used this place as a junkhouse and now Choat seemed to have toted everything he couldn't use or didn't want down from the main house. Boxes of pictures and memorabilia Ellen had saved. Now it was spilled and thrown about at random, and he was touched with a dull anger: his very past had been kicked about and discarded.

He set about arranging some kind of quarters. He carried boxes and chairs and garbage bags of clothing into the bedroom and set up Paul's old cot by the window for what breeze there was.

He sat for a time bemusedly studying snapshots. Dead husks of events that had once transpired. Strange to him now as if they'd happened on some other level of reality, in someone else's life. An entire envelope of photographs of dead folks. One of Ellen's father lying in his casket. His shock of black hair, great blade of a nose. Eighty years old and his hair black as a crow's wing. Another of

Ellen standing by the old man's grave. He studied her face carefully. It looked ravaged, tearstained, swollen with grief.

He put them away. He had not even known they existed. He had no use for them then or now, and why anyone would need to be reminded of so sad a time was beyond his comprehension.

He fared better in an old brass-bound trunk. Choat had missed a bet here, if he knew he'd kick himself. He found Paul's old pistol wrapped in a piece of muslin. He unfolded the cloth. An enormous Buntline Special–looking pistol but it was really just a .22 caliber target pistol on a .45 frame. He fumbled around in the trunk but he couldn't find any shells.

He shuffled through a stack of 78 rpm records reading the labels. Old Bluebird records by the Carter Family, Victor records by Jimmie Rodgers, the Singing Brakeman. "Evening Sun Yodel," "Away Out on the Mountain." He could remember hearing these songs in his youth, singing them himself, he and Ellen playing these selfsame records on the Victrola. Jimmie Rodgers was a blues singer and he remembered that Ellen hadn't been too high on him but she had been fond of the Carter Family. Jimmie Rodgers, dead of TB and still a young man after all these years and even turning a dollar or two off that: and that graveyard sure is a lonesome place, they lay you on your back and throw the dirt down in your face.

Well why the hell not, he thought. He moved stacks of folded quilts, old newspapers off the Victrola and wiped the dust off. The machinery creaked when he cranked it and he doubted it would work.

It did though. The needle hissed on the record and there was Rodgers' distinctive guitar lick then a dead voice out of a dead time still holding the same smoky sardonic lilt: *She's long, she's tall, she's six feet from the ground.*

The old man was lost in the song and didn't hear the girl until she was in the room. He turned and she was crossing the threshold. She had a plate in one hand and a tumbler of iced tea in the other. Jimmie Rodgers was singing: *I hate to see that evenin sun go down, cause it makes me think I'm on my last go-around.*

He arose and lifted the tonearm off the record.

Mama sent this.

He hadn't anticipated anything approaching human kindness out of the Choat family and he didn't quite know how to handle it.

She said she bet you was hungry and hot as it was you needed somethin cold to drink.

He took the plate awkwardly and cleared a spot for it on the coffee table. She set the tea beside it.

Well. You tell her I'm much obliged. What'd Lonzo have to say about it?

He was down at the barn. What's that you're listenin to?

That's Jimmie Rodgers, the Singin Brakeman. Evenin Sun Yodel.

What is that, country? Sure is some weird-soundin shit. Where's he out of, Nashville?

Hell if he's out of anywhere. He's been dead and gone from here over fifty years.

Oh. Well, how do you know he's in hell?

If drinkin whiskey and runnin other folks' women'll put you there then that's where he's at. Anyway he's in the ground with the dirt throwed in his face. That sounds a right smart like hell to me.

Lord you'd cheer a person up. Are you always in this good a mood?

Just when I get rooted away from the trough, the old man said. He was studying the plate. He was of two minds about it. He mistrusted Ludie Choat's cooking and figured her none too clean in her personal habits but then you didn't know what was in Vienna sausage, either. All he had was the Viennas and besides there was okra rolled in meal and fried. It had been a long time since he had eaten fried okra. The plate also held garden tomatoes peeled and sliced and he figured if everything else proved inedible he could always eat the tomatoes.

What are you doin, movin in here?

Yes I am. I'll have it right homey before I'm through. Curtains on the windows, bouquets of flowers to smell the place up. I may get me a dog.

Daddy won't allow a dog on the place. He can't stand to hear them bark.

Mmm, the old man mused. Say he can't?

I got to get back to the house before Daddy turns up. Just set the dishes out on the porch in the mornin, all right?

All right, he said irritably, peering closely at the dishes. But if I ain't badly mistaken they're mine anyway.

AT FIRST LIGHT HE WAS UP as was his custom and in the dewy coolness he went up the slope behind the tenant house following the meandering line of an old rail fence he himself had built long ago. At the summit he paused to catch his breath and stood leaning on his walking stick peering back the way he'd come. The slope tended away in a stony tapestry and the valley lay spread out below him in a dreamy pastoral haze and mist rose out of the distant hollows blue as smoke. The sky was marvelously clear and on this July morning each sound seemed distinct and equidistant: he could hear cowbells on the other side of the woods, a truck laboring up a hill on some distant road. These sounds and sights reminded him of his childhood long ago in Alabama, and they caused a singing in his blood and a rise in his spirits, he could hear his heart hammering strong and fierce as when he was a boy. He was alive and the world alive with him and he had come back to it without either of them being changed.

He entered the cool dappled green of the woods going down-hill now and when he came out of the trees into the light again he was in Thurl Chessor's pasture and approaching the barn and house. He went on past deceased tractors and rusting mowers and old mule-drawn planters like museum artifacts.

He was suddenly and against his will assailed by memory. It came to him that he was a repository of knowledge that was being lost, knowledge that no one even wanted anymore. The way the earth looked and smelled rolling off the gleaming point of a turn-ing plow, the smell of the mule and the feel of the sweat-hardened harness and the way the thunderheads rolled up in the summer and lay over the hills like malignant tumors and thunder booming along the timberline and clouds unfolding in a fierce and violent coupling and seeding in the furrows a curious gift of ice that lay gleaming in the black loam like pearls.

He remembered laying out all night as a young man and trudging woodenly behind the mule the next day, sleep-robbed and weary, jerky as a puppet the mule was controlling with the plowlines.

He shook these thoughts out of his head and went on. He could see Thurl walking back toward the house from the pig lot with a feed bucket in his hand. Thurl was his contemporary and he had known him forty years but they had never been close. Thurl was not a very good farmer but he had managed to survive. Thurl did not have a head for business, an eye for the small detail. He was apt to leave a tractor out in the weather with the intake filling with rainwater and pine needles then curse the folks in Illinois or wherever that made it and wonder why it wouldn't start. On the other hand, Meecham thought ruefully, he was not living in a tenant shack with Lonzo Choat reared back in the main house like the lord of the manor.

Chessor put the bucket on a slab shelf and turned and studied Meecham with no surprise. Well, I see you're back. Run off, did you.

Yeah.

Are they after you?

After me? Hellfire. It was a old folks' home, not a chain gang. Why would they be after me?

I don't know. I don't know anything about it. Where'd you sleep last night? Did Lonzo make you down a pallet on the floor?

That's mainly why I come down here. I need to use your telephone. I need to call Paul and see if I can't get this mess straightened out. I've got to get Choat out of there.

You'll play hell doin it. Or doin it quick anyway. He's got a foot in the door now. You get him evicted legal the law won't make him move for thirty days. They're not goin to throw him right out.

I need to use your telephone anyway. It's long distance but I got money.

That's all right. It's in the front room where it always was.

He spoke with a young woman who would make no commitment as to Paul's whereabouts. He was put on hold and treacly music began to play softly in the background. He was on hold for some time then she came back on the line. Mr. Meecham is engaged right at the moment, she said.

I'm fairly engaged myself, the old man said. You get him on here. I aim to clear this mess up and no mistake about it.

I'm sorry, sir. Mr. Meecham is tied up right now. His time is very valuable.

If I hadn't sold calves and pigs to send him through law school it wouldn't be worth fifteen cents. You get him on this phone.

There was the dawning of knowledge in the woman's voice. Are you Mr. Meecham's father by any chance?

There's rumors to that effect.

Well, I'm sorry, sir. I didn't understand. He's on his way to court but I'll have him paged. He has a beeper. Give me your number and I'll have him return your call in a moment.

Meecham read her the number and cradled the phone. Paul's got a beeper, he thought to himself. He was unsure exactly what a beeper was but he was vaguely impressed nonetheless. He tried to call Paul's face to mind but it was the child Paul had been that came swimming up from the depths of memory and the circles the adult Paul moved in were as strange to them both as some continent across the waters. He sat staring at the telephone as if he expected it to perform some bizarre and clever trick he had taught it.

He picked it up on the first ring.

Dad?

So you got you a beeper, the old man said.

Dad, what is this about?

I want them folks out of the house and I want them out today.

What?

That Choat bunch. Layin up there sleepin in your mama's bed and eatin out of her dishes. Looks like you'd be ashamed of yourself. I want em gone.

Where are you calling from?

Where do you think I'm callin from? Thurl Chessor's place, they've done broke my phone or somethin. Are you goin to get them out today or not?

There was a pause. What are you doing there? You're supposed to be in the nursing home in Linden.

Supposed to be? I'm supposed to be where I damn well please. Nobody tells me where I'm supposed to be, nobody ever did. What is this mess you've cooked up?

There was another pause, this one longer, and this time Paul's face did come to mind, like a slowly developing photographic plate, the thin face filled out with rich food and prosperity, perhaps tanned from the golf course, the pudgy fingers massaging his temples as if the old man was giving him a headache.

This is getting too complicated for me, Paul finally said. At any rate it's too complicated for the telephone. Use that phone to call a cab, and go back to the home. I'll come down there at— a pause again and the old man knew Paul was looking at his watch—five o'clock and explain everything about the sale.

Sale my ass. You can't sell what ain't yourn.

Well, obviously we need to discuss it, but as to what I can or can't do, I'm your legal guardian and the trustee of your estate. When you started acting erratic after Mama died I got worried about you. I figured you were a danger to yourself, and the court—

I'll be a danger to a whole hell of a lot more than myself unless you get your ass on the ball and unscramble this paperwork. I'll do it myself, I'm not penniless. Do you think you're the only lawyer that ever hit a golf ball?

Five o'clock, all right?

The old man slammed the phone so hard Chessor glanced at it sharply as if it might have broken. Meecham was lightheaded with rage. Black dots swam before his eyes like a swarm of gnats and he felt dizzy and strange, as if his very soul was packing up to flee his body. It seemed to him that he had scraped and cut corners and done without just to send Paul to an expensive school where he'd learned a trade that was doing him out of what he had taken a lifetime to accumulate.

He sat on the porch with Chessor drinking morning coffee and trying to think what to do. He had to formulate a plan.

Well? Chessor asked.

The old man sipped his coffee and sat staring across Chessor's yard toward the pear tree. The yard was littered with a motley of broken and discarded plunder, and dogs of varied and indeterminate breed lay about the yard like fey decorations some white-trash landscapist had positioned there with a critical eye.

He give me the runaround.

Ain't that the way of the world, Chessor said.

I got to have me a way of goin. You still got that old Falcon?

Yeah. It still runs but I had to quit drivin it. They took my license a while back cause I kept runnin into folks. I can't see like I used to.

What'll you take for it?

I don't know. I ain't got no use for it. Two hundred dollars? Would you give that?

Let's look at it.

He checked the oil and brake fluid. He checked the coolant level and listened to the engine idle with a critical ear. Thurl was apt to run an automobile without oil and use water for brake fluid and trust the radiator to take care of itself.

What was that place like?

It was all right.

All right. That's why you're livin in a sharecropper's cabin I reckon.

No, it was all right. They fed pretty good, nobody mistreated you. It was just . . . just a job to them, I guess. You had the feelin if you died in your sleep they'd just move you out and somebody else in and nobody would give much of a shit.

You want the car?

I guess. You throw in that lit old tan dog with one ear up and one ear down and I'll give you ten more bucks.

Why don't I just sell out lock, stock, and barrel and you move in here, Chessor said. Anyway that dog ain't worth ten dollars. That thing sets in barkin long about dark and don't let up till daylight.

He may just be a fifteen-dollar dog, Meecham said.

HE NAMED THE DOG NIPPER and set about immediately training it to bark at his command. Showing a great deal of aptitude for this, the dog was a brilliant pupil and seemed to need little instruction. He rewarded its efforts with bits of tinned mackerel and in no time at all he could command, You hush, Nipper, and the dog would erupt into a fierce grating bark as annoying as a fingernail scraped endlessly across a blackboard, leaping and growling with its black little eyes bulging, ugly as something alien, something left on a beach by receding tides.

The old man had been to Ackerman's Field and laid in supplies and he was feeling fairly complacent. He had bought bread and milk and tinned soup and a gallon of orange juice and he bought a hot plate to warm the soup on. As an afterthought he bought a box of shells for the pistol. He expected this night to pass far more pleasantly than the previous one. Sitting on the porch watching the day wane with the rusty green Falcon parked in his driveway and Nipper dozing at his feet he felt quite the country esquire.

Of course Choat noticed the dog right away, he could hardly have avoided it. He ignored it until nightfall then came in his shambling graceless walk down the slope from the main house. White trash right down to the ground, the old man thought. He even walks like it.

Where'd you get that thing?

The old man was sitting on the stoop cradling the dog as you might a child. The dog watched Choat with its eyes shiny as bits of black glass.

It followed me home, Meecham said. I guess you could say I found it.

You better lose it then. I ain't puttin up with no dog on this place.

It's my dog and my place and I guess you'll like it or lump it. He don't bark much.

Yeah. I heard it not barkin much most of the goddamned day. It'll come up with its neck wrung and you may not fare much better.

He's a good boy. He don't bother nobody. You hush now, Nipper.

The dog began to bark ferociously at Choat and snap its fierce little teeth and strain against the fragile shelter of the old man's arms.

You learnt that little son of a bitch to do that, Choat said viciously. I don't know how you found out a barkin dog drives me up the wall but by God you did and it's goin to cost you.

The old man felt an uncontrollable grin trying to break out on his face but he swallowed hard and fought it down. Then something in Choat's face sobered him. Choat had raised a fist and he looked as if he was going to attack man or dog or both, his flat porcine face was flushed with anger.

You touch me and I'll have you in jail for assault before good dark, the old man said.

Choat lowered the fist, he turned toward the main house. You need put in the crazy house. And that's where you'll be before this is over.

You hush there, Nipper, Meecham told the dog.

✦ ✦ ✦

HE WAS ABED EARLY but he awoke at eleven o'clock the way he had planned to do and went barefoot with the dog onto the porch. Lace filigrees of moonlight fell through the leaves, the main house was locked in sleep.

He sat on the stoop and packed the bowl of his pipe with Prince Albert. He could feel the warmth of the dog against his thigh. When he had the pipe going and the fragrant blue smoke rolling he opened a tin of mackerels.

Hush, Nipper.

The dog began to bark.

He forked out a mackerel and fed it to the dog. It stopped barking and snapped up the fish and looked about for more. Now I've done fed you, the old man said. You behave yourself, now.

The dog began a frenzy of barking. After a while the porch light came on at the farmhouse and the door opened and Choat came out onto the porch wearing only a pair of boxer shorts. Gross and misshapen against the dark doorway. How about shuttin up some of that goddamned racket, he called.

I can't get him to hush, the old man yelled. I don't believe he's used to the place yet.

He's about as used to it as he's goin to get. You bring him up here and I believe I might manage to quieten him down some.

He'll be all right. I expect he'll hush by daylight anyway.

You contrary old bastard. I'm just going to let you be and out-live you. You're oldern Moses anyway. You'll be in the ground before the snow flies and I'll still be here layin up in your bed.

He went back in and pulled the door to and cut off the light. After a while the old man went back in with Nipper. Before he went to bed he got out the pistol and loaded it. He found a can of machine oil and oiled the action and when he spun the cylinder it whirled, clicking with a smooth lethal dexterity.

✦ ✦ ✦

SOME TIME PAST MIDNIGHT he awoke to such bedlam that for a moment he was disoriented and thought he must have dozed off in a crazy house somewhere. Looking out the window into the moonlit yard did little to refute this view. What on earth, he asked himself. Choat was beating someone with what looked like a length of garden hose. His wife Ludie was swinging onto his arm and trying to wrest away the hose. He paused and turned and shoved her and she fell onto her back with all her limbs working like some insect trying frantically to right itself. All of them seemed to be screaming simultaneously at the top of their lungs. The hose made an explosive whopping sound each time it struck. You little slut, Choat was screaming. Then Meecham saw that it was the girl, such clothes as she had on torn away by the hose.

There was a car parked in the edge of the yard with the driver's-side door open and of a sudden someone streaked into Meecham's vision running full tilt toward it. A young man trying to haul up his pants and at the same time trying to avoid the hose that was falling with metronomic regularity.

Choat flung the girl aside and ran in pursuit of the fleeing boy. The boy had one hand behind him flailing about for the hose and the other hauling at his breeches and he was screaming Yow, Yow, every time the hose struck. He leapt into the car and slammed the door and cranked the engine. The hose was bonging hollowly on the roof when the engine caught and the car went spinning sideways wildly in the gravel. Glass broke when it glanced off the catalpa tree in the corner of the yard. It righted itself and one light came on as he shot off down the road.

Choat did not even skip a beat in his flailing. He fetched Ludie a blow or two and turned his attention back to the girl. She was on her knees with her arms locked about her head and face and the old man could see by moonlight her naked back laced with thick red welts.

Hold it, Meecham yelled. He had the window raised and the pistol barrel resting on the sill. He raised it pointed into the yard.

Choat whirled, the hose hanging limply at the end of his arm. He looked confused for a moment, as if he couldn't fathom where he was or what he was doing with the hose or why somebody was pointing a two-foot pistol at him.

You nosy bastard. I might of knowed you'd put into this.

I'm tired of watchin you beat folks, Meecham said. That's a child there, not a dumb brute. You raise that hose one more time and if what passes for a brain in you is big enough to hit then I aim to lay a slug in it.

You ain't got the balls, Choat said.

Meecham lowered the pistol and fired and when the bullet thocked into the ground a little divot of earth flew and showered Choat's bare feet. Choat dropped the hose and stepped abruptly back.

I aim to law you too, first thing in the mornin. There's bound to be laws about beatin young girls with garden hoses.

Choat opened his mouth to speak. Then he closed it. Finally he said, You'll regret this, Meecham. You'll be sorry ever day of your life you shot towards me.

Meecham waved the pistol barrel. Get this circus out of my yard so a man can get some sleep.

THE NEXT DAY was a veritable beehive of activity on the Choat place. In the morning the old man drove into town. He was back before noon seated on a Coke crate in the shade of the catalpa like a spectator awaiting the onset of some bizarre show.

Shortly after noon a white service truck with SOUTH CENTRAL BELL on the side drove into the yard and a man with a toolbox got out and went into the house. Meecham guessed they were having the phone hooked up and he was pleased at this for once he was back in his own house he might have need for a telephone.

Then in midafternoon a dusty Plymouth from the sheriff's department pulled up and a deputy in cop's khaki got out with a folded paper in his hand. He went up the steps. Choat explaining, making expansive hand gestures. How this was all just some misunderstanding. All this in silent pantomime. Finally he gave up and got in the car and the deputy slammed the door and they drove away.

Almost immediately Ludie and the girl followed in the Choat car. None of them looked at him. It was quiet the balance of the day until just before dark when the Choat family returned. Choat himself was driving. He got out with a six-pack of beer under his arm. He unlocked the trunk and took out a red five-gallon can and lifting one-sided with its weight strode to the porch. When he set the can on the porch he turned and gave Meecham a look so malevolent the old man expected tree leaves to char and the grass around him to burst into flame. Choat turned and trudged on to the house.

MEECHAM THAT NIGHT had difficulty in falling asleep. He'd found an old man's sleep chancy at best but tonight he had begun thinking about Ellen and try as he might he could not get his mind off her. He remembered when they were young, when they couldn't keep their hands off each other and the nights were veined with heat. The way he wore Aqua Velva shaving lotion to this day because she had liked the smell of it when they were going together. Then the swift inevitable squandering of days and the last time he saw her alive.

It was on a Saturday and they were getting ready to go to town. He was in a hurry to get to a cattle sale and she kept dragging around. Trying to decide this dress, that dress, something. I just don't know which one to wear.

Well, you best be for wearin one of them, Meecham said. I'm goin out to the truck and if you're not there in five minutes I'm gone and you'll have the rest of the day to make up your mind.

He had laid his pocket watch in the seat beside him and when five minutes were gone he cranked the truck. He saw her hand pull aside the kitchen curtain, her face lean palely to the glass. Then he drove away.

He'd done such things a thousand times with no payoff but this time the cards fell wrong. When he returned she was dead on the kitchen floor with one glazed eye studying the linoleum as if there was some profound message encoded there.

When finally he slept he dreamed of her, strange tortured fever dreams a madman might have. He was in the undertaker's office and they were discussing arrangements. Backhoe fees, the price of caskets. They were sitting on opposite sides of a limed oak desk and the undertaker was backlit so starkly his vulpine face was in shadow, just the sinister suggestion of a face. The light gleamed off his brilliantined hair. Curving horns grew out of his skull like bull's horns and his yellow eyes seemed to be watching Meecham out of thick summer bracken.

Of course, there's an option we haven't considered, the undertaker said. We could animate her.

Animate her?

Of course. It's a fairly expensive process but it's done frequently. The motor functions would be somewhat impaired and the speech a little slurred, but it's immeasurably preferable to the grave. As I said, it's done regularly, mostly for decorative purposes.

Then animate her, Meecham cried. He was hit by a wave of joy, an exalted relief so strong it made him lightheaded. He would not have to give Ellen up at all, an animated Ellen was immeasurably preferable to the grave.

Then it's settled, the hollow voice said out of the bracken.

Meecham dreamed he turned over and his arm lay across the animated Ellen and he abruptly awoke.

Animate her, he was saying aloud. He was crying, tears were streaming down his cheeks, he could taste them hot and salty in his throat.

The dog was lying on the edge of the old man's pillow. Its fierce little teeth were bared and its eyes bulbous and its tongue swollen and distended. There was a piece of plowline knotted around its neck and the covers were tucked neatly about its chin.

Jesus Christ, Meecham said. He jerked backward, forgetting the cot was scooted against the wall, and slammed the back of his head against the window frame. He sat rubbing his head for a moment then he crawled over the foot of the bed and fumbled his pocketknife out of his pants.

He cut the plowline and sat massaging the dog's chest. The body was still warm and limp but it quickly became obvious the dog was not going to take another breath. Meecham was seized with enormous sorrow. He had killed the dog as surely as if he had knotted the plowline himself. If he had left well enough alone the dog would still be fighting over scraps in Thurl Chessor's front yard.

He laid the dog on the floor and got the pistol out of the night table and cocked it and went through the house making sure Choat was not hidden somewhere watching. Hoping all the time that he was. The house was empty. By the time he had replaced the pistol and made his morning coffee on the hot plate he had come to see things in a different light. He was still going to make Choat pay but he had come to see Nipper as more than a dog. Nipper was a sacrificed pawn in a game that he and Choat were playing, and Choat had simply upped the ante.

THERE WAS NO TAXIDERMIST in Ackerman's Field that Meecham could locate but he heard of one in Waynesboro and so drove there. As deer season was still months away this was a slow season for taxidermy, but the process was more involved than he had thought and he had to stay overnight in a motel. The bill for preparing and mounting the dog was one hundred and seventy-five dollars but the old man counted it out with a willing hand. He knew he was spending money like a furloughed sailor but he figured every nickel he threw away would be a nickel that Paul could not get his pale manicured hands on. In fact the old man wished that Paul could have been with him. He would love to tell Paul that he had paid a taxidermist a hundred and seventy-five dollars to stuff a ten-dollar dog for no other reason than to aggravate Lonzo Choat.

The taxidermist was gifted in his art and this new and improved Nipper transcended lifelike: he had been lent a dignity he had not possessed in life. His mouth was closed, his little glass eyes thoughtful and intelligent. The expression on his face was exactly as if he was thinking over some philosophical remark that had been made and was preparing in his mind a rebuttal.

Meecham drove back to Ackerman's Field with Nipper in the passenger seat across from him. He'd positioned the dog so that Nipper's little agate eyes faced the window.

Wish I could of got some kind of barker put in you, he said. Maybe I'll get you a beeper.

Nipper sat motionless watching the scenery slide by the glass, ripe summer fields fading slowly into autumn.

WHEN CHOAT GLANCED UP from the circular he had taken from the mailbox and saw the old man and the dog on the porch his left foot seemed to forget it was in the process of taking a step and he stumbled and almost fell. He did an almost comical double take, then his face took on a look of studied disinterest and he went back to reading the circular.

When he glanced up again Meecham was tossing sticks into the yard. Fetch, boy, he was saying.

I wouldn't hold my breath till he brought that stick back, Choat said.

He's a slow study, Meecham agreed. I believe he's got some Choat in his family tree somewhere.

You smartmouthed old bastard. If I could buy you for what you're worth and sell you for what you think you're worth I'd retire. I'd never hit another lick at nothin.

You ain't hit that first lick yet, Meecham pointed out.

Choat was looking closely at the dog. I bet that little son of a bitch is a light eater, he said.

He don't eat much but he's a hell of a watchdog, Meecham said. Lays right across my feet and never shuts his eyes all night. One of these nights the fellow that tied that plowline will come easin through the door and I'll make him a date with the undertaker.

WHEN THE BLACK LEXUS stopped in the yard of the tenant house the front door of the main house opened and Choat came out onto the porch with a can of beer. He sat down in the swing and propped his feet against a porch stanchion.

The car gleaming in the packed earth before the tacky share-cropper's shack looked out of place, as if somewhere there was some mistake, some curious breakdown in the proper placement of things. Then the door opened and Paul got out. He smoothed down the blond wing of his hair. He took off his sunglasses and folded the earpieces down and tucked them into the pocket of his sport shirt.

Hey, Dad.

I was wonderin when you'd show up. Come up and get a seat.

Paul came over to the edge of the porch and brushed invisible dust off the boards with a hand and pulled up the cuffs of his trousers and seated himself. How you making it, Dad?

I'm makin it fine.

That's not what I'm hearing. I was talking to Alonzo Choat this morning. He tells me you're cutting a pretty wide swath around here.

Well. I was never one to let things slide.

No. You never were that.

Did you come out here to straighten this mess out?

In a way. I came out here to pick you up and drive you back to the nursing home.

Then you've wasted gas and a good bit of your valuable time drivin out here. It'll be a cold day in hell when you guile me into that place again. I get mad ever time I think about it.

Dad, it's just till we get this straightened out. I've signed a lease and it has to run its course. When the ninety days are up I'll get out of the sale and you can move back in. If we need a practical nurse to look after you then I'll hire one.

The old man was silent a time. He marveled at how different

they were, how wide and varied the gulfs between them. It saddened him that he no longer had the energy or even the inclination to try and broach them. But it amused him that Paul had not improved much in his ability to lie. Being unable to lie convincingly to a jury must be a severe handicap in the lawyer trade.

I don't need a nurse, he finally said.

Perhaps not. You need something though. Shooting a pistol at a man. Having him arrested so that his family has to go bail him out. Setting dead dogs around the porch like flower pots. For God's sake, Dad.

Well, I can't say I didn't do it. But you got the wrong slant on it. I'm not goin to argue with you, arguin with you was always a waste of time. You'd just lie out of it. Do you think I don't know you? Do you think I can't see through your skin to ever lie you ever told?

I'm not leaving here without you. You're a danger to yourself and you're a danger to other people. Goddamn it. Why do you have to do everything the hard way? Can't you see you've played this string out as far as it will go? You know that if you don't go with me voluntarily I'll have to get papers and send people out here after you. Is that what you want?

The old man was suddenly seized with weariness, a weight of torpor bearing down on him as if all the things he'd done and all the things he'd said and all the things he'd heard in all the years he'd lived had suddenly come due all at once. It took an enormous effort to reply, just to breathe. He sat packing the bowl of his pipe and staring at the red kerosene can on Choat's porch.

Goodbye, Paul, he said at last. You take care of yourself.

I'LL TELL YOU WHAT he did do one time, Thurl Chessor said. He was in Long's grocer store and when they wasn't nobody watchin him he poked a mouse down into a Co-Cola bottle and acted like he drunk off of it. Oh he cut a shine. Spittin and gaggin. He throwed such a fit with Long and the bottlin company they give him a world of cold drinks just to shut him up. Cases and cases of em, they drunk on em all summer. That bunch like to foundered theirselves on Co-Colas.

But do you reckon he'd burn a man out?

I wouldn't think so. I never heard tell of him doin anybody any real harm. He'll steal anything ain't tied down or on fire but he's too triflin and lazy to make much effort.

Well. He said he was goin to. He said that tenant house would go up like a stack of kindlin and me with it. I may have leaned a little hard on him, shootin at him and all. Anyway I believe he'll try it. He strangled that dog.

You ought to get the law then. Tell the high sheriff.

Choat would just deny it. He's tryin to make Paul believe I'm crazy. All I want you to do is just speak up if anything does happen. You go tell the law I told you ahead of time he threatened to do it. Will you do that?

Yeah. I'll do that.

I wouldn't want him to get clean away with it.

No. You can have another one of them pups if you want it.

No I believe I'll pass, the old man said. I'm a little hard on dogs. Besides, I've still got the other one.

Maybe, Chessor said tentatively. Maybe it would be the best all the way around if you just went back. You said it was all right.

I lied, the old man grinned. It's a factory where they make dead folks and I ain't workin there no more.

Chessor was silent a time. As if he was considering his own bleak future as well as Meecham's. We all got to work somewhere, he finally said.

Meecham drove back and sat on the porch smoking his pipe and waiting for full dark so that he could steal the kerosene can. At last the day began to fail. Dark rising out of the earth like vapors. Against the sky the main house looked black and depthless as a stage prop. Beyond the Rorschach trees the heavens were burnished with metallic rose so bright it seemed to pulse. As if all the light there was was pooling there and draining off the rim of the world like quicksilver.

HE WORKED VERY FAST. He figured if he faltered he'd quit, give it up, let Paul be a daddy to him. He upended a box of photographs and threw on old newspapers and lit it all with a kitchen match and when the photographs began to burn with thin blue flames he picked up the can and began to pour kerosene around the room.

Except when he threw it the fire leapt toward him like something he'd summoned by dark invocation and even as he hurled the can from him he was thinking how like Choat it was to keep lawn mower gas in a can clearly labeled kerosene. His lashes and eyebrows were singed away and he could feel his hair burning and when the can blew the room filled up with liquid fire. The walls were flaming and on the foot of the burning bed Nipper watched him calmly out of the smoke with his glass eyes orange with refracted fire.

Meecham covered his face with his hands and fell to the floor. Far off he could hear somebody screaming Help me, help me, and then he realized it was he himself.

WHEN HE CAME TO he was lying on his back staring upward into the stars. His body seemed to be absorbing the heat from the wheeling constellations, he rocked on a sea of molten lava. He could hear a voice and an ambulance wailing and after a while he figured out the voice was Lonzo Choat's.

He's damn lucky these houses is so close or I never would of heard him. Beats the hell out of me what he thought he was doin. He's been actin funny, I believe his mainspring may have busted. I reckon he thought it was winter and he was just buildin a fire.

That's a hell of a brave thing you did, Choat, another voice said. Let's go with him, Ray.

Then the stars were gone and he was rocking down the sleek wall of the night. He could feel the ambulance beneath him wild and fierce as a beast, the heavy shocks taking stockgap and curve, then there was a sharp pain in his wrist and a voice was saying, Lay back, old-timer, this'll cool you off.

He was in a cold glacial world of wind-formed ice, ice the exact blue of frozen Aqua Velva, a world so arctic and alien life was not even rumored and he struggled up to see.

Help me hold him, Ray, he's trying to get up.

But the frieze of night was familiar. Why I believe we've crossed over into Alabama, he said to himself in wonder, and in truth they were descending into a landscape sculpted by memory. The ambulance rocked on past pastoral farmhouses whose residents' dust these sixty years still dreamed their simple dreams behind darkened windows, past curving lazy creeks he had fished and waded as a boy, past surreal cotton fields white as snow in the moonlight.

He pressed his face to the glass as a child might and watched the irrevocable slide of scenery, tree and field and sleeping farmhouse, studying each object as it hove into view and went slipstreaming off the dark glass as if it might have something to tell him, might give him some intimation as to his destination.

A Death in the Woods

CARLENE WAS STANDING naked before the window when Pettijohn awoke. She was holding the curtains aside with an upraised arm and she was peering into the night, the flesh of her left breast lacquered by a pulsing light that cycled red to blue, red to blue, and back again.

What the hell is that? Pettijohn asked.

I don't know, she said. Lights.

When she turned from the window, her eyes were just dark slots in the shadows of her face and lit so by the strobic light she might have been some erotic neon succubus he'd conjured from a fever dream.

What woke you up?

I don't know. I was just looking toward those woods and there were lights everywhere.

There was no way there could have been any lights. Beyond the glass lay only fallow fields, deep woods. He got out of bed and crossed the carpet to stand beside her. Her hair brushed his shoulder. Silver beads of rain strung off the eaves. Past the dark stain of the fields that were more sensed than seen, moving lights turned and swayed and darted through the slanting rain in a curious ballet that seemed senseless, profoundly alien.

What the hell is it? he asked again.

She just shook her head.

He was pulling on pants and a shirt, looking about for his shoes. She was watching him.

What in the world are you doing?

He looked up sharply, as if she'd taken leave of her senses. He'd found both shoes and now he was tying them. I'm going to see what that is.

In this rain? Why don't you just let it alone? It's nothing to us.

The way I see it, it's something to us. Those are our woods. Nobody's got any business even being there.

He went out of the house and around the side in the rain and to the edge of the backyard. Here he climbed a woven-wire fence and descended in the grown-up field. All the time, he was staring toward the dark blur where the woods began and his face was half perplexed and half angry.

Lights twisted and turned, smaller white lights like flashlights strung out of the woods. Soon vehicles began to shape themselves out of the blue murk—police cars, ambulances. A pickup truck. An emptiness swung in the pit of his stomach. He couldn't fathom what might have happened. A wind was blowing the rain in slant gusts. He buttoned his shirt and wished he'd worn a jacket.

An ambulance was backed to the edge of the woods, lights revolving, rear door sprung. Attendants were carrying a stretcher out of the trees. They loaded it and its plastic-wrapped freight into the rear: All this in a silent tableau, then in a rush the sound came up. The first sound he heard through the muting rain was the slam of the ambulance door. As he approached, he became aware of the detached and mechanical crackling of voices from the police radio, the rush of windy rain in the dripping woods.

The high sheriff that year was a man named Holly Roller. Folks when they kidded him called him Holy Roller, but none were kidding him tonight. When he finished with the radio, Pettijohn asked, What's going on back here, Sheriff?

Roller hung the microphone back in its rack on the dash. Couple of coon hunters found a body back in here last night.

A what?

A body, a dead man.

Pettijohn stared toward the woods. The coon hunters stood in the shelter of an enormous cedar. Denim jumpered, felt hatted, wet. Rifles kept dry under their coats. Coonhounds were curled at their feet like curious black-and-tan familiars. The two men looked as if they wished they were anywhere but here. Like unwilling passersby called up to witness or attest something.

One of the attendants knelt against the bole of a tree. He was very young. A green surgical mask hung from his neck. He'd vomited into it, and as Pettijohn watched, he vomited on his shoes. His hands were encased in translucent plastic gloves and he kept trying to strip them off.

A dead man, Pettijohn said.

I hope I never see one deader. He's deader than I ever want to get. Who was he?

His driver's license said he was a Waters. You couldn't prove it any other way, or I couldn't. He must have been there two or three weeks and everything from dogs on down had been eating on him. Where'd you come from, anyway?

I live right across that field.

Where that light is?

Yes.

These woods belong to you?

Yes, Pettijohn said again.

That's pretty damn close. What, a couple of hundred yards? You ain't seen or heard anything out of the way?

Out of the way? Like what?

I don't know. Like folks wandering around back in here. Shots. You ain't even seen buzzards after him?

No, Pettijohn said.

Who else lives over there?

Just my wife. He wondered was she still standing against the window, watching him, or watching where he was.

She say anything about seeing anything unusual?

No. What killed him?

Best I can tell a twelve-gauge shotgun. There was one laying by a log, back in that thick brush. Come on, I'll show you.

Pettijohn wasn't sure he wanted to see, but he went anyway. It seemed to be required; new rules seemed to apply here. All these official comings and goings had padded out a trail through the sodden leaves. He went through a tangle of winter huckleberry bushes. They entered a shadowed glade. The light flitted about, fixed on a dead beech tree the winds had taken, and abruptly the woods altered, became somber, like an abandoned graveyard, like a church where the religion has no name.

What I think he done was set on that beech yonder and study about it a long time. We found a Marlboro pack and seventeen cigarette butts, all Marlboros. He was doing some serious studying. That black spot's where he was, where the torso was. The head was over yonder where that smaller round spot is. I reckon dogs or something drug it there.

The light moved. Pettijohn's eyes followed it.

He had one boot on and one boot off. That TBI man said that's how he pulled the trigger.

A dull anger ached in Pettijohn. He'd loved these woods. He could walk in summer dusk, watch silent winter snowfalls. Now they had a quality of unease. Perhaps they were not even his woods anymore. Possession seemed to have shifted subtly to the dead man. They felt defiled.

I need to get back to the house, Pettijohn said.

Well, if anything comes up, I guess I know where you live.

I won't know any more then than I do now.

Halfway across the field, he noticed day was coming. Shapes accruing bleakly out of the gray, rainy dawn. After a while, he could see the green roof of his house. The black truck he drove to work and the blue Ford he'd bought Carlene last year. They seemed commonplace, no part of the woods he'd been in, and there was something vaguely reassuring about them.

SHE OFFERED BREAKFAST, but he wanted no part of it. All he could handle was coffee. The woods were too much with him.

He's ruined the damned woods, he said. There's something different about them. Something . . . I don't know, I can't put my finger on it. Just different.

She ate unperturbed. She dipped a triangle of toast delicately into egg yolk. You're just too sensitive, she told him. She put the toast in her mouth and began to chew. He couldn't tell if she was being sarcastic or not.

Well, he said, I was back there, you weren't. What I can't figure is why he picked our woods to blow himself away. Those woods run all the way to Deerlick Creek. Why couldn't he do it there?

You see everything from your own selfish perspective, she said.

I'm sure that while he was thinking about shooting himself he didn't stop to consider whether it was an inconvenience to you.

Inconvenience? That's not what I mean and you know it.

I never know what you mean anymore. Sometimes I wonder if I ever did.

What I want to know is why he did it and why he did it there.

You never know when to leave a thing alone. Maybe he was hunting there when the impulse or whatever hit him. Maybe it was an accident. Maybe he was on drugs. Besides, it's none of our business. Let it go, Bobby.

It was Sunday and he didn't have to go to work. After noon the rain ceased and the sun broke through and burnt away the clouds. The sky was marvelously blue and it held an autumnal look of distances. A warm wind looping up from the south brought them distant voices and children's laughter. They went out to see. Across the field, the edge of the woods thronged with people. A family strung out across the field like miswandered carnival folk. Young girls in Sunday dresses bright as cut flowers.

Why, goddamn, he said. I wish you'd look at those morbid freaks. All I need is a roll of tickets.

She didn't answer.

HE DROVE THROUGH THE GATE in the chain-link fence at the hose factory where he worked and parked in the lot and cut the switch and pocketed the keys. He dreaded going in. He always did. He told himself if he could make it another year he would have enough money saved to buy a few horses and he was going to say to hell with industrial hose and try to make it raising horses and farming. Live simple. Just him and Carlene and the farm. The world seemed to have gone volatile and unpredictable, but there was something timeless and reassuring about horses. He sat with his hands on the steering wheel and thought about horses for a while and then got out of the truck and walked toward the brick factory. It looked like a prison. A dull hammering emanated from it. Ceaseless, rhythmic. Here the machinery ground metal on metal twenty-four hours a day. He showed his pass at the guardhouse and went through gray steel doors into the din and clocked in and went to the break room.

Reuben and Stayrook were already sitting at a red Formica table, drinking coffee from paper cups. The three of them formed the crew that operated the number three press. Reuben was an enormous, gentle man shaped like a round-shouldered mountain, and winter and summer he wore overalls and long-sleeve khaki shirts that were perpetually sweated through.

There he is, Stayrook sang out. There's the infamous shotgunner of meter readers. And we didn't even know they had a bounty on them.

Pettijohn put coins in a Coke machine, then sat down at the table across from Reuben and Stayrook. What the hell are you talking about?

That Waters feller they found in the woods behind your house worked for the power company. Went round readin folks' meters, how much electricity they used. Did you not know him?

Pettijohn was making interlocking circles with the wet bottom of the Coke can. No, he said. Anyway, it wasn't all that close.

Not that close? What I heard, you could of stood on your back doorstep and pissed on him.

Reuben glanced at the clock and took out a package of Bugler smoking tobacco and a packet of papers and began to build himself a cigarette. I guess you know them woods is haunted now.

What?

They're ruined. Something happening like that ruins a place. He'll be tied to wherever he done it and you won't never be able to look at them woods without thinking of Waters.

Oh, for Christ's sake. Give me a break, Reuben.

Say, Pettijohn, Stayrook said. When're we going out to Goblin's Knob and drink a few cold ones? Get out amongst em and run some wild women?

Pettijohn studied him. His last friend out of the wild lost years. Beneath the flesh of the man Stayrook had become, Pettijohn could see the face of the child he'd been and in some curious way the old man he'd be if he was lucky enough to live that long.

I quit all that.

Yeah. I had a wife looked like Carlene I might stay home with her, too. Keep a eye on her. I ever marry I aim to marry some old gal so ugly nobody else'd ever try to take her away from me. That way I could rest easy and she'd be grateful for any passin kindness I might offer.

Reuben glanced at the clock. About time to get it, he said.

We had some wild times though, didn't we? Stayrook asked.

Pettijohn nodded, but he didn't think about all that much anymore. The high times were blurred in mist, sharp edges already rounded off by time. Wild times had come and gone like telephone poles veering up drunkenly in speeding headlights, but they seemed to have little to do with this new and improved Pettijohn.

As they rose from the table, Stayrook punched him in the ribs and grinned. Tell Reuben about that time in Chicago when we saw that drunk Indian throw that piano down the stairs.

Pettijohn, try though he might, could call no such incident to mind, and there was something mildly disquieting about it. You ought to remember a thing like that. Maybe he'd seen one too many drunk Indians throw one too many pianos down one too many stairways and it was time to get on to something else.

He just smiled his noncommittal smile, taking no position at all, and Stayrook shook his head. You ain't been no fun since you got married, he said.

THAT NIGHT HE GOT HURT for the first time in the three years he'd worked there. It happened as they were changing the die in the press. He was thinking about the black oval of earth in the woods and holding the wrench positioned on the die for Reuben to hit with the sledgehammer. Something he'd done a thousand times before. The wrench weighed fifty or sixty pounds and had always reminded Pettijohn of something lost from the toolbox of a giant.

He must have been standing off-balance, for when the clang of steel on steel came and the wrench slipped, he fell headfirst into the press, the wrench ringing again when it struck the concrete floor. He felt no pain when his head struck the press, just a dull, sick concussion and a wave of red behind his eyelids and the sensation that his knees had turned to water. A hand stabbed at the floor to break his fall, index finger splayed out beneath his boneless weight. He felt that. A rush of nausea washed over him and he could taste sour bile at the back of his mouth.

When he came to himself, he had arisen to his knees and Reuben was stooped peering down at him. Reuben leaned forward with his enormous hands cupping his knees and his face was very close to Pettijohn's. Behind the thick twin layers of safety glass, his eyes were rabbitlike and benign. His entire face was rabbitlike, Pettijohn suddenly saw—the soft twitching nose, the magnified eyes pinked-rimmed and myopic. Behind Reuben other workers had gathered, but Pettijohn saw no face he could put a name to and they might have been strangers staring down at some mishap in the street.

Goddamn, Bobby. Are you all right?

I think I hurt my finger, he said.

Finger, hell. You may be hurt bad. You knocked the shit out of your head and you're bleedin like a stuck hog. Stayrook, help me get him to the nurse's station.

I believe he's busted that press, Stayrook said.

In the infirmary a middle-aged woman with a beehive of purple hair and an air of professional detachment cleaned and bandaged his cut. You're going to need a few stitches in the corner of that eye, she said. I'm afraid you're going to have a scar there, too. I'm sending you out to the hospital.

No. I'm not going to any hospital.

You don't have a choice. It's company policy. You have to go.

I don't have to do anything. It's my head. He felt dull and angry. He should not have fallen. He'd never done anything this foolish before.

Very well, then. Suit yourself. But your medical insurance won't pay any expenses you might incur later. And you'll have to sign a release.

Get it.

Coming out of the infirmary, he saw Reuben still awaiting him, cap in hand, out of place in this antiseptic world of steel and spotless tile.

They sendin you out to the hospital? he asked solicitously.

No. I'm taking the rest of the day off. Maybe a day or two.

Oh, Reuben said, crestfallen. Pettijohn knew that Reuben had been counting on driving him out to the hospital and waiting on him, thirty minutes or more of idle time that he'd be paid for and that he could easily stretch to an hour.

Ain't you in no pain?

She gave me a bunch of pain pills. Anyway, my head's all right. It's my damn finger that's giving me a fit.

You ought to have it X-rayed, Reuben said, trying one last time.

No. They're liable to just sew me up and slap me into the hospital overnight. I'm going home.

That's the ticket. Go home and soak it inside her; that's the best thing for it.

In cider?

Yeah, inside her, Reuben said. That'll draw the soreness out of it. A leering eye closed in a lewd wink.

Halfway to the parking lot and for no good reason, the remark angered him. Reuben hadn't meant anything by it; that was just the way people talked. Still, it made an assumption he wasn't comfortable with. It assumed an intimacy that he wasn't sure existed anymore.

HIS HEAD HURT TOO MUCH for sleep and he sat beside the bed where she lay, his feet propped on the hearth of the dead fireplace.

Can you not sleep, Bobby?

Not right now.

Do you want me to get you a pain pill?

No, I'm all right. The one pill he'd taken had eased the pain but had made him lightheaded and drunk. He felt curiously off balance, out of sync, as if something somewhere needed to be adjusted half a turn. Everything looked and felt skewed; the level and plumb of the world seemed subtly off. He wasn't sure though how much of it was caused by the accident. He'd been feeling eerie and disassociated ever since he'd stood peering down at the dark oval in the woods.

They said Waters was a meter reader. Do you remember ever seeing him up here?

Who?

Waters. The man they found in the woods. Did you ever see him?

I don't know. I may have. They all wear those yellow hardhats and they all look alike to me. Why?

Well, everybody has been talking about him.

They certainly have around here, she said. Why don't we just let it be.

He fell silent. He studied her where she lay. He'd never thought about her leaving, the rest of his life without her. Her still somewhere in the world getting up in the morning and going to bed at night, living her life and yet no part of his. He'd always felt that she had saved him from something. Who knew what, perhaps she'd saved him from himself. Yet she'd always been a person of silences, of dark places you couldn't see into. He would have liked to see the world through the eyes she saw it with, but her vision of it seemed posted off-limits, no trespassing. It seemed as best he could judge a serene world of chrome and ice and you went through it unscathed. Nothing touched you, nothing hurt you, nothing branded you with its mark to show you'd even been there.

I wonder what he was thinking while he was smoking nearly a pack of cigarettes, he said aloud. She didn't answer. He knew she was awake. He could tell by the pitch of her breathing. She was lying naked in the warm dark. Her breathing changed when she slept. He used to lie awake and listen to it, a sort of reassurance that she was there.

He hadn't been talking to her anyway. He had just thought of Waters, sitting on the dead beech, perhaps the gun in his lap. Was it dark? Was the sun in his eyes? Staring at nothing, then at the drifted leaves between his boots that had shifted to reveal a chasm of unreckonable depth.

Suddenly, she turned to face him and reached her arms to enfold him. She raised on one elbow and kissed his throat. Bobby, she said, just let it alone. It's nothing to us. We didn't even know him. It's nobody's fault. Can't you see that none of it even matters? We've got our own lives to go on with. She took his hand and placed it on her naked breast. Marvelously, his hand passed through it into nothing, past the brown nipple and the soft flesh and the almost imperceptible resistance of the rib cage and into a vast gulf of space where winds blew in perpetuity and the heart at its center was seized in bloody ice. Rolling against him and sliding her hand up his thigh, she was a ghost, less than that, like nothing at all.

THE HIGH SHERIFF'S CAR sat idling noiselessly in Pettijohn's front yard. With his cup of morning coffee, Pettijohn crossed the lawn toward it. A flicker of annoyance crossed his face, then there was no look there at all.

Mornin, son. I get you up?

I've been up.

What happened to your face?

I got hurt at work.

What do you work at, sortin wildcats?

Pettijohn didn't reply.

I thought you might want to know how it all came out.

How did it all come out?

They decided there's no question he shot himself. The angle of the shot and all.

Roller was sitting with his hands clasping the steering wheel and he was peering through the windshield toward the distant woods as intently as if they touched him with the same vague sense of unease Pettijohn had been feeling.

Well? Pettijohn said.

Well what?

I appreciate all this news coverage or whatever it is. But I can't help wondering what makes me important enough for the high sheriff to drive out and report the result of an inquest.

The truth is, I wanted to talk to you some more. It occurred to me you might have remembered something. Seeing him pass your house, hearing a shot, anything.

No. I told you. I'm not here all the time. I have to make a living. Some folks can't drive around the county asking questions and get paid for it. My wife's here all the time. You could ask her.

Actually, I figured she told you I was out here Monday morning. And if there's a soul on this round earth that knows less about Randy Waters than you do, you're married to her.

Pettijohn was silent.

Oh well, it's a small thing anyway, Roller said. It just sticks in my craw, where he was. How he got there.

He came in on those log roads. The way you got him out.

The problem for me is no vehicle. Did somebody let him out to hunt, and if they did, why don't they speak up? He lived in Ackerman's Field. Did he tote that shotgun all the way from town just looking for enough privacy to shoot himself? Now, what gets me about them woods is what he was doing there in the first place.

Hunting. Scouting a place to put up a deer stand. You hear gunfire back in there every weekend, when deer season opens.

I don't know. Maybe. Like I said, it's a small thing. The Tennessee Bureau of Investigation don't care. He shot himself. His wife has no idea why. I just have a fondness for stories, and that's not a story. It might be a beginning, or an end, but it's damn sure not a story.

Maybe he didn't even kill himself. Maybe somebody blew him away and hauled him back in there and dumped him out and went about their business.

Roller eased the car into reverse, stopped it with a foot on the brake. The pitch of the engine changed.

Oh, I'm satisfied he did it. Our boy Waters had problems. He'd tried it all and none of it worked. Drugs, booze, women. Did I say he tried it a few years back? His folks or whoever got him up and carried him to old Doc Epley. There had been a bad car wreck over by Mormon Springs and Epley had blood all the way to his elbows and he was busy as a one-legged man in a ass-kickin contest. "Put him over on that cot and I'll get to him when I can," Epley told them. "I got folks here tryin to live." There'd been a kid in that wreck and Epley done everything he could and then it died anyway. After he got Waters patched up, he got a tube of lipstick off his nurse's desk and drew a big X right over Waters' heart. "There, by God," he told him. "You ever try it again, there's you a map to go by."

God Almighty.

It might have been harsh, but it did the trick. He didn't have no trouble findin it this time.

WOODS HERE SOMBER and ancient. Pettijohn passed under great live oaks and cypresses and beeches with distended groping arms like gothic trees in a fairy-tale wood. The glade was sepulchral. Light came falling through the latticework of branches and it had the quality of light filtered through stained glass. It stood in green-gold columns, shimmered with the movement of the trees.

Dark oval of earth, so stained with the body's seepings. So unhallowed a resting place. In the nights, the beasts would quarrel and contest territorial rights, how'd a body sleep? By day the sun would sear the flesh and scald the blind eyes, vultures tilt on the updrafts and glitter in the sun like some hybrid of flesh and chrome.

He sat on the windfall beech and smoked cigarettes and thought about things. As if by placing himself where Waters had been and echoing his motions he'd gain some insight into the workings of his mind. There were clues could he but find them. A story could he but read it. It sticks in my craw, too, Roller, he thought. And I like a story as well as the next one.

He arose and toed the cigarette out in the dirt and looked about. Directly, he wound through the winter huckleberries following a path so faint it might have been a ghost path, a dream of a footpath. He moved along with confidence for he now knew where he was going: They were his woods. The ground began to climb gently in an earth bulwark and leveled out, and he came through a spinney of sassafras onto the rim of the abandoned pond.

There seemed clues in abundance here. What to make of all this? Two old lawn chairs tilted by the wind. Nestled in the roots of an elm half a liter of a red wine called Tokay rosé and in the brush a folded blanket, still sodden and mildewed from the fall rains. An empty plastic bottle that had contained suntan lotion. A glint of the sun off metal drew him farther, to where a tiny gold crucifix lay half buried in the packed clay. He dipped it in the water and wiped it clean on the tail of his shirt. An earring. He dropped it into a shirt pocket and stood up. He remembered what Reuben had said about haunted woods and he grinned a rueful grin and figured him right. He reckoned these woods haunted, but he could not have said by what.

✦　✦　✦

SHE WAS SITTING on the sofa with a book open on her lap, and she had her legs stretched out across the coffee table. He leaned and laid the crucifix between her smooth tan calves. You must have lost an earring, he said.

She leaned forward and picked it up. Thanks, she said. You gave me those. Where was it?

He had no way of knowing what look he had on his face, but when she looked up at him hers went opaque and guarded, as if a curtain had fallen behind her eyes.

He went into the kitchen and made a glass of iced coffee. He held the cold glass against his forehead. He had a headache he seemed to have been born with, and the ice seemed to help it.

She went with her book through the doorway to the bedroom. When he'd drunk half the coffee, he followed her into the room. Her book lay on the night table, a torn strip of paper to mark her place, and she had a suitcase open on the bed and she was stacking clothes in it. He could see his reflection in the mirror across. His image was dark and warped looking in the faulted glass.

Don't start, she said.

I'm not going to start. I just want to know one thing.

She turned. She looked at him as if she'd never seen him before. No, she said. You never want to know just one thing. You have to know it all. That's what's the matter with you, and it's been the ruin of you.

The ruin of me? What about you? You knew all the goddamn time he was out there. There in the brush with the dogs fighting over him, pulling him apart. What made him do it? Did he get in over his head and you brushed him off? Did he break it off and you were about to tell his wife? Or did you shoot him yourself?

She went on serenely packing clothes. By my count, that's way

47

more than one thing, she said. She glanced up at him and smiled. Besides, I sort of got the impression that that sheriff thought you knew a lot more than you were saying. Perhaps you did it yourself.

All right. Forget all that. It doesn't matter who killed him. The only thing I want to know is what you thought about.

What I thought about?

After all he'd been to you. Lying on that blanket with you. Nights when you were in bed with me and he was lying out there with things crawling over his face, what did you think about?

She gave him a slight frown of incomprehension. I never did think of that at all, she said.

He had crossed the room before he knew what he was doing. Perhaps he'd meant to strike her, but the motion that started as a blow ended with a hand laid gently on her shoulder. His thumb could feel the small knob of bone beneath the flesh. The hand subsided, dropped uselessly to his side. He couldn't think of anything to say. He went back and leaned against the wall and watched her.

After a time, she went out with the suitcase. As she went through the doorway, she picked up the book from the night table. The screen door slapped to on its keeper spring. The Ford cranked. He heard it turning in the driveway, retreating down the hill. Everything grew very quiet. The house seemed to be listening intently. It seemed to be waiting for him to make the next move.

He went out and sat down on the stone steps. The day seemed to grow still and he sat and smoked and grew still along with it. Suddenly, he realized it was almost night. He'd sat down in broad daylight and now it was the darkest shade of twilight and the cries of whippoorwills were washing over him from out of the trees.

At length he rose and went around the house and through the backyard. He stood at the fence and watched. The horizon had almost merged with the darkness. It was dissolving rapidly, like a horizon cut from paper and dropped into acid. The spiky tops of the cypresses marked the spot where the body had lain. Where the bodies had lain. In an uneasy moment of revelation, he divined that the woods were not yet finished with him, that he had barely tapped the reservoir of their knowledge. It seemed to him that this dark quarter acre of death and assignation would go on and on whispering to him secrets he did not want to hear as long as he had the strength to listen.

Bonedaddy, Quincy Nell, and the Fifteen Thousand BTU Electric Chair

*B*ONEDADDY BOWERS had not had a driver's license since 1989 but that did not deter him on his appointed rounds. Cops he met raised a casual hand, Hey, Bonedaddy. He was a laidback good old boy of twenty-seven who was not going to hurt anybody or cause any real harm unless you were a sixteen-year-old virgin or a factory worker on the nightshift with a restless wife home listening for the sound of the gutted mufflers of Bonedaddy's truck.

Bonedaddy liked George Jones, the Buffalo Bills, professional wrestling, cold longneck bottles of Bud with water beading on the side. He liked pliable young girls he could mold to his liking, soft summer nights beside the Tennessee River, consoling the distraught wives of inattentive young husbands. That Bonedaddy, folks said, shaking their heads. Women sensed something in Bonedaddy that men did not that went beyond his dark good looks, an unpredictable thread of danger that ran through his character like a faultline, a bright streak of precious metal in a fissured strata of rock. Had Bonedaddy not met his comeuppance he might have continued running sixteen-year-old virgins until he had to hobble after them with a walking stick, waylay them on the way to the mailbox after his social security check.

His comeuppance, though he had no way of knowing her as such, was sitting at the Sonic drive-in drinking a cherry Coke the first time he noticed her. She was a girl named Quincy Nell Qualls, five months past her sixteenth birthday, and she was a virgin. She had blondwhite hair and Nordic blue eyes and she was sitting behind the wheel of a little red Gremlin hatchback and when Bonedaddy looked down at her from the window of his pickup truck something passed between them tangible as an electric shock.

Good God, Bonedaddy said. He had scooted across the truck seat and rolled the glass down on the passenger side.

She didn't reply. She looked up at him with her guileless blue eyes as clear as springwater. Bonedaddy had no way of knowing that he had been under observation, that she had kept up with his comings and goings as studiously as an ornithologist might ponder the migratory habits of birds. It was the first warm day of May and she could feel the weight of the sun on her face and she knew she looked good in it.

You're Candace Qualls' little sister, right?

I'm Candace's sister.

God. You grew up. I never noticed you before. I guess I never paid any mind to you after me and Candace broke up.

Bonedaddy could do that and had done it, work his way through a whole family of sisters. In his ten years on the road he'd gone through as many as three or four stairstep sisters. Folks grinned and said that Bonedaddy was a caution, the moment a girl was out of pigtails Bonedaddy would be standing at the front door, his hand raised to knock.

Where's she at now?

Up at UT Martin taking premed.

Me and her were pretty hot stuff there for a while.

All the time Bonedaddy and Candace were pretty hot stuff Quincy Nell had been watching from the sidelines. She had already determined that she was going to marry Bonedaddy. She loved him, and Candace didn't. Candace was marking time and waiting to go away for college. Quincy Nell loved everything about him. She loved the straight fall of his long hair that was as black and shiny as a raven's wing. She loved the thin scar curving down his left cheek that never tanned and that he told everyone he got knife fighting although in actuality it had been caused by a bumper jack kicking out when he was fifteen years old. Everybody in Clifton knew that he had not been in a knife fight so he mostly used that story picking up women in the string of honkytonks across the Perryville bridge. She loved him with a childlike devotion, and she would have died for him, though she didn't figure she'd have to go nearly that far.

Last time I paid you any mind you was a kid. You still get hot playin softball and pull your T-shirt off?

No, she said. I don't do that anymore.

Say me and you ought to get together tonight. You want to ride over cross the river where they have that dance?

No, she said. I can't. I've got a date tonight.

Bonedaddy studied her in bemused silence. She knew she had him. Bonedaddy could never stand the sound of the word no, it aroused in him enormous efforts of acquisition, and she knew that before the weekend was gone Bonedaddy would have his bone-white Toyota truck parked in her front yard and he himself would be parked on the shady end of the porch talking up her father.

SHE HAD A DATE THAT NIGHT with Robert Earl Crouch. They drove to Columbia and went to the bowling alley but there was no one there they knew. There was no movie she wanted to see at the multiplex either so they drove back to Clifton and parked on a long point of land grown up with wild mimosa that overlooked the river. Under the starlight the rimpled surface of the river looked hammered and it glittered with a thousand points of light. Sometimes a tug went upriver pushing a barge, the sound of the tug's motor and distant foreign voices drifted to them on the soft warm wind.

Robert Earl kissed her and she kissed him back. He had always smelled like Dentyne chewing gum but lately she had noticed that he smelled like Stetson aftershave. He cupped her right breast and she moved his hand.

Quit it, she said.

Do what? he asked in disbelief. His voice carried a tinge of quiet outrage, he'd been disenfranchised of a privilege that had been a given for some months.

What's the matter with you, Quincy Nell?

There's nothing the matter with me. You don't care what I want. You never want to do what I want to do. All you care about is yourself.

He was silent a time. Finally he said: Just what is it you want to do?

You never know what I'm thinking about. I'm just a body to you. I think we might as well break up.

Why Jesus Christ, Robert Earl said.

✦ ✦ ✦

HER FATHER SAT on the front porch and passed the time of day with Bonedaddy. Bonedaddy had a graceful easy charm, it didn't matter to whom he was talking. Old ladies confided in him and children trusted him with their secrets and dogs had been known to follow him home. Quincy Nell's father was not even a suitable challenge and Bonedaddy was humming along on half power.

Quincy Nell's father was an English teacher at the high school and though they lived in a veritable warren of Republicans he was of a liberal bent of mind and he liked to think that guidance rather than discipline was what he should be dispensing. He liked to say, Well, I'm of a liberal bent of mind myself and I can't say that the position you're taking is very compassionate. He was fond of saying that blood would tell, that he'd let Candace decide things for herself and things had turned out fine.

The upshot of it was that he let her go. He said Quincy Nell was a lot younger but that she had a good head on her shoulders and a mind of her own. Quincy Nell's mother had reservations but she ultimately deferred to the father. Quincy Nell's father privately felt that he could see down the road a lot farther than Quincy Nell could and he foresaw a day of enlightenment when the revelation that she had been wasting her time on Bonedaddy would hit her and she would get on to other things. Privately her mother thought that Bonedaddy would make a good-looking son-in-law.

That evening she rode in the off-white Toyota for the first time. They drove down to Clifton and had cheeseburgers and cherry Cokes at the Sonic and drove around the sleepy-looking town for a while. He took her home early. His behavior was exemplary. She was slightly disappointed.

That night she took down a pristine notebook and opened it to the first page. She licked the tip of her pencil and wrote the word OBJECTIVES. She wrote: Marry Bonedaddy Bowers and then she underlined it. She thought awhile and then made two subheadings, one, two. Beneath one she wrote: Become whatever he wants me to be. Then she wrote and underlined, Take the place of everyone he knows.

Came then hot honeysuckle nights of eros. Whispers in the dark by the river. They'd take blankets and lie beneath the trailing fronds of mimosa, scented blossoms falling on their bodies in the moonlight. Urgent entreaties and urgent denials and engagements fought over millimeters of bare sweating flesh. Every calculated liberty she permitted just drove him wilder until his entire body seemed tumescent with desire and night by night he was getting more difficult to handle. Candace had told her once, It's funny the way he does it. He just goes along assuming you're going to and before you know it you have. Forewarned is forearmed and that wasn't working this time and there were nights they fought their private war until the world seemed to have fallen asleep and forgotten them, the lights of the town folding one by one and the last drunken carouser home in bed and even the insects hushed and the moon about to set, tracking palely above the surface of the river like the luminescent husk of a dead world.

Some afternoons he would sit about the Quallses' porch after he got off work at the pallet mill or he'd lounge about the living room watching a football game. He had quit drinking he told her and as summer drew on he drank vast quantities of a beverage called Sharp's, brown bottles of it that looked and tasted like beer but were supposed to have the alcohol removed. But all this was mere preamble. Just necessary overture for the hot sweaty darkness when she wanted to as much as he did but fought him bitterly until she cried with frustration.

By the middle of June she was still a virgin she guessed but even she had to admit it was territory she claimed by the sheerest of technicalities.

She heard about the appliances on a radio show called Tradetime and she called the number they'd given immediately. The man said he had a washer and a dryer and a refrigerator and a fifteen thousand BTU air conditioner and that his wife had left him and that he would take five hundred dollars for the lot.

Consider them sold, she told him. And don't sell them to anybody else until you hear from me.

Are you crazy, Bonedaddy said that afternoon. I don't need that shit.

We may not now, Quincy Nell said. We will when we're married. We'll need all that stuff and this'll save us a lot of money.

I got nowhere to keep all that crap, he said. I live in a house trailer, you know.

She'd listened for his reaction when she mentioned the word marriage. This was a subject that had come up during the hot sweaty nights but this was its first mention when they were, as it were, cold sober. He didn't deny it.

We'll put it in Daddy's shed, she said. I'll keep it there and when we're married we'll get one of those apartments out on Cisco Pike. The one I looked at had kind of lime-green walls. They're real nice.

They are? he asked. There was the first trace of disquiet in his voice.

Yeah. You get to decorate them any way you want to.

You don't have any idea of the time it's took me to save up five hundred dollars. I ought to have kept my mouth shut about it, too.

It's for us, she said. Our money, you said. Didn't you say that?

Sure I did, he said, thinking of the river, the scent of her flesh. I'll talk to Daddy about putting it in the shed.

I'd be careful about what I talked to Daddy about, Bonedaddy said. We're trying to keep this quiet, right?

Sure. I'd just feel better about what we've been doing if there was some kind of a definite commitment. Five hundred dollars is a big commitment and I'd know you haven't been just lying to me. See?

I see all right, Bonedaddy said.

WE JUST NEED A PLACE to keep it until we get married, Quincy Nell said.

Her father was reading a copy of *Harper's* and he glanced at the page number he was on and laid the magazine aside with some reluctance.

Married?

Well, not right now. When I'm eighteen. We're going to save our money until then. I'm going to get a part-time job at the Sonic and Bonedaddy's got his job at the pallet mill. It doesn't take much for him to live.

Her father looked indulgent. That had always been his way. He would listen carefully to every word she said as if weighing each word separately and when she was finished he would take off his glasses and wipe them with a tissue studying her thoughtfully with his soft aesthete's eyes and then he would tell her how full of shit she was. His way had been to warn her and let her go, he'd warned her about older men, younger men, sex, drugs, life itself.

I believe I've heard all this before from Candace, he said. This is like a summer rerun.

Candace turned out all right.

Candace hasn't turned out yet. Candace is in the process of turning out.

Whatever.

Two years from now you'll be admitting that you were every bit as foolish as you sound to me right this minute.

Maybe so. But what do you have to lose? At the very worst you'll gain a shedful of appliances. They're mine. Ours. He's buying them for me.

I need my shed.

For what? All there is in there are spiderwebs and old fruit jars.

All right all right, he said. Just don't bother me with it. Do what you want.

BONEDADDY COUNTED THE MONEY out carefully. You sure you won't come off that five hundred a little?

But the little bespectacled man had already divined more of the way of things than even Bonedaddy had and he wasn't about to come off. He hooked his thumbs in his suspenders. He winked at Quincy Nell.

That's about the least dollar I could take, he said regretfully.

All right, here then, Bonedaddy said, shoving the money at him. He looked at his Toyota loaded to the tailgate with five hundred dollars' worth of used coppertone appliances. Let's get the hell out of here, he said.

The shed was a converted storm cellar dug out of a hillside and faced with poplar logs. It had a heavy door framed up out of sawmill oak and a hasp and lock. They tore out the shelves and boxed the fruit jars and unloaded the appliances with a dolly Bonedaddy had borrowed from his friend Clarence, who lived just down the road and made deliveries for a furniture store. When the appliances were stored inside and the lock secured through the hasp they were hot and sweaty.

Let's go swimming, Bonedaddy said. I aim to buy me a Budweiser about waist high and just wallow around in it.

You quit drinking, remember?

I reckon a five-hundred-dollar commitment entitles me to drink a goddamned beer, Bonedaddy said. Right?

I guess so, Quincy Nell said.

I would reckon that it entitles me to a lot of things.

NIGHT ON THE RIVER. Boats passed below unseen in the sweet floral darkness. Laughter floated by sourceless, laughter from nowhere, all these lovers faceless in the dark. The Toyota was parked on the point with the radio tuned to a country station. Earl Thomas Conley. Quincy Nell? Bonedaddy said. She clung to him with a stricken urgency. She started to say something. He put himself inside her. She knotted her fingers in his long black hair. On the radio Earl Thomas Conley sang, *Love don't care whose heart it breaks, it don't care who gets blown away.*

SHE HAD THOUGHT THAT that would do it. According to such spotty information as she had accumulated and hoarded she should have hooked him like a bad drug, strung him out like an addict with a vicious little monkey clinging to his back. It didn't seem to change things much. Life went on. Summer turned hot, then hotter. He used the nail gun at the pallet mill. He drank long-necked beers with his friend Clarence when they got off work in the afternoon. He won forty dollars in a pool tournament and with ten dollars of it bought her a ragged panda that already looked secondhand, as if it had come from a yard sale. He became interested in baseball and said that the Atlanta Braves were going to take it right down to the wire.

In the meantime Bonedaddy sang in her blood like electricity. She couldn't stop thinking about him. She thought about where he was and what he was doing every minute of the day, the thought of him going to bed with another woman took her to the point of madness. She couldn't quit thinking about him. She lived for the sweaty nights under the mimosas when she would cling to him desperately and think she was going to die in his arms and not caring if she did.

Having fought so long and hard and ultimately successfully for something Bonedaddy seemed to dismiss it as a thing of no moment. Goddamn, Quincy Nell, he said. You're going to wear me right down to the ground. I have to work tomorrow. I can't lay up and sleep like you do.

She felt her grip on him loosening, her fingers tiring. She clung to him as if she'd absorb him. She dreamed lime-green walls, yellow chintz curtains she'd seen at Wal-Mart, a baby in a highchair saying Daddy for the first time and her telling Bonedaddy about it the minute he came through the door. While Bonedaddy spoke of the Atlanta pitching staff, the merits of Mike Tyson as opposed to Muhammad Ali.

July drew on to August. She prayed and waited. Something was happening to her. One morning she was sick and fear and anticipation mingled like oil and water.

By now Bonedaddy had talked her into drinking a beer now and again. Two beers made her giggly. I'm missing a period, she giggled. And I can't find it anywhere.

Don't joke about such shit as that, Bonedaddy said.

I'm not joking. I think I'm pregnant.

You can't be.

This was so specious an argument she didn't even pursue it. She didn't even reply.

Are you serious, Quincy Nell.

Yes I am.

Well. I guess all we can do is wait and see. Likely it'll come to nothing.

She knew it already had come to something. Over a month ago she had had a prophetic dream. She had dreamt that her life was overseen by two angels. These angels looked rather like middle-aged old-maid schoolteachers and they oversaw her life with a system of awards and demerits, checks and balances. All right, she's done it five times, the first angel said. Let's give her a baby. The second angel had said, No we'd better wait. That time out by the pallet mill doesn't count.

We're going to get married anyway, Quincy Nell said. I guess we can just do it sooner.

I guess, Bonedaddy said.

HE GOT A REAL DEAL on the washer and dryer and refrigerator. Someone at work had offered him five hundred dollars for them. He was going to take it.

No you're not, she said. They're ours. For our apartment.

Look, he said. It's all the money back and the air conditioner free and clear. We can buy another set of appliances.

There's no use buying something you've already got, she said.

They stood arguing in the yard before the shed. Clarence waited in the truck. From time to time he'd take a drink of his beer. There were other beers iced down in a cooler. Bonedaddy argued with vehemence, there was something sinister about him. The parents watched from the porch, vaguely embarrassed. The father looked wan and ineffectual, like a cardboard cutout of a father.

The damn things are mine and I'm getting them and that's all there is to it, Bonedaddy said. Clarence, get out and help me.

Clarence got out.

THEN THERE WERE DAYS when she walked on the edge of the abyss. Her parents watched her with hooded eyes. Nothing was yet said, everything was left open-ended. Life was a dark torrent moving beneath her feet and everything that was left unsaid moved inaudibly beneath the waters. Pregnant, statutory rape, courts and lawsuits. Her life seemed unending and she couldn't see anymore the way that it would go. Maybe he thinks it will just go away, she thought viciously.

Nights he didn't come and he didn't call. She called the trailer and the telephone rang and he didn't answer. She cried into her pillow and her body ached for him and her mind replayed the things he'd said when the mimosa blossoms fell in the windless dark and Earl Thomas Conley warned, It don't care who gets blown away. Someone saw him at the dance across the river with a black-haired girl from Coble and she beheaded the panda with a single-edge razor and set the truncate corpse on the bureau, poor piebald panda with its jaunty air of yard-sale innocence.

The worst was when she slipped out at night and waited on him at his trailer, listening to the radio in the Gremlin and watching the stars pulse and quake in the hot dark.

When he came he was in a black Lexus with a woman older than he was. He leaned to kiss her when he got out. Either he hadn't noticed the Gremlin or more likely he just hadn't cared.

Quincy Nell was out before he was and she closed on him before he could even shut the door of the Lexus.

You son of a bitch, she said.

What on earth, the woman in the Lexus wanted to know. She looked mildly amused, as if this were some diversion staged for her benefit.

Quincy Nell and Bonedaddy swayed like graceless dancers in the patchy yard of the house trailer. She tried to slap him, but he shoved her hard backward and she fell and cried out.

You'll hurt the baby, she cried.

Baby? the woman in the Lexus said. The window powered up on the Lexus and the woman vanished behind smoked glass. The motor cranked and the car backed up the driveway.

Goddamn it, Quincy, Bonedaddy said. Do you have to tell everyone you see? You're going to ruin me in this town.

I'm going to ruin you in every town there is on a map, she said.

A porch light came on next door. The front door of the trailer opened and a man stood on a makeshift stoop of stacked concrete blocks in the harsh light. Insects spiraled in the electric helix. He was a fat man naked to the waist holding a can of beer. His belly looped over the waistband of his slacks.

I ain't puttin up with no more of this crap, Bonedaddy, the man said. You ain't beatin up on no little slip of a girl while I'm around to stop it.

Then stop it or call the fucking law, Bonedaddy said.

I done called them, the fat man said.

A middle-aged deputy sheriff came to put things to rights. An authoritative presence in khaki. She glanced at his holstered pistol. What's the trouble here, Bonedaddy, he asked.

Bonedaddy was all polite deference. A touch of self-deprecation in his voice. Well, she just kind of attacked me, he said. Jumped right out of the bushes on me. She seen me with Jewel Seiber and I reckon she's jealous. Everything's all right now.

Quincy Nell felt small and far away, so far you couldn't see her.

Let me drive you home, the cop told her. His voice was curiously gentle.

I've got my car, she said. I have to drive.

I believe we'll send someone for it, the cop said. Just get in the squad car there.

I have to drive my car.

I believe we'll send someone for it, he said again. Get in the car, please.

She got in the car.

He drove back through Clifton. He seemed not to know what to say to her. She watched his reflection in the glass. His face looked strangely ambiguous. She thought he might begin to lecture her, or pull over at a roadside table and rape her.

Finally he cleared his throat. I've got a daughter myself about your age, he began.

That's nice, she said, and that was the end of that.

IN AUGUST THE HEAT turned malign. It didn't rain and it didn't rain. In the bottomlands corn withered and the blades twisted upon themselves then turned yellow and sere. The thermometer at midday hovered at 110 degrees for ten days in a row. The sky was absolutely cloudless and about the sun it seemed to quake and tremble like molten metal.

Bonedaddy labored shirtless with the nail gun shooting eight-penny nails into oak pallets. He worked in cutoff jeans and a red bandanna tying back his wet black hair and the sun hammered him fiercely as a weapon the God of his childhood had turned against him for his sins.

Nights were no cooler. At night far-off upriver you could see heat lightning flicker soundless and rim-light such clouds as there were with brief flashes of rose and white but it would come to nothing and in the morning the clouds would be gone and the hot bowl of sky as smooth and seamless as a china cup.

Quincy Nell was home alone when he came. He came backing the Toyota up across the yard to the door of the storm cellar. He got out. She was standing on the porch with her arms crossed over her stomach watching him across the porch railing.

Hey babe, he said. I come after my air conditioner. That trailer's like trying to sleep in a microwave oven.

You don't have an air conditioner.

Oh come on don't give me that. I paid good money for it and you seen me do it.

You got every nickel of that money back. By now I guess you've spent it on that Seiber woman.

No I never.

Then buy you an air conditioner.

I bought something a whole lot cheaper but just as good, he said.

He was opening the toolbox on the truck. He took out a wrecking bar almost three feet long. It was new-looking and a price tag still dangled from a string tied to it. He started toward the door of the storm cellar. She was already off the porch coming around the corner of the house. The only weapon she'd come across was a garden rake and she was carrying that. Get off my property, she was yelling.

I'm taking it.

Then you'll take it to a jail cell if you break that lock. Daddy's by a telephone right now and he can have the law here in fifteen minutes. Everybody knows it's mine anyway.

Come on, Quincy Nell.

No. It goes in our apartment.

Quincy Nell, there ain't any apartment. I live in a house trailer, remember. Get it through your head. And I believe I'll go to the law myself. I'll get a paper says that air conditioner's mine and I'll have a deputy sheriff to help me unload it, too.

Then go on and do it, she said.

After he left she unlocked the door. She knelt in the door looking at the air conditioner. She could feel her swelling stomach pressing against her thighs. The thing sat on stacked bricks. It was no longer an air conditioner, and hadn't been for some time. It was pale lime-green walls and yellow chintz curtains, a baby in a highchair saying Daddy for the first time and her telling Bonedaddy about it the minute he came through the door. She began to cry, for all that was lost, for all that had never been.

THE JADE-GREEN station wagon stopped in the driveway and a man got out and opened the rear door. He was a tall thin man in baggy twill pants and a T-shirt and he had thin black hair combed to cover a bald spot. He was grinning at her. He looked vaguely familiar and by the time he was halfway to the doorstep she had recognized him.

How stupid do they think I am? she asked herself.

He was at the foot of the doorstep. He took out a bright red bandanna and mopped his face with it.

You the little lady got the air conditioner I heard about on the radio? Sure is fine weather for one.

Yeah. I called it in on Tradetime. It's a hundred and twenty-five dollars.

Well, that's fine, that's fine, the man said. He appeared nervous.

Say don't I know you? Aren't you Bonedaddy Bowers's brother that lives over at Coble?

Well, yeah, that's me all right. But I wanted the air conditioner for me, not him.

Whoever it's for it's a hundred and twenty-five dollars.

Well what I was thinking see I don't even know if it works. I was planning on taking it and making sure everything was all right then bringing you back the money. I know your daddy.

She was shaking her head. I'm sorry, she said. It don't leave here till the money's in my hand. If it don't work you can bring it back. It's guaranteed.

He stood twisting the handkerchief in his hands.

You can tell Bonedaddy I wasn't born yesterday, she said. I didn't just fall off some hay truck that was passing through town.

Yes ma'am, Bonedaddy's brother said.

IT WAS THREE DAYS later when Clarence called. Clarence lived a quarter mile or so below Quincy Nell in a doublewide house trailer with his momma.

I got it sold, he said.

What?

I been hearing you every day on Tradetime. There's a friend of mine down here, Cecil, he's got the money in his pocket and he wants that air conditioner.

Send him up here then.

I can't. Cecil won't come. Bonedaddy whipped him a week or

two ago over something and he's afraid Bonedaddy'll catch him hauling off that air conditioner.

This is the last place he's likely to see Bonedaddy. He's more likely to be at your house than mine.

He's pissed at me. He got mad at me cause I said he was running over you.

I can't load it by myself anyway, she said.

That's no problem. I'll run up there and help you.

When they had loaded the air conditioner into the Gremlin the shed looked curiously empty. She left the door standing ajar and it held only shadows.

Clarence laid a hand on her arm. Me and you ought to get together one of these nights, he said.

No. Me and Bonedaddy'll probably get back together.

I don't think so. You want to know what he said?

No, she said. She leaned against the side of the Gremlin and wiped the sweat out of her eyes with a sleeve. All right. What did he say?

He said you was a free agent. He said he reckoned you was anybody's dog wanted to go hunting.

No he never.

He damn sure did.

He's a liar then.

The driveway curved downhill and she followed Clarence's truck. Where the driveway came out onto the county road there was an old abandoned farmhouse set in the corner with a yardful of pecan trees and here Clarence stopped in the middle of the road. She braked and sat in momentary confusion. Clarence's truck must have died. She could hear a flat popping sound.

She turned to look. The yard was grown up knee-high with grass and there were old cast-off car parts and machinery jutting out of it. Bonedaddy was standing under one of the pecan trees looking up. He was wearing frayed denim cutoffs and no shirt and his hair was tied back in a ponytail and he was burned dark by the sun. He had a little chrome-plated pistol and he was shooting pecans off the tree branches with it.

Quincy Nell had a queasy feeling in the pit of her stomach. She thought she might throw up, or perhaps faint. She got out of the car without cutting the switch. Clarence had gotten out of his truck too and stood there grinning sheepishly into the sun. He looked ashamed, but not much.

Hey baby, Bonedaddy said. What you got in there? Why, I do believe it's that new air conditioner I ordered.

He came across the grassy yard grinning at her. His teeth were white against the dark flesh of his face. He had swung out the cylinder of the revolver and he was feeding copper-colored cartridges into it as he came. He was wearing sunglasses, the mirrored kind that turned the world back at you and she could see herself twinned in them.

Clarence told me what you said about me.

What I said? Who knows what that might be. Clarence is a terrible liar. Ain't you Clarence?

I lie all the time, Clarence agreed.

I hope you kill somebody with that thing and they send you to the penitentiary, Quincy Nell said. I hope they send you to the electric chair.

Boy the cold wind'll blow on me tonight, he said. I feel a cold front approaching already.

Don't even think about taking that air conditioner.

Clarence, help me load it.

Clarence was looking at Quincy Nell. No, he said almost inaudibly.

Do what?

I ain't touchin it, Clarence said.

Bonedaddy studied him for a moment. He laid the pistol on the tailgate of Clarence's truck. Suit yourself then. I'll load it my damn self.

He strode to the rear of the Gremlin. He fastened a hand to either side and gave a mighty heave and the air conditioner came free and he turned tottering under its unexpected weight and grinning foolishly. When he came around in the road Quincy Nell was standing against the tailgate of Clarence's truck pointing the little chrome-plated pistol at him. She was standing feet apart and arms extended straight out holding the pistol both-handed and staring down its barrel.

Put it back in my car, she said.

He stood with his jaw dropped and the thing clasped in front of him like some curious and inadequate offering he was making.

You stupid cunt, he finally said.

Quincy Nell could see herself in the sunglasses. She could feel the hard hot edge of the tailgate against the flesh of her upper thighs.

Clarence had started to run. He ran silent and intent, like a quarterback who sees an opening and takes it, across the grass-grown yard and into the sedge leaping a cast-off turning plow and disappearing into a thin spinney of cypress. The first shot whanged off the steel case of the air conditioner and shattered the point of Bonedaddy's collarbone. It exploded in a fine pink mist and he dropped the air conditioner on his feet. The corner of the case struck his shin just below the knee and cut a long curving welt in his leg. He looked as if he was struggling to pick up the air conditioner. She shot him just below the left nipple and a tiny blue hole appeared, another, another, little pocks in the dark flesh where blood slowly welled black and viscous as tar and tracked down his rib cage. He sat in the road hugging the air conditioner. She lowered the gun. She stepped toward him and sat in the dusty road. His eyes were closed. She clasped the pistol loosely in her right hand and with her left forefinger traced the pale line of scar tissue down his cheek.

Up the road at the doublewide Clarence's mother came out to see what in the world was going on. She shaded her eyes with a hand and peered down the road. Then she went back in and the door slapped hard behind her.

Quincy Nell sat in the dust, her legs folded under her. The back of her right hand lay in the roadbed, the little pistol resting on her palm. She could hear the Gremlin idling. She guessed she'd just have to sit here until someone came along who knew what to do about all this.

The Paperhanger

THE VANISHING of the doctor's wife's child in broad daylight was an event so cataclysmic that it forever divided time into the then and the now, the before and the after. In later years, fortified with a pitcher of silica-dry vodka martinis, she had cause to replay the events preceding the disappearance. They were tawdry and banal but in retrospect freighted with menace, a foreshadowing of what was to come, like a footman or a fool preceding a king into a room.

She had been quarreling with the paperhanger. Her four-year-old daughter, Zeineb, was standing directly behind the paperhanger where he knelt smoothing air bubbles out with a wide plastic trowel. Zeineb had her fingers in the paperhanger's hair. The paperhanger's hair was shoulder length and the color of flax and the child was delighted with it. The paperhanger was accustomed to her doing this and he did not even turn around. He just went on with his work. His arms were smooth and brown and corded with muscle and in the light that fell upon the paperhanger through stained-glass panels the doctor's wife could see that they were lightly downed with fine golden hair. She studied these arms bemusedly while she formulated her thoughts.

You tell me so much a roll, she said. The doctor's wife was from Pakistan and her speech was still heavily accented. I do not know single-bolt rolls and double-bolt rolls. You tell me double-bolt price but you are installing single-bolt rolls. My friend has told me. It is cost me perhaps twice as much.

The paperhanger, still on his knees, turned. He smiled up at her. He had pale blue eyes. I did tell you so much a roll, he said. You bought the rolls.

The child, not yet vanished, was watching the paperhanger's eyes. She was a scaled-down clone of the mother, the mother viewed through the wrong end of a telescope, and the paperhanger suspected that as she grew neither her features nor her expression would alter, she would just grow larger, like something being aired up with a hand pump.

And you are leave lumps, the doctor's wife said, gesturing at the wall.

I do not leave lumps, the paperhanger said. You've seen my work before. These are not lumps. The paper is wet. The paste is wet. Everything will shrink down and flatten out. He smiled again. He had clean even teeth. And besides, he said, I gave you my special cockteaser rate. I don't know what you're complaining about.

Her mouth worked convulsively. She looked for a moment as if he'd slapped her. When words did come they came in a fine spray of spit. You are trash, she said. You are scum.

Hands on knees, he was pushing erect, the girl's dark fingers trailing out of his hair. Don't call me trash, he said, as if it were perfectly all right to call him scum, but he was already talking to

her back. She had whirled on her heels and went twisting her hips
through an arched doorway into the cathedraled living room. The
paperhanger looked down at the child. Her face glowed with a
strange constrained glee, as if she and the paperhanger shared
some secret the rest of the world hadn't caught on to yet.

In the living room the builder was supervising the installation
of a chandelier that depended from the vaulted ceiling by a long
golden chain. The builder was a short bearded man dancing about,
showing her the features of the chandelier, smiling obsequiously.
She gave him a flat angry look. She waved a dismissive hand toward
the ceiling. Whatever, she said.

She went out the front door onto the porch and down a
makeshift walkway of two-by-tens into the front yard where her
car was parked. The car was a silver-gray Mercedes her husband
had given her for their anniversary. When she cranked the engine
its idle was scarcely perceptible.

She powered down the window. Zeineb, she called. Across the
razed earth of the unlandscaped yard a man in a grease-stained T-
shirt was booming down the chains securing a backhoe to a lowboy hooked to a gravel truck. The sun was low in the west and
bloodred behind this tableau and man and tractor looked flat and
dimensionless as something decorative stamped from tin. She
blew the horn. The man turned, raised an arm as if she'd signaled
him.

Zeineb, she called again.

She got out of the car and started impatiently up the walkway.
Behind her the gravel truck started, and truck and backhoe pulled
out of the drive and down toward the road.

The paperhanger was stowing away his T square and trowels
in his wooden toolbox. Where is Zeineb? the doctor's wife asked.
She followed you out, the paperhanger told her. He glanced about,

as if the girl might be hiding somewhere. There was nowhere to hide.

Where is my child? she asked the builder. The electrician climbed down from the ladder. The paperhanger came out of the bathroom with his tools. The builder was looking all around. His elfin features were touched with chagrin, as if this missing child were just something else he was going to be held accountable for.

Likely she's hiding in a closet, the paperhanger said. Playing a trick on you.

Zeineb does not play tricks, the doctor's wife said. Her eyes kept darting about the huge room, the shadows that lurked in corners. There was already an undercurrent of panic in her voice and all her poise and self-confidence seemed to have vanished with the child.

The paperhanger set down his toolbox and went through the house, opening and closing doors. It was a huge house and there were a lot of closets. There was no child in any of them.

The electrician was searching upstairs. The builder had gone through the French doors that opened onto the unfinished veranda and was peering into the backyard. The backyard was a maze of convoluted ditch excavated for the septic tank field line and beyond that there was just woods. She's playing in that ditch, the builder said, going down the flagstone steps.

She wasn't, though. She wasn't anywhere. They searched the house and grounds. They moved with jerky haste. They kept glancing toward the woods where the day was waning first. The builder kept shaking his head. She's got to be *somewhere,* he said.

Call someone, the doctor's wife said. Call the police.

It's a little early for the police, the builder said. She's got to be here.

You call them anyway. I have a phone in my car. I will call my husband.

While she called, the paperhanger and the electrician continued to search. They had looked everywhere and were forced to
search places they'd already looked. If this ain't the goddamnedest
thing I ever saw, the electrician said.

The doctor's wife got out of the Mercedes and slammed the
door. Suddenly she stopped and clasped a hand to her forehead.
She screamed. The man with the tractor, she cried. Somehow my
child is gone with the tractor man.

Oh Jesus, the builder said. What have we got ourselves into
here.

THE HIGH SHERIFF that year was a ruminative man named Bellwether. He stood beside the county cruiser talking to the paperhanger while deputies ranged the grounds. Other men were inside
looking in places that had already been searched numberless
times. Bellwether had been in the woods and he was picking
cockleburs off his khakis and out of his socks. He was watching
the woods, where dark was gathering and seeping across the field
like a stain.

I've got to get men out here, Bellwether said. A lot of men and
a lot of lights. We're going to have to search every inch of these
woods.

You'll play hell doing it, the paperhanger said. These woods
stretch all the way to Lawrence County. This is the edge of the
Harrikin. Down in there's where all those old mines used to be.
Allens Creek.

I don't give a shit if they stretch all the way to Fairbanks,
Alaska, Bellwether said. They've got to be searched. It'll just take
a lot of men.

The raw earth yard was full of cars. Dr. Jamahl had come in a sleek black Lexus. He berated his wife. Why weren't you watching her? he asked. Unlike his wife's, the doctor's speech was impeccable. She covered her face with her palms and wept. The doctor still wore his green surgeon's smock and it was flecked with bright dots of blood as a butcher's smock might be.

I need to feed a few cows, the paperhanger said. I'll feed my stock pretty quick and come back and help hunt.

You don't mind if I look in your truck, do you?

Do what?

I've got to cover my ass. If that little girl don't turn up damn quick this is going to be over my head. TBI, FBI, network news. I've got to eliminate everything.

Eliminate away, the paperhanger said.

The sheriff searched the floorboard of the paperhanger's pickup truck. He shined his huge flashlight under the seat and felt behind it with his hands.

I had to look, he said apologetically.

Of course you did, the paperhanger said.

FULL DARK HAD FALLEN before he returned. He had fed his cattle and stowed away his tools and picked up a six-pack of San Miguel beer and he sat in the back of the pickup truck drinking it. The paperhanger had been in the Navy and stationed in the Philippines and San Miguel was the only beer he could drink. He had to go out of town to buy it, but he figured it was worth it. He liked the exotic labels, the dark bitter taste on the back of his tongue, the way the chilled bottles felt held against his forehead.

A motley crowd of curiosity seekers and searchers thronged the yard. There was a vaguely festive air. He watched all this with a dispassionate eye, as if he were charged with grading the participants, comparing this with other spectacles he'd seen. Coffee urns had been brought in and set up on tables, sandwiches prepared and handed out to the weary searchers. A crane had been hauled in and the septic tank reclaimed from the ground. It swayed from a taut cable while men with lights searched the impacted earth beneath it for a child, for the very trace of a child. Through the far dark woods lights crossed and recrossed, darted to and fro like fireflies. The doctor and the doctor's wife sat in folding camp chairs looking drained, stunned, waiting for their child to be delivered into their arms.

The doctor was a short portly man with a benevolent expression. He had a moon-shaped face, with light and dark areas of skin that looked swirled, as if the pigment coloring him had not been properly mixed. He had been educated at Princeton. When he had established his practice he had returned to Pakistan to find a wife befitting his station. The woman he had selected had been chosen on the basis of her beauty. In retrospect, perhaps more consideration should have been given to other qualities. She was still beautiful but he was thinking that certain faults might outweigh this. She seemed to have trouble keeping up with her children. She could lose a four-year-old child in a room no larger than six hundred square feet and she could not find it again.

The paperhanger drained his bottle and set it by his foot in the bed of the truck. He studied the doctor's wife's ravaged face through the deep blue light. The first time he had seen her she had hired him to paint a bedroom in the house they were living in while the doctor's mansion was being built. There was an arrogance about her that cried out to be taken down a notch or two. She flirted with him, backed away, flirted again. She would treat him as if he were a stain on the bathroom rug and then stand close by him while he worked until he was dizzy with the smell of her, with the heat that seemed to radiate off her body. She stood by him while he knelt painting baseboards and after an infinite moment leaned carefully the weight of a thigh against his shoulder. You'd better move it, he thought. She didn't. He laughed and turned his face into her groin. She gave a strangled cry and slapped him hard. The paintbrush flew away and speckled the dark rose walls with antique white. You filthy beast, she said. You are some kind of monster. She stormed out of the room and he could hear her slamming doors behind her.

Well, I was looking for a job when I found this one. He smiled philosophically to himself.

But he had not been fired. In fact now he had been hired again. Perhaps there was something here to ponder.

At midnight he gave up his vigil. Some souls more hardy than his kept up the watch. The earth here was worn smooth by the useless traffic of the searchers. Driving out, he met a line of pickup trucks with civil defense tags. Grim-faced men sat aligned in their beds. Some clutched rifles loosely by their barrels, as if they would lay to waste whatever monster, man or beast, would snatch up a child in its slaverous jaws and vanish, prey and predator, in the space between two heartbeats.

Even more dubious reminders of civilization as these fell away. He drove into the Harrikin, where he lived. A world so dark and forlorn light itself seemed at a premium. Whippoorwills swept red-eyed up from the roadside. Old abandoned foundries and furnaces rolled past, grim and dark as forsaken prisons. Down a ridge here was an abandoned graveyard, if you knew where to look. The paperhanger did. He had dug up a few of the graves, examined with curiosity what remained, buttons, belt buckles, a cameo brooch. The bones he laid out like a child with a Tinkertoy, arranging them the way they went in jury-rigged resurrection.

He braked hard on a curve, the truck slewing in the gravel. A bobcat had crossed the road, graceful as a wraith, fierce and lantern-eyed in the headlights, gone so swiftly it might have been a stage prop swung across the road on wires.

BELLWETHER AND A DEPUTY drove to the backhoe operator's house. He lived up a gravel road that wound through a great stand of cedars. He lived in a board-and-batten house with a tin roof rusted to a warm umber. They parked before it and got out, adjusting their gun belts.

Bellwether had a search warrant with the ink scarcely dry. The operator was outraged.

Look at it this way, Bellwether explained patiently. I've got to cover my ass. Everything has got to be considered. You know how kids are. Never thinking. What if she run under the wheels of your truck when you was backing out? What if quicklike you put the body in your truck to get rid of somewhere?

What if quicklike you get the hell off my property, the operator said.

Everything has to be considered, the sheriff said again. Nobody's accusing anybody of anything just yet.

The operator's wife stood glowering at them. To have something to do with his hands, the operator began to construct a cigarette. He had huge red hands thickly sown with brown freckles. They trembled. I ain't got a thing in this round world to hide, he said.

Bellwether and his men searched everywhere they could think of to look. Finally they stood uncertainly in the operator's yard, out of place in their neat khakis, their polished leather.

Now get the hell off my land, the operator said. If all you

think of me is that I could run over a little kid and then throw it off in the bushes like a dead cat or something then I don't even want to see your goddamn face. I want you gone and I want you by God gone now.

Everything had to be considered, the sheriff said.

Then maybe you need to consider that paperhanger.

What about him?

That paperhanger is one sick puppy.

He was still there when I got there, the sheriff said. Three witnesses swore nobody ever left, not even for a minute, and one of them was the child's mother. I searched his truck myself.

Then he's a sick puppy with a damn good alibi, the operator said.

THAT WAS ALL. There was no ransom note, no child that turned up two counties over with amnesia. She was a page turned, a door closed, a lost ball in the high weeds. She was a child no larger than a doll, but the void she left behind her was unreckonable. Yet there was no end to it. No finality. There was no moment when someone could say, turning from a mounded grave, Well, this has been unbearable, but you've got to go on with your life. Life did not go on.

At the doctor's wife's insistence an intensive investigation was focused on the backhoe operator. Forensic experts from the FBI examined every millimeter of the gravel truck, paying special attention to its wheels. They were examined with every modern crime-fighting device the government possessed, and there was not a microscopic particle of tissue or blood, no telltale chip of fingernail, no hair ribbon.

Work ceased on the mansion. Some subcontractors were discharged outright, while others simply drifted away. There was no one to care if the work was done, no one to pay them. The half-finished veranda's raw wood grayed in the fall, then winter, rains. The ditches were left fallow and uncovered and half filled with water. Kudzu crept from the woods. The hollyhocks and oleanders the doctor's wife had planted grew entangled and rampant. The imported windows were stoned by double-dared boys who whirled and fled. Already this house where a child had vanished was acquiring an unhealthy, diseased reputation.

The doctor and his wife sat entombed in separate prisons replaying real and imagined grievances. The doctor felt that his wife's neglect had sent his child into the abstract. The doctor's wife drank vodka martinis and watched talk shows where passed an endless procession of vengeful people who had not had children vanish, and felt, perhaps rightly, that the fates had dealt her from the bottom of the deck, and she prayed with intensity for a miracle.

Then one day she was just gone. The Mercedes and part of her clothing and personal possessions were gone too. He idly wondered where she was, but he did not search for her.

Sitting in his armchair cradling a great marmalade cat and a bottle of J&B and observing with bemused detachment the gradations of light at the window, the doctor remembered studying literature at Princeton. He had particular cause to reconsider the poetry of William Butler Yeats. For how surely things fell apart, how surely the center did not hold.

His practice fell into a ruin. His colleagues made sympathetic allowances for him at first, but there are limits to these things. He made erroneous diagnoses, prescribed the wrong medicines not once or twice but as a matter of course.

Just as there is a deepening progression to misfortune, so too there is a point beyond which things can only get worse. They did. A middle-aged woman he was operating on died.

He had made an incision to remove a ruptured appendix and the incised flesh was clamped aside while he made ready to slice it out. It was not there. He stared in drunken disbelief. He began to search under things, organs, intestines, a rising tide of blood. The appendix was not there. It had gone into the abstract, atrophied, been removed twenty-five years before, he had sliced through the selfsame scar. He was rummaging through her abdominal cavity like an irritated man fumbling through a drawer for a clean pair of socks, finally bellowing and wringing his hands in bloody vexation while nurses began to cry out, another surgeon was brought on the run as a closer, and he was carried from the operating room.

Came then days of sitting in the armchair while he was besieged by contingency lawyers, action news teams, a long line of process servers. There was nothing he could do. It was out of his hands and into the hands of the people who are paid to do these things. He sat cradling the bottle of J&B with the marmalade cat snuggled against his portly midriff. He would study the window, where the light drained away in a process he no longer had an understanding of, and sip the scotch and every now and then stroke the cat's head gently. The cat purred against his breast as reassuringly as the hum of an air conditioner.

He left in the middle of the night. He began to load his possessions into the Lexus. At first he chose items with a great degree of consideration. The first thing he loaded was a set of custom-made monogrammed golf clubs. Then his stereo receiver, Denon AC3, $1,750. A copy of *This Side of Paradise* autographed by Fitzgerald that he had bought as an investment. By the time the Lexus was half full he was just grabbing things at random and stuffing them into the backseat, a half-eaten pizza, half a case of cat food, a single brocade house shoe.

He drove west past the hospital, the country club, the city-limit sign. He was thinking no thoughts at all, and all the destination he had was the amount of highway the headlights showed him.

IN THE SLOW RAINS of late fall the doctor's wife returned to the unfinished mansion. She used to sit in a camp chair on the ruined veranda and drink chilled martinis she poured from the pitcher she carried in a foam ice chest. Dark fell early these November days. Rain crows husbanding some far cornfield called through the smoky autumn air. The sound was fiercely evocative, reminding her of something but she could not have said what.

She went into the room where she had lost the child. The light was failing. The high corners of the room were in deepening shadow but she could see the nests of dirt daubers clustered on the rich flocked wallpaper, a spider swing from a chandelier on a strand of spun glass. Some animal's dried blackened stool curled like a slug against the baseboards. The silence in the room was enormous.

One day she arrived and was surprised to find the paperhanger there. He was sitting on a yellow four-wheeler drinking a bottle of beer. He made to go when he saw her but she waved him back. Stay and talk with me, she said.

The paperhanger was much changed. His pale locks had been shorn away in a makeshift haircut as if scissored in the dark or by a blind barber and his cheeks were covered with a soft curly beard.

You have grown a beard.

Yes.

You are strange with it.

The paperhanger sipped from his San Miguel. He smiled. I was strange without it, he said. He arose from the four-wheeler and came over and sat on the flagstone steps. He stared across the mutilated yard toward the treeline. The yard was like a funhouse maze seen from above, its twistings and turnings bereft of mystery.

You are working somewhere now?

No. I don't take so many jobs anymore. There's only me, and I don't need much. What has become of the doctor?

She shrugged. Many things have change, she said. He has gone. The banks have foreclose. What is that you ride?

An ATV. A four-wheeler.

It goes well in the woods?

It was made for that.

You could take me in the woods. How much would you charge me?

For what?

To go in the woods. You could drive me. I will pay you.

Why?

To search for my child's body.

I wouldn't charge anybody anything to search for a child's body, the paperhanger said. But she's not in these woods. Nothing could have stayed hidden, the way these woods were searched.

Sometimes I think she just kept walking. Perhaps just walking away from the men looking. Far into the woods.

Into the woods, the paperhanger thought. If she had just kept walking in a straight line with no time out for eating or sleeping, where would she be? Kentucky, Algiers, who knew.

I'll take you when the rains stop, he said. But we won't find a child.

The doctor's wife shook her head. It is a mystery, she said. She drank from her cocktail glass. Where could she have gone? How could she have gone?

There was a man named David Lang, the paperhanger said. Up in Gallatin, back in the late 1800s. He was crossing a barn lot in full view of his wife and two children and he just vanished. Went into thin air. There was a judge in a wagon turning into the yard and he saw it too. It was just like he took a step in this world and his foot came down in another one. He was never seen again.

She gave him a sad smile, bitter and one-cornered. You make fun with me.

No. It's true. I have it in a book. I'll show you.

I have a book with dragons, fairies. A book where Hobbits live in the middle earth. They are lies. I think most books are lies. Perhaps all books. I have prayed for a miracle but I am not worthy of one. I have prayed for her to come from the dead, then just to find her body. That would be a miracle to me. There are no miracles.

She rose unsteadily, swayed slightly, leaning to take up the cooler. The paperhanger watched her. I have to go now, she said. When the rains stop we will search.

Can you drive?

Of course I can drive. I have drive out here.

I mean are you capable of driving now. You seem a little drunk.

I drink to forget but it is not enough, she said. I can drive.

After a while he heard her leave in the Mercedes, the tires spinning in the gravel drive. He lit a cigarette. He sat smoking it, watching the rain string off the roof. He seemed to be waiting for something. Dusk was falling like a shroud, the world going dark and formless the way it had begun. He drank the last of the beer, sat holding the bottle, the foam bitter in the back of his mouth. A chill touched him. He felt something watching him. He turned.

From the corner of the ruined veranda a child was watching him.
He stood up. He heard the beer bottle break on the flagstones. The
child went sprinting past the hollyhocks toward the brush at the
edge of the yard, a tiny sepia child with an intent sloe-eyed face,
real as she had ever been, translucent as winter light through dirty
glass.

THE DOCTOR'S WIFE'S HANDS were laced loosely about his
waist as they came down through a thin stand of sassafras, edging
over the ridge where the ghost of a road was, a road more sensed
than seen that faced into a half acre of tilting stones and fading
granite tablets. Other graves marked only by their declivities in
the earth, folk so far beyond the pale even the legibility of their
identities had been leached away by the weathers.

Leaves drifted, huge poplar leaves veined with amber so
golden they might have been coin of the realm for a finer world
than this one. He cut the ignition of the four-wheeler and got off.
Past the lowering trees the sky was a blue of an improbable intensity, a fierce cobalt blue shot through with dense golden light.

She slid off the rear and steadied herself a moment with a hand
on his arm. Where are we? she asked. Why are we here?

The paperhanger had disengaged his arm and was strolling
among the gravestones reading such inscriptions as were legible,
as if he might find forebear or antecedent in this moldering earth.
The doctor's wife was retrieving her martinis from the luggage
carrier of the ATV. She stood looking about uncertainly. A graven
angel with broken wings crouched on a truncated marble column
like a gargoyle. Its stone eyes regarded her with a blind benignity.
Some of these graves have been rob, she said.

You can't rob the dead, he said. They have nothing left to steal.

It is a sacrilege, she said. It is forbidden to disturb the dead. You have done this.

The paperhanger took a cigarette pack from his pocket and felt it, but it was empty, and he balled it up and threw it away. The line between grave robbing and archaeology has always looked a little blurry to me, he said. I was studying their culture, trying to get a fix on what their lives were like.

She was watching him with a kind of benumbed horror. Standing hip-slung and lost like a parody of her former self. Strange and anomalous in her fashionable but mismatched clothing, as if she'd put on the first garment that fell to hand. Someday, he thought, she might rise and wander out into the daylit world wearing nothing at all, the way she had come into it. With her diamond watch and the cocktail glass she carried like a used-up talisman.

You have broken the law, she told him.

I got a government grant, the paperhanger said contemptuously.

Why are we here? We are supposed to be searching for my child.

If you're looking for a body the first place to look is the graveyard, he said. If you want a book don't you go to the library?

I am paying you, she said. You are in my employ. I do not want to be here. I want you to do as I say or carry me to my car if you will not.

Actually, the paperhanger said, I had a story to tell you. About my wife.

He paused, as if leaving a space for her comment, but when she made none he went on. I had a wife. My childhood sweetheart. She became a nurse, went to work in one of these drug rehab places. After she was there awhile she got a faraway look in her eyes. Look at me without seeing me. She got in tight with her supervisor. They started having meetings to go to. Conferences. Sometimes just the two of them would confer, generally in a motel. The night I watched them walk into the Holiday Inn in Franklin I decided to kill her. No impetuous spur-of-the-moment thing. I thought it all out and it would be the perfect crime.

The doctor's wife didn't say anything. She just watched him.

A grave is the best place to dispose of a body, the paperhanger said. The grave is its normal destination anyway. I could dig up a grave and then just keep on digging. Save everything carefully. Put my body there and fill in part of the earth, and then restore everything the way it was. The coffin, if any of it was left. The bones and such. A good settling rain and the fall leaves and you're home free. Now that's eternity for you.

Did you kill someone, she breathed. Her voice was barely audible.

Did I or did I not, he said. You decide. You have the powers of a god. You can make me a murderer or just a heartbroke guy whose wife quit him. What do you think? Anyway, I don't have a wife. I expect she just walked off into the abstract like that Lang guy I told you about.

I want to go, she said. I want to go where my car is.

He was sitting on a gravestone watching her out of his pale eyes. He might not have heard.

I will walk.

Just whatever suits you, the paperhanger said. Abruptly, he was standing in front of her. She had not seen him arise from the headstone or stride across the graves, but like a jerky splice in a film he was before her, a hand cupping each of her breasts, staring down into her face.

Under the merciless weight of the sun her face was stunned

and vacuous. He studied it intently, missing no detail. Fine wrinkles crept from the corners of her eyes and mouth like hairline cracks in porcelain. Grime was impacted in her pores, in the crepe flesh of her throat. How surely everything had fallen from her: beauty, wealth, social position, arrogance. Humanity itself, for by now she seemed scarcely human, beleaguered so by the fates that she suffered his hands on her breasts as just one more cross to bear, one more indignity to endure.

How far you've come, the paperhanger said in wonder. I believe you're about down to my level now, don't you?

It does not matter, the doctor's wife said. There is no longer one thing that matters.

Slowly and with enormous lassitude her body slumped toward him, and in his exultance it seemed not a motion in itself but simply the completion of one begun long ago with the fateful weight of a thigh, a motion that began in one world and completed itself in another one.

From what seemed a great distance he watched her fall toward him like an angel descending, wings spread, from an infinite height, striking the earth gently, tilting, then righting itself.

THE WEIGHT OF MOONLIGHT tracking across the paperhanger's face awoke him from where he took his rest. Filigrees of light through the gauzy curtains swept across him in stately silence like the translucent ghosts of insects. He stirred, lay still then for a moment getting his bearings, a fix on where he was.

He was in his bed, lying on his back. He could see a huge orange moon poised beyond the bedroom window, ink-sketch tree branches that raked its face like claws. He could see his feet bookending the San Miguel bottle that his hands clasped erect on his abdomen, the amber bottle hard-edged and defined against the pale window, dark atavistic monolith reared against a harvest moon.

He could smell her. A musk compounded of stale sweat and alcohol, the rank smell of her sex. Dissolution, ruin, loss. He turned to study her where she lay asleep, her open mouth a dark cavity in her face. She was naked, legs outflung, pale breasts pooled like cooling wax. She stirred restively, groaned in her sleep. He could hear the rasp of her breathing. Her breath was fetid on his face, corrupt, a graveyard smell. He watched her in disgust, in a dull self-loathing.

He drank from the bottle, lowered it. Sometimes, he told her sleeping face, you do things you can't undo. You break things you just can't fix. Before you mean to, before you know you've done it. And you were right, there are things only a miracle can set to rights.

He sat clasping the bottle. He touched his miscut hair, the soft down of his beard. He had forgotten what he looked like, he hadn't seen his reflection in a mirror for so long. Unbidden, Zeineb's face swam into his memory. He remembered the look on the child's face when the doctor's wife had spun on her heel: spite had crossed it like a flicker of heat lightning. She stuck her tongue out at him. His hand snaked out like a serpent and closed on her throat and snapped her neck before he could call it back, sloe eyes wild and wide, pink tongue caught between tiny seed-pearl teeth like a bitten-off rosebud. Her hair swung sidewise, her head lolled onto his clasped hand. The tray of the toolbox was out before he knew it, he was stuffing her into the toolbox like a rag doll. So small, so small, hardly there at all.

He arose. Silhouetted naked against the moon-drenched window, he drained the bottle. He looked about for a place to set it, leaned and wedged it between the heavy flesh of her upper thighs. He stood in silence, watching her. He seemed philosophical, possessed of some hard-won wisdom. The paperhanger knew so well that while few are deserving of a miracle, fewer still can make one come to pass.

He went out of the room. Doors opened, doors closed. Footsteps softly climbing a staircase, descending. She dreamed on. When he came back into the room he was cradling a plastic-wrapped bundle stiffly in his arms. He placed it gently beside the drunk woman. He folded the plastic sheeting back like a caul.

What had been a child. What the graveyard earth had spared the freezer had preserved. Ice crystals snared in the hair like windy snowflakes whirled there, in the lashes. A doll from a madhouse assembly line.

He took her arm, laid it across the child. She pulled away from the cold. He firmly brought the arm back, arranging them like mannequins, madonna and child. He studied this tableau, then went out of his house for the last time. The door closed gently behind him on its keeper spring.

The paperhanger left in the Mercedes, heading west into the open country, tracking into wide-open territories he could infect like a malignant spore. Without knowing it, he followed the self-same route the doctor had taken some eight months earlier, and in a world of infinite possibilities where all journeys share a common end, perhaps they are together, taking the evening air on a ruined veranda among the hollyhocks and oleanders, the doctor sipping his scotch and the paperhanger his San Miguel, gentlemen of leisure discussing the vagaries of life and pondering deep into the night not just the possibility but the inevitability of miracles.

The Man Who Knew Dylan

*H*E WOKE IN a yellow room. Yellow walls, a print of van Gogh's saffron sunflowers, pale winter light through the window. For a moment he didn't know where he was, but Crosswaithe had woken in far stranger places than this one, and soon everything clicked into focus: the hissing and sighing that was keeping the woman in the bed across the room alive or what passed for it, the sallow husk of the woman herself, a foam cup half full of cold coffee on the table beside his chair.

He drank the coffee and sat watching the still form beneath the folded coverlet. He set the cup aside and wiped a hand across the sandpaper stubble on his face and stood up. He approached the bed and stood looking down at the woman. What had been a woman. The skin was pulled tightly over the delicate framework of bones. The eyes were closed and the lids were bluely translucent like those of hatchling birds. He tried to feel pain, pity. If he felt anything at all it was a sort of detached interest in the way she seemed to be receding from sight. Everything was sliding from her, and nothing was coming back. Nothing mattered. No one expected her to do anything at all and whatever was going to happen was going to happen no matter what she did or if she did nothing whatever. The machine breathed on, breathed on.

He went out of the room and softly closed the door behind him. He went down a waxed tile hallway past the nurses' station and out into the early December day. He lit a cigarette and walked two blocks down Main Street then turned right and went four down Maple to a long low building with a huge Plexiglas sign that said PETTIGREW MAGNAVOX. He unlocked the door and went in clicking on lights and walked on past long lines of sofas and easy chairs and silent flickering television sets.

In the office he put on a pot of coffee and stood before it with a cup in his hand waiting for the trickle to start and when it did he moved the pot aside and placed his cup beneath the stream. When it filled he replaced the pot and went with the cup to a desk and sat drinking the coffee and idly reading yesterday's newspaper. After a while he looked at his watch and went into the bathroom and took from beneath the lavatory a shaving kit. He lathered his face and shaved, the face looking back at him hollow-eyed and angular and somehow sinister, like a nighttime predator's face peering at him through a backlit window.

At five minutes before eight Crosswaithe's erstwhile brother-in-law arrived. J. C. Pettigrew was a heavyset jowly man wearing a tan tweed topcoat and a golfing cap. He hung up coat and cap then took a folded document from the topcoat pocket. He unfolded it and slapped it hard onto the desk before Crosswaithe.

You've got a little run this morning, he said. He waited for Crosswaithe to look at the paper.

Crosswaithe went on drinking coffee and he didn't look. What is it? he finally asked.

The bank sent this note back. You've got to go to the Harrikin and pick up that projection TV you sold that old son of a bitch with the hole in his throat. I told you that son of a bitch was no good.

He seemed all right.

You felt sorry for him because he had that hole in his throat and that damned microphone he held to it when he talked. Buzz, buzz, buzz. You sold a two-thousand-dollar television set to a man just because he had a hole in his throat.

You told me to use my own judgment.

I also told you he was a bootlegger and a dopegrower and he was no good. You assured me you'd work the note. It's four months behind and not worked and the bank's kicked it back. I don't know whether it was the old man or that daughter of his that kept sidling around and showing you her black drawers. But whichever it was I want my TV.

Crosswaithe drained his cup and stood up. I'll get your TV, he said. He folded the note and shoved it into his hip pocket.

You look like hell, Pettigrew said. What'd you do, stay out all night? Was you by the hospital? How's Claire?

Crosswaithe shrugged. How she always is, he said. He was putting on his coat. Pettigrew was watching him. Pettigrew had tiny piglike eyes that were not liking what they were seeing. I don't doubt you give her some disease that you picked up somewhere, he said. You only married her for what little money Daddy had. It's a crying shame she didn't divorce you before you run through it.

One of these days the time is going to come when I have to stomp your ass, Crosswaithe said. It's just inevitable. I won't be able to help myself. It may not be today and it may not be tomorrow but it's going to come. You're going to get sideways with me some morning before I've had all my coffee and I'm going to kick hell out of you. What do you think about that?

Pettigrew had taken a step or two back. You're only here because of Claire, he said. Now get on the move. Get there and get back, the weatherman's talking about snow.

CROSSWAITHE DROVE the company pickup truck into the far southern part of the county. A waste of a country ravaged and scarred by open-pit mines and virtually abandoned, leftover remnants of landscape, the tailings of a world no one would have. At a beer joint called Big Mama's he stopped and asked directions and set out again. He drove on and on over rutted switchback roads. Jesus Christ, he said. He was driving into a world where the owls roosted with the chickens, where folks kept whippoorwills for pets and didn't get the Saturday Night Opry till Monday morning.

The house when he found it was set at the mouth of a hollow. A tin-roofed log house canted on its stone foundation and leant as if under the pressure of enormous perpetual winds. Blown-out autos set about the yard as if positioned with an eye for their aesthetic value. A black cat elongated like running ink down the side of a crumpled Buick and vanished silently in the woods.

He knocked on the door. After a while he knocked again. A curtain was pulled aside and the girl's face appeared. She stood regarding him through the glass. He had been thinking about her on the drive out here, remembering not individual features but the sum expression, a sort of sullen eroticism.

The door opened. Hey, she said. I remember you. Come on in.

Hey, Crosswaithe said. He had the note in his hand. I came about the television set.

What about it?

Crosswaithe was by now standing in the front room looking about. A clean simple room, cheap vinyl trailer-park furniture.

The television set looked like something that been teleported there from more opulent surroundings.

Well, he said, you didn't pay for it. I had to come pick it up. He was studying it with an eye toward handling it and loading it into the bed of the truck. It had a distinctly heavy look.

How much do I owe?

He looked at the note. A little over a thousand dollars, he said. Is your father not at home?

There's nobody here but me, the girl said. She had long dark hair and eyes that in the room's poor light seemed to vary from gray to a deep sea-green. Every move the girl made had undercurrents: the hip-slung way she stood too close to him, even the way she said, There's nobody here but me. Long attuned to nuance and shadings he could turn to his own advantage, Crosswaithe picked all this up immediately but there were subtle connotations here he wasn't prepared to deal with just yet.

Where's he at?

Not here, she said. Come on in and let's sit down and talk about it. I've got some money.

Crosswaithe at the mention of money crossed and sat with his elbows on his knees on the edge of the sofa. He was thinking that maybe he wouldn't have to wrestle with a projection TV after all. Even with the two-wheeler it would be difficult for one man to handle it without dropping it.

She went through a curtained doorway into another room. He could hear her rummaging around, opening and closing drawers. Perhaps she was looking for money. The room was cold; he shivered involuntarily and sat hugging his knees. He wondered what they used for heat around here, they didn't seem to be using anything today.

When the curtain parted she came back into the room carrying a whiskey bottle by the neck and in her other hand a brown envelope. She sat on the sofa beside him and laid the whiskey bottle in his lap. Get you a drink, she said. I've got to see how much money I've got here.

Crosswaithe sat clasping the bottle loosely. I've about quit doing this, he said.

Daddy made it, it's supposed to be good.

Crosswaithe shook the bottle and watched the glassine bead rise in it. The girl had withdrawn from the envelope a thin sheaf of checks. They looked to Crosswaithe like government checks. He unscrewed the cap of the bottle. It's cold in here, he said. Maybe I will have just a sip.

He drank and swallowed. He swallowed rapidly a time or two to keep it down. Hot bile rose in his throat. Great God, he said. What's in this stuff?

I don't know. Whatever you make whiskey out of. Daddy made it, it's supposed to be good.

Crosswaithe's eyes were watering, he could feel it in his sinus passages. I can taste old car radiators and maybe an animal or two that fell in the mash but there's something I can't quite put my finger on.

She was laughing. She hid her mouth with a hand when she laughed and he wondered if her teeth were crooked. She stopped laughing and wiped her eyes. A curving strand of black hair lay across her forehead like a comma.

You're a good-looking thing, she said. I noticed it right off the day we bought the TV. Did you sell it to us because of the way I was flirting with you?

My brother-in-law said I sold it because your father had a hole in his throat.

What do you say?

It could have been a little of both. What's with all these checks?

She fanned them out like a poker hand. There were six of them. They're social security checks, she said. Daddy drawed them one a month after he got that cancer. I just saved these up. You'll have to give me a ride into town to cash them, though. None of these cars around here works and I never was much of a mechanic.

Crosswaithe was taking cautious little sips of the whiskey against the cold. His feet felt numb and he kept stamping them to keep the circulation going. The whiskey was giving him a vague ringing of the ears. Why is it so cold in here? he asked. They've got this stuff out now they call fire, and it's the very thing. Have you not heard of it?

Me and my boyfriend broke up, she said.

Crosswaithe searched for some connection however tenuous but he couldn't find one.

I'm out of wood, she said. He used to bring me a load of wood now and then but he quit when we broke up. I'm going to Florida on part of this money anyway. Somewhere it's warm.

There must be three or four thousand dollars there.

Four thousand and eighty dollars.

Since you had this money you could have just paid the note and saved everybody a lot of trouble.

The girl had the checks spread out and was holding them beneath her chin in the manner of an oriental fan. It's no trouble to me, she said, giving him a sly smile above the fan. Besides, I knew if I waited you'd be coming to get it. He didn't want to sell it anyway, and I knew he'd send you instead of coming himself.

Well let's decide something one way or another. No offense, but I'm freezing my butt off in here, and there's a heater in my truck.

If I'm going to Florida I don't even need it. Over a thousand dollars is a lot of money for a TV I don't even need.

Suit yourself, Crosswaithe said. It's all the same to me. I suspect this might be my last day in the TV hauling business anyway.

I thought you looked like a man with a bridge on fire, she said.

BY TWO O'CLOCK they had the checks cashed and were sitting in a booth in Big Mama's drinking long-necked bottles of Coors. The check cashing had taken place without their being set upon by federal agents as he'd secretly expected, Crosswaithe sitting in the truck keeping the motor running like the driver of a getaway car, watching the frozen streets and wondering how he knew there was something peculiarly amiss about the money. Something in her manner, some kind of bad news that just radiated off her. Or maybe Crosswaithe just had his radar turned up too high: for days he had divined machinations behind the curtains, tugs on the strings that controlled him, and he had to be on the road. Somewhere his name was being affixed to papers that needed only the serving to alter his life forever, and even the low-grade heat from the four thousand eighty dollars in his left front pocket did nothing to comfort him.

Beyond the rain-streaked window in the bar the day had gone gray and desolate. The sky had smoothed to uniform metallic gray and a small cold rain fell, a few grains of sleet rattled off the glass like shot. A flake of snow, listing in the wind and expiring to a pale transparency on the warm glass. There was an enormous coal heater in the middle of the room and from time to time one of the orange-clad deer hunters that peopled Big Mama's would stoke it from a scuttle and with an iron poker roil sparks from its depths that snapped in the air like static electricity.

The girl's name was Carmie and everyone seemed to know her. She seemed a great favorite here. Everyone bought her a beer and asked her if her old man had ever showed up and wanted to know if she was going to the dance at Goblin's Knob.

What's Goblin's Knob? Crosswaithe asked.

A beer joint over on the Wayne County line. It's a real mean place, they're always having knockdown dragouts over there. Knifings. A fellow was shot and killed over there a week or two ago. I was thinking we might go over there tonight.

And then again we might not, Crosswaithe said.

It always amazed him and scared him a little how easily he fell into the way of things. For seven years he had walked what he considered the straight and narrow, a sober member of the business community, an apprentice mover and shaker. Yet it felt perfectly normal to be drinking Coors in a place called Big Mama's with four thousand dollars in his pocket and a young girl sitting so close he could feel the heat of her thigh and whose nipples printed indelibly not only against the fabric of her pullover but on some level of Crosswaithe's consciousness as well.

She kept talking about Florida as if their heading out there was a foregone conclusion and Crosswaithe did nothing to deter her. Part of it was the attraction of a world drenched in Technicolor, green palm trees and white sand and blue water: he felt stalemated by this monochromatic world of bleak winter trees, as if he'd been here too long, absorbed all the life and color out of the landscape.

There's something that has to be done before we can go to Florida or anywhere else, she said.

Crosswaithe waited.

She had been making on the red Formica tabletop a series of interlocking rings with the wet bottom of her beer bottle and now sat studying the pattern she'd made as if something of great significance was encoded there.

Daddy's dead, she said.

Well, I'm sorry your father died but I don't see what it has to do with leaving. Seems to me that would be just one less thing keeping you here.

She was silent a time. I just can't have anybody finding him, she finally said. She was peering intently, almost hypnotically into Crosswaithe's eyes, and he divined that truth from her would vary moment to moment, and there was something so familiar in her manner that for a dizzy moment it was like looking into a mirror and seeing his reflection cast back at him smooth and young and marvelously regendered.

I went to see about him one morning and he was just stiff and dead. Just I guess died in his sleep and never made a sound. I didn't know what to do. I didn't have any money. Daddy kept all the money and he ran through it as fast as he got it. I took out running toward the highway to find help. Then I stopped. I sat down by the side of the road and thought it over.

You thought what over?

It was the thirtieth of the month. If I waited three more days there'd be a check in the mailbox for six hundred and eighty dollars. If I told anybody there'd be death certificates and funerals and all that and the government would just keep the check. I thought about it from every angle and it just didn't seem like I had a choice.

If you considered all those angles it must have occurred to you that sooner or later they might lock your ass up.

Of course it did.

And it also might have occurred to you that at some point six hundred and eighty dollars would become thirteen hundred and sixty.

That too.

Crosswaithe lit a cigarette he didn't want. There was already a blue shifting haze to the room like battlefield smoke and the air had become hot and close.

Just what month are we talking about here?

The thirtieth of June, Carmie said.

Crosswaithe was silent a time. He sat staring out the window past the gravel parking lot. Bare winter trees, bleak fading horizons folding away to blue transparency. It had begun to snow, a few flakes then more, drifting toward the window almost horizontally in the heavy wind. He rose and dropped the cigarette into an empty beer bottle and started pulling on his coat.

Billy, she said.

What?

It's not what you think.

Probably not, Crosswaithe said.

He went out the front door and stood with his hands in his pockets. The day had turned very cold. Snow snaked across the parking lot in shifting windrows. He felt a little drunk. He'd had a few beers and more of the old holethroated alchemist's potion than he wanted to think about and he wasn't used to it.

He was standing on the doorstep staring at a dead deer in the bed of someone's pickup truck when she came out the door behind him. The deer had blood matted in its hair and its eyes were open. The eyes had gone dull and snowflakes lay on them without melting and when they reminded him of Claire's eyes behind their blue bird's lids he was seized with a sourceless dread, an almost palpable malaise that cut to the core of his being. The Grim Reaper had leaned to him face to face and laid a hand to each of his shoulders and kissed him hard on the mouth, he could smell the carrion breath and taste graveyard dirt on his tongue. He suddenly saw that all his youthful optimism was long gone, that his time had come and gone to waste. That things were not all right and would probably not be all right again.

I've had days when I could have raised that deer from the dead like Lazarus, he told the girl.

She linked an arm through his and stood hunched in her thin coat. The wind spun snow into her dark hair. She looked very young. Crosswaithe abruptly realized that she might be the very last one, the last young girl who would stand arm in arm with him with her head leaned against his shoulder. He could smell her hair.

Have you ever drank a strawberry daiquiri? she asked him.

I don't think so. His breath smoked in the cold air.

What's in them?

Probably strawberries and some of that stuff your daddy made out of old car radiators.

We could be in Key West lying on the hot sand drinking them, she said.

We could be up at Brushy Mountain cranking out Tennessee license plates on a punch press, Crosswaithe said. I know where this conversation is going and you can just forget it.

When I was fourteen or fifteen Daddy used to make me go sit with these old men he was playing poker with. Fat old men in overalls with their tobacco money folded up in the bib pockets and their gut full of beer and Daddy's whiskey. They stank, I can still smell them. They smelled like snuff and sweat and they all had black greasy dirt under their fingernails. I'd sit and play up to them while Daddy dealt himself aces off the bottom of the deck. When I was sixteen he sold me to a cattle farmer from Flatwoods. I was supposed to be a cherry but Daddy had the last laugh there. What do you think about that?

I don't think about it at all, Crosswaithe said. I'm not a social worker. And I'm for goddamned sure not an undertaker.

But you do begin to see why I'm not all tore up about his dying, don't you? They owed me that money for taking care of him. Somebody did. For changing all those dirty bedclothes and putting up with him till he died. I was owed. Do you see?

I might if I believed any of it, he said.

A pickup truck pulled into the parking lot and a short pudgy man in a denim jumper got out of it. He stood for a time behind Crosswaithe's truck staring at the lashed-down television set. Finally he turned and came on toward the steps.

Hey Carmie.

Hey Chessor.

Whose big TV is that? The man had on a checked cap with huge earflaps and the flaps stood out to the side like a dog's ears. He seemed a little drunk.

It's mine, Crosswaithe said.

I need me one like that. Where'd you get it?

I found it where it lost off a truck, Crosswaithe said.

Was there just the one?

Crosswaithe stood and listened to the buzz of alcohol in his head. To the remorseless ticking of a clock that had commenced somewhere inside him, and to a voice that whispered Let's go, let's go, what are we wasting time here for? He'd already decided to call Robin but the time wasn't yet right.

There was just the one, he said.

I need me one. You wouldn't want to sell it, would you?

It might not even work, Crosswaithe said.

Chessor turned to study it. Hell, I'd make a stock feeder out of it if it didn't. Use it for something. My dope crop come in pretty well and I need to buy something.

To Crosswaithe the conversation seemed to have turned surreal. He stood looking at his truck. It would probably start, he could just drive away, drive all the way across the country to San Francisco where Robin was.

I better hang on to it, he said.

When Chessor shrugged and went into Big Mama's Carmie shoved a hand into his pocket and laced her fingers into his. Nobody would ever know, she said. Nobody would even think anything about it. Daddy was always just walking off and staying gone for weeks at a time. Everybody knew he had the cancer, he could just have died somewhere. All we'd have to do is get him up that hollow behind the house and bury him.

Why the hell haven't you already done it, then? If you needed help any one of these good old boys would have been glad to furnish it.

I was waiting on you, she said.

Like fate.

What?

You were just lying in wait for me like fate. All the time I was going to work and going home and living my dull little life all this was up around a bend. You were just killing time and waiting for me to come along and tote a dead man up a hollow and bury him.

I guess. That's a funny way to look at it.

How would you look at it?

I never really thought about it. It sort of happened a little at a time.

Well where have you got him?

She leaned her mouth closer to Crosswaithe's ear though there was no one else around. Her breath was warm. He's in the freezer, she said.

Of course he is, Crosswaithe said. I don't know why I even bothered to ask.

THE PICK WHEN IT STRUCK the frozen earth rang hollowly like steel on stone and sent a shock up Crosswaithe's arms like high-voltage electricity. Hellfire, he said. He slung the pick off into the scrub brush the hollow was grown up with and took up the shovel. Beneath the black leaves the earth was just whorls of frozen stone and the shovel skittered across it. He leaned on the shovel a moment just feeling the cold and listening to the silence then hurled it into the woods after the pick and turned and walked back down the hollow.

You can forget this digging business. The ground's frozen hard as a rock.

The girl seemed to be sorting through clothing, packing her choices and discarding the rest, occasionally drinking from a pint of orange vodka. Is there not any way you can get a hole dug? she asked. He's not very big.

Not unless you've got a stick or two of dynamite. Do you?

No.

You had this all planned out so well I thought you might have laid a few sticks by.

No.

I guess we could just burn the goddamned house, Crosswaithe said. At least we'd get warm.

He fell silent a time, thinking. Finally he said, Did he have a gun, did he ever go hunting?

He had a rifle he used to squirrel hunt with. Stillhunt. He'd sit right still under a tree until a squirrel came out.

He'll be still all right, Crosswaithe said. Go get the gun.

He smashed a rickety ladderback chair and in a half-dark bedroom found an old wool Navy peacoat. He crammed the peacoat into the wood heater and laid the oak dowels and slats atop it and lit the coat with his cigarette lighter. He hunkered before it cupping his hands over a thin blue wavering flame. The hell with all this, Crosswaithe said.

He crossed a windy dogtrot to a spare room used to store oddments of junk. His head struck a lowhanging lightbulb shrouded with a tin reflector and the fixture swung like a pendulum, streaking the walls with moving light. He opened the freezer. Jesus Christ, he said. The old man lay on his side half covered with plastic bags of green beans and blackberries. He was wrapped in some sort of stained swaddling and only the top of his head was visible. He had a blue-looking bald spot the size of a baseball iced over with silver frost. Crosswaithe shuddered. He took a deep breath. He grasped the old man where he judged his shoulder might be and jerked as hard as he could.

Nothing happened. The old man wouldn't budge. There was an inch or so of ice in the bottom of the freezer as if the whole mess had thawed and refrozen. He stood studying it. Finally he grasped the front edge of the freezer with both hands and tilted everything over onto the floor. There was a horrific din and bags of frozen food went skittering like bowling balls, Crosswaithe falling and scrambling up. When the freezer struck the floor there was an explosion of ice and the old man shot out like a tobogganist blown crazed and flashfrozen out of a snowbank. He went sailing across the room and fetched up hard against the opposite wall and careened off it with a hollow thud and lay spinning lazily on the linoleum.

Crosswaithe went outside to the dogtrot and sat with the logs hard against his back. He lit a cigarette and sat smoking it. He tried to get his mind under some kind of control. To force order onto chaos. He tried to think of the girl, the curving line of a hip, a rosebud nipple on a field of white.

The girl herself came out of the living room. What's the matter? she asked.

Get away from me, Crosswaithe said.

It's about dark, she said. We're going to have to do something.

Get away from me, he said again. She went back into the room and pulled the door to. Crosswaithe rose and spun the cigarette at the snowy dark and went back into the room. He grasped the old man by the edge of the twisted sheet and went dragging him out of the room like some demented pulltoy.

We've got to get this mess off him and clothes on him, Crosswaithe said. I'm going to take him back in the woods and lean him against a tree like he was out hunting and just died. It'd look kind of peculiar next spring if some hunter walked up on him and he was still wearing this bedsheet. And find him some shoes.

He dragged a recliner next to the heater and propped the old man in it. The sides of the sheet-iron heater were cherry red. He went looking for something else to feed it. The old man crouched steaming and smoking in his chair and they sat before the fire watching him like necromancers trying to raise something from the dead.

HE WENT WITH THE GUN hauling the old man along into deepening dark. Trees like runs of ink on a white page, a shifting curtain of billowing snow. His feet creaked on the snowy earth and everything gleamed with a faint phosphorescence. When he got to the head of the hollow he could drag the old man no farther. He was forced to wrap gun and body in the blanket and shoulder the whole loathsome package and climb pulling himself from sapling to sapling up the slope. Halfway up he paused to rest, leaned with the old man balanced on him like something dread that had sprung upon him out of the dark and just would not let go. He crouched listening to his ragged breathing, to the soft furtive sound of the woods filling up with snow.

AT GOBLIN'S KNOB the parking lot blazed with light and there was the dull thump of a bass guitar feeding out of the white frame building like something you felt rather than heard. The graveled parking lot was filled with pickup trucks, with racked deer rifles in the back windows, and most of them festooned with tags with messages on them. Crosswaithe read a few of them on the way to the porch. This vehicle protected by Smith and Wesson. I'll give up my gun when they pry it from my cold dead fingers. Kill them all and let God sort them out.

Let's get the hell out of here, Crosswaithe said.

We'll just stay a minute. I need to get some more vodka for the road and I might see somebody I need to say goodbye to.

I need to say goodbye to every son of a bitch I've met in this sorry godforsaken place, Crosswaithe said.

Inside it was hot and loud and smoky. One enormous room with booths set about the walls and a bare wood dance floor where bodies jerked spasmodically to a bluesy shuffle amplified from a raised bandstand.

They found a corner booth and Crosswaithe wended his way to the bar and bought two bottles of beer and wended his way back through a crowd that seemed a cross section of Harrikin society. There were fat men in baseball caps turned backwards and overalls stained with deer blood or blood from more dubious sources and rawboned Marlboro men in cowboy hats and girls in beehive hairdos and formal gowns and girls in jeans and boots. Some of the men were carrying pistols, for Crosswaithe could see more than one imprinted against fabric pockets and once he bumped against one in a jumper pocket that swayed heavily and the man carrying it pulled away and eyed Crosswaithe with a long speculative look.

Let's get the bottle and go find a motel room, Carmie said. Head out for Florida in the morning.

Just a minute, Crosswaithe said. Did you see that guitar? He must have went down and met the devil at the crossroads for one like that.

The lead guitar player of the band was playing a National steel guitar that Crosswaithe drunk as he was had to feel in his own hands. He drained his bottle and set it aside and rose and picked his way around the crowd's perimeter to the bandstand. He stood with his hands in his coat pockets letting the wave of rehashed Lynyrd Skynyrd wash over him until the band took a break between numbers and the man leant the guitar against an amplifier.

Mind if I fool with your guitar?

The guitar player had pale shoulder-length hair and he smoothed it back both-handed and looked at Crosswaithe. It was my daddy's and I don't want it busted over somebody's head. Can you play one?

I tried a lot of years.

Hell, sit in with us then. We need all the help we can get around here.

Crosswaithe began tentatively with the band feeling its way behind him, bass and drums and second guitar looking for a way into the song then falling silent one by one. There was no way in. The song was a scratchy old 78 from the bottom of someone's trunk, his fingers feeling around and into a past that was realer and more imminent than the present, his fingers exploring the cracked linoleum and raw pine boards and faded rose wallpaper of Robert Johnson's fabled kitchen. They read Son House's "Death Letter Blues" and halfway through a song by Reverend Gary Davis the old magic seized him, a tide of power that rolled over him and made him omnipotent, invulnerable to kryptonite and bullet-proof, someone who could make or destroy worlds at his whim or simply bend them to his liking the way his fingers bent the snaking strings.

When he handed the guitar back the man just looked at him. Goddamn, he said.

At least they didn't throw bottles.

Where'd you learn to play like that?

All over the place, Crosswaithe said. Is there a pay phone here?

There's one here but it's outside. For some damn reason they put it on the porch.

At the bar he exchanged a five-dollar bill for quarters and went out the door into the cold. In the phone booth he stood for a moment with the receiver in his hand waiting for the number to rise up from his subconscious the way he knew it would do. When it did he put in money and dialed, and in San Francisco, in a room he'd never been to, a room his mind had imbued with myth, a phone began to ring. It rang and rang. At length he hung up and tried for another number. This one came harder but it did come. The phone was picked up on the third ring.

Hello?

Richie?

Who is this?

Billy Crosswaithe.

Crosswaithe? Goddamn. Where are you, are you here in town?

I'm in Tennessee.

What are you doing in Tennessee?

Freezing my butt off and thinking about warmer climates, Crosswaithe said. What's going on?

You mean in the six or seven years it's been since you called? I don't know if there's time enough to tell you all that.

Just in the few minutes before you answered the phone, Crosswaithe said.

I was working. Are you in Nashville, is that what you're doing in Tennessee? Are you famous yet?

Not yet.

I keep waiting to see you on the cover of *Rolling Stone* or to read a record review somewhere.

Any day now.

There was a quickening of interest in Richie's voice so that Crosswaithe wondered for a cynical moment what he had ever done to make Richie think that something entertaining was going to happen just because he had called. Things happen around you, Richie had said once long ago. You never know what's going to happen next. As if Crosswaithe's life was a story Richie read a chapter of every few years.

What's going on in your life, Richie?

Crosswaithe listened awhile. Richie had a computer company, he had started on a shoestring but things were beginning to boom. Crosswaithe glanced at his watch. He stared out the glass into the world of night. All the world there was a black vacuum sucking whirling snow up into it.

When Richie fell silent Crosswaithe said, I called Robin a few minutes ago but nobody answered. Has she moved?

For the first time Crosswaithe's radar detected caution, hesitation. Robin's in Tupelo, Richie said.

In Tupelo, Mississippi? What's she doing there?

Well, Father's there. He's old. He's a lot older than he was the last time you called. He's not able to care for himself and Robin moved in with him. She is a nurse, you know.

I know. Do you have the number there?

There was silence for a time. Finally Richie said, Of course I have it, but I don't think I'm going to give it to you.

Why not?

Why not? I don't think you're good for her. I know damn well you're not good for her. She has problems and you make them worse. You turn up every few years and knock her off balance. We've been through a lot and I love you like a brother but frankly I think you ruined her life a long time ago. I think she expects things from you that you're not capable of doing. She was just a kid, for Christ's sake, what, sixteen years old?

I just wanted to talk to her.

Come on out and talk to me. We'll go out on the town like we used to. Set em up and knock em down. It's warm out here.

Hey, Crosswaithe said. I've been meaning to call and tell you this. You remember that time we went up to Woodstock looking for that place Dylan lived after the motorcycle accident?

Yeah. Then we made a pilgrimage to Big Pink.

I saw him.

You saw Dylan? What, in concert? So did I, several times.

No, not in concert. In New Orleans. He was coming out of a bar on Bourbon Street. I was drunk and he was drunk or on something and I bumped into him.

You actually bumped into him? What did he say?

He said, Hey, man, watch where you're going, or something like that.

Hey, man, watch where you're going, Richie said, laughing. That's real profound. How would you interpret that, what do you suppose it means? Did you ask him anything?

No. He had his, whatever, entourage. He was with that Byrd, Roger or Jim McGuinn. His eyes looked stoned, out there.

I'd have asked him something.

He wouldn't have known.

The hell he wouldn't.

You know how we always thought he had a handle on things? How he knew where the answers were in the back of the book? He doesn't. He's just wandering around this sideshow like everybody else. Trying to make it through to daylight the best way he can.

The hell he is. He knows.

He doesn't know, Crosswaithe said. And you can take that to the bank.

Listen, about Robin, she's been through some rough times. The messy divorce, and then a messier custody trial for her son because of her drinking problem. She's got everything under control now, but I don't know if you ought to talk to her.

Divorce, Crosswaithe thought. Child, custody fight. Drinking problem. How time flies.

I don't see how talking to me could make it any worse.

Just don't promise a bunch of shit you can't deliver, all right? Do you have a pen?

I can remember it.

He hung up and dialed the number. He wondered what time it was in Mississippi. Early, late, ten years ago, twenty years ago. He suddenly noticed that his knuckles clutching the phone were bloodless and white and he loosened his grip. When the voice came on he felt it like a physical shock, a palpable and three-dimensional remnant from his past.

She recognized his voice immediately. I don't think I want to talk to you, she said. Anyway I don't have time. I was up with Father, he's frail and sick.

Crosswaithe thought of Father, frail and sick, remembering the violent weight of him, the strong carpenter's arms closed on him in a headlock, remembering the smell of him, Old Spice and Red Man chewing tobacco and the smell of violence, like the smell of an enraged animal.

I just woke up this morning wanting to see you, Crosswaithe said, hearing his voice but not the words, Crosswaithe on automatic pilot, hearing the buzz of his voice but seeing a Mexican hotel room with panic spreading, blood spreading in the center of a white sheet like a malignant flower blooming, her abortion turning into a car crash. Today just seemed different, Crosswaithe went on. I knew I'd have to call you before the day was over. Why do you suppose that is?

I don't know, unless it's because you've used up all the people wherever you are and need to move on. Maybe it's because you're a cold-blooded bastard who uses people then flushes them like toilet paper. Could that be it?

Maybe, but I don't think so. I think I just want to see you.

There was silence for a time. What's the matter with you? she finally asked, and this time there was a different tone to her voice, perhaps imperceptible to one less attuned than Crosswaithe: here was malleable clay to sculpt, a slate upon which to write.

I don't know exactly, he said, and a part of him seemed to split off from the whole and watch cynically, a tiny Crosswaithe standing with head cocked sidewise and a look of sardonic amusement on his face, a look that said, there he goes again, where does he get this stuff? can you believe this guy?

It's no one thing, Crosswaithe said. I just can't seem to get my life together. Things were running along pretty good and then it all just blew apart. My wife divorced me but I could handle that, the worst thing was my son. I've got this six-year-old the sun rises and sets on and I just lost a bloody custody battle. I'm not even certain about any kind of visitation rights. I guess I just don't know where to turn.

Crosswaithe recounting this tale felt his vision blur, felt real pain for the fictional son he had lost, for a dizzy moment lost control over which emotions were real and which manufactured, what events were true and what dreamed.

Don't bullshit me, you can't manipulate me, he imagined her screaming. But she said quite calmly, This doesn't sound at all like you, Billy. Are you leveling with me?

Listen, I was thinking about driving down to Natchez, he said. If I stopped in Tupelo do you think I could see you?

No. I don't have the time or inclination for this.

Just for a little while.

If I said yes I'd be a fool, she said. If I said no I'd be a liar. I prefer to be neither.

That's good enough for me, Crosswaithe said, and broke the connection. His face felt hot and flushed and he leaned it against the cold glass. I heard the news, there's good rockin tonight, he said aloud.

At the bar he drank a cup of coffee. There was a subtle difference in the atmosphere of the room. An undercurrent of unease, he could smell violence like the scent of ozone in an electrical storm. In the far corner a fight erupted in a cascade of overturned tables and flying bottles and spread toward him like ripples on water. Hey good buddy, a voice said. He turned. It was Chessor with the checked cap with doglike earflaps. He put a proprietary arm about Crosswaithe's shoulders. Let's get drunk and kill somebody, he said.

Crosswaithe twisted away. He drained his coffee cup and set it on the bar and started toward the corner Carmie was in. Halfway there someone hit him in the side of the head and he went down and went the rest of the way to the door on his hands and knees, through a forest of denim-clad legs, buffeted by thrashing bodies, the brawl following him like a plague.

He was already in the truck with the engine running when she came out. She got in and offered him a half-pint bottle. Get you a drink, she said. You've got blood on your mouth.

He took a drink and rinsed it around in his mouth and rolled down the window and spat bloody vodka onto the snow.

Did we eat today, she said. I'm beginning to feel awfully peculiar.

I think we had a steak somewhere this morning.

We never did make it to bed though, and that was sort of the point of this whole thing. Why don't we find a warm motel and a warm meal and a warm bed and start out for Key West in the morning?

Why don't we, Crosswaithe said.

HE BACKED THE TRUCK carefully up the incline to the loading dock at PETTIGREW MAGNAVOX. It was drifted with snow and the rear wheels began to spin sideways, whining wildly on the ice. The hell with it, he said. He got out and slammed the truck door and lowered the tailgate. He got the two-wheeler lifted and the television set onto the tailgate but he couldn't get it turned properly and he couldn't decide what to do with it. His hands were freezing and finally he lowered the two-wheeler back onto the bed of the pickup. You heavy son of a bitch, he told it. Carmie stood in the snow watching him.

At last he leaned his back against the truck railing and braced his feet against the television and shoved. It went freewheeling off the icy tailgate and slammed onto the asphalt, striking on one corner and settling heavily onto its back with the screen collapsing inward and snow drifting into it.

Jesus, the girl said.

Crosswaithe was shaking with silent laughter.

What the hell's the matter with you? Carmie asked.

Oprah Winfrey came out of that thing when it hit like a bat out of hell, he said. Did you not see her?

You're crazy as shit, the girl told him.

At least that crazy, Crosswaithe agreed.

WHEN HE PULLED INTO the hospital parking lot the girl was asleep but she awoke and looked wildly about. Where are we? This is not a motel.

I have to see somebody a minute.

Who?

My ex-wife.

Weeks seemed to have passed since he had left her at six o'clock in the morning but here the clock hands seemed not to have moved at all. His coffee cup was still in the wastebasket, the machines that lived for her had not missed a beat, van Gogh's sunflowers tilted toward a sun that had not moved in the sky. He studied her face remembering for a moment things she had said and the nights when she had clung to him with sweet urgency, like drowning, like dying. What's it like over there? he asked her silently, but her face had no secrets to tell him and if she knew what it was like over there she was keeping it to herself.

Outside he stood on the concrete steps breathing deeply, sucking his lungs full of the cold air until he could feel the oxygen run in his veins like ice. Snowflakes melted in his lashes, on his face, he could feel them in his lungs.

The girl was asleep with the bottle of orange vodka clasped loosely in her hands and her head resting against the window glass where she'd jury-rigged a pillow with a folded sweater but halfway to Waynesboro she awoke and looked about as if she'd see where she had got to. Crosswaithe was thinking about where the old man leant again: the beech with the rifle propped against him and the world going to ice when as if she'd read his mind or simply judged what he'd be thinking she said,

I guess Daddy's about snowed under by now.

All day long Crosswaithe had wondered how the girl could switch back and forth from beer to vodka with no apparent sign of it but now it seemed to have caught up with her. Her voice coming out of the darkness was slurred and after a while she began to chuckle softly to herself.

Crosswaithe lit a cigarette from the dash lighter. The snow blew into the headlights and went looping weightlessly away and the road melted out by the lights looked like a tunnel into a perpetual ice storm.

The last few weeks with Daddy were just hell, Carmie said. Pure hell. He stayed on to me all the time. Like I had give him that cancer or could take it away if I wanted to and just wouldn't. He used to call me names with his talker, bitches and whores, worse names than that. If I was a whore he made me one, didn't he?

Crosswaithe could feel her eyes on him demanding an answer but he didn't say anything. He cranked the window down for the cold air to clear his head.

Can you keep a secret? she asked.

I've already got more than I need, Crosswaithe said. I've got secrets people have given me I haven't even taken out of the box yet.

Finally I took his talker away from him and threw it in the stove. One day he was mouthing names at me while I was changing his sheets and I just picked up a pillow and laid it across his face. Just to keep his mouth from working. But then I caught both sides of the pillow and leaned on him as hard as I could. He fought awhile but he was real weak and after a little bit he just quit.

I'll bet he did, Crosswaithe said.

They were coming into Waynesboro, strings of neon night lights, no other traffic about. On the square there was a bus station with a running greyhound outlined in blue neon and he pulled the truck up to the curb.

Why are we stopping here? What's this place?

Go get us a couple of cups of coffee. I'm running down or something. Driving through this shit's hard on the nerves.

Can't we get some at the motel?

We've got to find one first. Crosswaithe was fumbling out money. He handed her a five and she got out bunching her shoulders against the cold. Keep the heater going, she said.

She was halfway to the bus station when he leaned across the seat and called her back. He slid two one-hundred-dollar bills from the rubber-banded money and pocketed them. He reached the money to the girl. Put this in your purse before I lose it, he said. We need to hang on to it.

HE THOUGHT FOR A MOMENT she was going to refuse it but then she shrugged and walked away stowing it in her purse. He watched her. She went in. The windows of the bus station were steamed from condensation and she looked gray and spectral walking away, as if she were fading out, not real at all.

He eased the truck in gear and drove away. He turned onto the Natchez Trace Parkway five miles out of Waynesboro and the first thing he saw was a sign that said TUPELO MISS 121 MILES. He was a believer in signs and portents and took this as an omen. He rolled on. He drove with the windows cranked down for the cold astringent air and when he crossed the Mississippi line it was hardly snowing at all and a band of rose light lay in the east like a gift he hadn't expected and probably didn't deserve.

Those Deep Elm Brown's Ferry Blues

I HEARD A WHIPPOORWILL last night, the old man said.

Say you did? Rabon asked without interest. Rabon was just in from his schoolteaching job. He seated himself in the armchair across from the bed and hitched up his trouser legs and glanced covertly at his watch. The old man figured Rabon would put in his obligatory five minutes then go in his room and turn the stereo on.

It sounded just like them I used to hear in Alabama when I was a boy, Scribner said. Sometimes he would talk about whippoorwills or the phases of the moon simply because he got some perverse pleasure out of annoying Rabon. Rabon wanted his father's mind sharp and the old man on top of things, and it irritated him when the old man's mind grew preoccupied with whippoorwills or drifted back across the Tennessee state line into Alabama. Scribner was developing a sense of just how far he could push Rabon into annoyance, and he fell silent, remembering how irritated Rabon had been that time in Nashville when Scribner had recognized the doctor.

The doctor was telling Rabon what kind of shape Scribner was in, talking over the old man's head as if he wasn't even there. All this time Scribner was studying the doctor with a speculative look on his face, trying to remember where he had seen him. He could almost but not quite get a handle on it.

Physically he's among the most impressive men of his age I've examined, the doctor was saying. There's nothing at all to be concerned about there, and his heart is as strong as a man half his age. But Alzheimer's is irreversible, and we have to do what we can to control it.

Scribner had remembered. He was grinning at the doctor. I've seen you before, ain't I?

Excuse me?

I remember you now, the old man said. I seen you in Alabama.

I'm afraid not, the doctor said. I'm from Maine and this is the farthest south I've ever been.

Scribner couldn't figure why the doctor would lie about it. Sure you was. We was at a funeral. You was wearing a green checked suit and a little derby hat and carrying a black shiny walkin stick. There was a little spotted dog there lookin down in the grave and whinin and you rapped it right smart with that cane. I hate a dog at a funeral, you said.

The doctor was looking sympathetic, and Scribner was going to try to lie out of it. Rabon was just looking annoyed. Who were you burying? he asked.

This confused Scribner. He tried to think. Hell, I don't know, he said. Some dead man.

I'm afraid you've got me mixed up with someone else, the doctor said.

Scribner was becoming more confused yet, the sand he was standing on was shifting, water rising about his shoes, his ankles.

I reckon I have, he finally said. That would have been sixty-odd years ago and you'd have to be a hell of a lot older than what you appear to be.

In the car Rabon said, If all you can do is humiliate me with these Alabama funeral stories I wish you would just let me do the talking when we have to come to Nashville.

You could handle that, all right, the old man said.

Now Scribner was back to thinking about whippoorwills. How Rabon was a science teacher who only cared about dead things and books. If you placed a whippoorwill between the pages of an enormous book and pressed it like a flower until it was a paper-thin collage of blood and feathers and fluted bone then Rabon might take an interest in that.

You remember that time a dog like to took your leg off and I laid it out with a hickory club?

No I don't, and I don't know where you dredge all this stuff up.

Dredge up hell, the old man said. I was four days laying up in jail because of it.

If it happened at all it happened to Alton. I can't recall you ever beating a dog or going to jail for me. Or acknowledging my existence in any other way, for that matter.

The old man was grinning slyly at Rabon. Pull up your britches leg, he said.

What?

Pull up your britches leg and let's have a look at it.

Rabon's slacks were brown-and-tan houndstooth checked. He gingerly pulled the cuff of one leg up to the calf.

I'm almost sure it was the other one, Scribner said.

Rabon pulled the other leg up. He was wearing wine-colored calf-length socks. Above the sock was a vicious-looking scar where the flesh had been shredded, the puckered scar red and poreless and shiny as celluloid against the soft white flesh.

Ahh, the old man breathed.

Rabon dropped his cuff. I got this going through a barbed-wire fence when I was nine years old, he said.

Sure you did, the old man said. I bet a German shepherd had you by the leg when you went through it, too.

LATER HE SLEPT FITFULLY with the lights on. When he awoke, he didn't know what time it was. Where he was. Beyond the window it was dark, and the lighted window turned the room back at him. He didn't know for a moment what room he was in, what world the window opened onto. The room in the window seemed cut loose and disassociated, adrift in the space of night.

He got up. The house was quiet. He wandered into the bathroom and urinated. He could hear soft jazzy piano music coming from somewhere. He went out of the bathroom and down a hall adjusting his trousers and into a room where a pudgy man wearing wire-rimmed glasses was seated at a desk with a pencil in his hand, a sheaf of papers spread before him. The man looked up, and the room rocked and righted itself, and it was Rabon.

The old man went over and seated himself on the side of the bed.

You remember how come I named you Rabon and your brother Alton?

Yes, the man said, making a mark on a paper with a red-leaded pencil.

Scribner might not have heard. It was in Limestone County, Alabama, he said. I growed up with Alton and Rabon Delmore, and they played music. Wrote songs. I drove them to Huntsville to make their first record. Did I ever tell you about that?

No more than fifty or sixty times, Rabon said. But I could always listen to it again.

They was damn good. Had some good songs, "Deep Elm Blues." "Brown's Ferry Blues." "When you go down to Deep Elm keep your money in your shoes," the first line went. They wound up on the Grand Ole Opry. Wound up famous. They never forgot where they come from, though. They was just old country boys. I'd like to hear them songs again.

I bought you a cassette player and all those old-time country and bluegrass tapes.

I know it. I appreciate it. Just seems like I can't ever get it to work right. It ain't the same anyway.

I'll take Brubeck myself.

If that's who that is then you can have any part of him.

It's late, Papa. Don't you think you ought to be asleep?

I was asleep. Seems like I just catnap. Sleep when I'm sleepy. Wake up when I'm not. Not no night and day anymore. Reckon why that is?

I've got all this work to do.

Go ahead and work then. I won't bother you.

The old man sat silent a time watching Rabon grade papers. Old-man heavy in the chest and shoulders, looking up at the schoolteacher out of faded eyes. Sheaf of iron-gray hair. His pale eyes flickered as if he'd thought of something, but he remained silent. He waited until Rabon finished grading the paper he was working on and in the space between his laying it aside and taking up another one the old man said, Say whatever happened to Alton, anyway?

Rabon laid the paper aside ungraded. He studied the old man. Alton is dead, he said.

Dead? Say he is? What'd he die of?

He was killed in a car wreck.

The old man sat in silence digesting this as if he didn't quite know what to make of it. Finally he said, Where's he buried at?

Papa, Rabon said, for a moment the dense flesh of his face was transparent so that Scribner could see a flicker of real pain, then the flesh coalesced into its customary opaque mask and Rabon said again, I've got to do all this work.

I don't see how you can work with your own brother dead in a car wreck, Scribner said.

SOMETIME THAT NIGHT, or another night, he went out the screen door onto the back porch, dressed only in his pajama bottoms, the night air cool on his skin. Whippoorwills were tolling out of the dark and a milky blind cat's eye of a moon hung above the jagged treeline. Out there in the dark patches of velvet, patches of silver where moonlight was scattered through the leaves like coins. The world looked strange yet in some way familiar. Not a world he was seeing, but one he was remembering. He looked down expecting to see a child's bare feet on the floorboards and saw that he had heard the screen door slap to as a child but had inexplicably become an old man, gnarled feet on thin blue shanks of legs, and the jury-rigged architecture of time itself came undone, warped and ran like melting glass.

NAKED TO THE WAIST Scribner sat on the bed while the nurse wrapped his biceps to take his blood pressure. His body still gleamed from the sponge bath and the room smelled of rubbing alcohol. Curious-looking old man. Heavy chest and shoulders and arms like a weightlifter. The body of a man twenty-five years his junior. The image of the upper torso held until it met the wattled red flesh of his throat, the old man's head with its caved cheeks and wild gray hair, the head with its young man's body like a doctored photograph.

Mr. Scribner, this thing will barely go around your arm, she said. I bet you were a pistol when you were a younger man.

I'm still a pistol yet, and cocked to go off anytime, the old man said. You ought to go a round with me.

My boyfriend wouldn't care for that kind of talk, the nurse said, pumping up the thingamajig until it tightened almost painfully around his arm.

I wasn't talking to your boyfriend, Scribner said. He takin care of you?

I guess he does the best he can, she said. But I still bet you were something twenty-five years ago.

What was you like twenty-five years ago?

Two years old, she said.

You ought to give up on these younger men, he said, studying the heavy muscles of his forearms, his still-taut belly. Brighten up a old man's declinin years.

Hush that kind of talk, she said. Taking forty kinds of pills and randy as a billy goat.

Hellfire, you give me a bath. You couldn't help but notice how I was hung.

She turned quickly away but not so quickly the old man couldn't see the grin.

Nasty talk like that is going to get a soapy washrag crammed in your mouth, she said.

WITH HIS WALKING CANE for a snakestick the old man went through a thin stand of half-grown pines down into the hollow and past a herd of plywood cattle to where the hollow flattened out then climbed gently toward the roadbed. The cattle were life-size silhouettes jigsawed from sheets of plywood and affixed to two-by-fours driven in the earth. They were painted gaudily with bovine smiles and curving horns. The old man passed through the herd without even glancing at them, as if in his world all cattle were a half-inch thick and garbed up with bright lacquer. Rabon had once been married to a woman whose hobby this was, but now she was gone, and there was only this hollow full of wooden cattle.

He could have simply taken the driveway to the roadbed but he liked the hot astringent smell of the pines and the deep shade of the hollow. All his life the woods had calmed him, soothed the violence that smoldered just beneath the surface.

When he came onto the cherted roadbed he stopped for a moment, leaning on his stick to catch his breath. He was wearing bedroom slippers and no socks and his ankles were crisscrossed with bleeding scratches from the dewberry briars he'd walked through. He went on up the road as purposefully as a man with a conscious destination though in truth he had no idea where the road led.

It led to a house set back amid ancient oak trees, latticed by shade and light and somehow imbued with mystery to the old man's eyes, like a cottage forsaken children might come upon in a fairy-tale wood. He stood by the roadside staring at it. It had a vague familiarity, like an image he had dreamed then come upon unexpectedly in the waking world. The house was a one-story brick with fading cornices painted a peeling white. It was obviously unoccupied. The yard was grown with knee-high grass gone to seed and uncurtained windows were opaque with refracted light. Untrimmed tree branches encroached onto the roof and everything was steeped in a deep silence.

A hand raised to shade the sun-drenched glass, the old man peered in the window. No one about, oddments of furniture, a woodstove set against a wall. He climbed onto the porch and sat in a cedar swing for a time, rocking idly, listening to the creak of the chains, the hot sleepy drone of dirt daubers on the August air. There were boxes of junk stacked against the wall, and after a time he began to sort through one of them. There were china cats and dogs, a cookie jar with the shapes of cookies molded and painted onto the ceramic. A picture in a gilt frame that he studied until the edges of things shimmered eerily then came into focus, and he thought: This is my house.

He knew he used to live here with a wife named Ellen and two sons named Alton and Rabon and a daughter named Karen. Alton is dead in a car wreck, he remembered, and he studied Karen's face intently as if it were a gift that had been handed to him unexpectedly, and images of her and words she had said assailed him in a surrealistic collage so that he could feel her hand in his, a little girl's hand, see white patent-leather shoes climbing concrete steps into a church, one foot, the other, the sun caught like something alive in her auburn hair.

Then another image surfaced in his mind: his own arm, silver in the moonlight, water pocked with light like hammered metal, something gleaming he threw sinking beneath the surface, then just the empty hand drawing back and the muscular freckled forearm with a chambray work shirt rolled to the biceps. Somewhere upriver a barge, lights arcing over the river like searchlights trying to find him. That was all. Try as he might he could call nothing else to mind. It troubled him because the memory carried some dark undercurrent of menace.

With a worn Case pocketknife he sliced himself a thin sliver of Apple chewing tobacco Rabon didn't know he'd hoarded, held it in his jaw savoring the taste. He walked about the yard thinking movement might further jar his memory into working. He paused at a silver maple that summer lightning had struck, the raw wound winding in a downward spiral to the earth where the bolt had gone to ground. He stood studying the splintered tree with an old man's bemusement, as if pondering whether this was something he might fix.

SAY, WHATEVER HAPPENED to that Karen, anyway? he asked Rabon that night. Rabon had dragged an end table next to the old man's bed and set a plate and a glass of milk on it. Try not to get this all over everything, he said.

Scribner was wearing a ludicrous-looking red-and-white-checked bib Rabon had tied around his neck, and with a knife in one hand and a fork in the other he was eyeing the plate as if it were something he was going to attack.

Your sister, Karen, the old man persisted.

I don't hear from Karen anymore, Rabon said. I expect she's still up there around Nashville working for the government.

Workin for the government? What's she doin?

They hired her to have one baby after another, Rabon said. She draws that government money they pay for them. That AFDC, money for unwed mothers, whatever.

Say she don't ever call or come around?

I don't have time for any of that in my life, Rabon said. She liked the bright lights and the big city. Wild times. Drinking all night and laying up with some loafer on food stamps. I doubt it'd do her much good to come around here.

I was thinkin about her today when she was a little girl.

She hasn't been a little girl for a long time, Rabon said, shutting it off, closing another door to something he didn't want to talk about.

PAST MIDNIGHT Scribner was lying on top of the covers, misshapen squares of moonlight thrown across him by the windowpanes. He had been thinking about Karen when he remembered shouting, crying, blood. When he pulled her hands away from her face they came away bloody and her mouth was smashed with an incisor cocked at a crazy angle and blood dripping off her chin. One side of her jaw was already swelling.

Where is he?

I don't know, she said. He's left me. He drove away. No telling where he's gone.

Wherever it is I doubt it's far enough, he said, already leaving, his mind already suggesting and discarding places where Pulley might be.

Don't hurt him.

He gave her a long, level glance but he didn't say if he would or he wouldn't. Crossing the yard toward his truck he stepped on an aluminum baseball bat that belonged to Alton. He stooped and picked it up and went on to the truck, swinging it along in his hands, and threw it onto the floorboard.

He wasn't in any of his usual haunts. Not the Snowwhite Café, the pool hall. In Skully's City Café the old man drank a beer and bought one for a crippled drunk in a wheelchair.

Where's your runnin mate, Hudgins?

Bonedaddy? He was in here a while ago. He bought a case of beer and I reckon he's gone down to that cabin he's got on the Tennessee River.

Why ain't you with him? The old man did not even seem

angry. A terrible calm had settled over him. You couldn't rattle him with a jackhammer.

He's pissed about somethin, said he didn't have time to fool with me. I know he's gone to the river though, he had that little snake pistol he takes.

The night was far progressed before he found the right cabin. It set back against a bluff and there was a wavering campfire on the riverbank and Bonedaddy sat before it drinking beer. When Scribner approached the fire, Bonedaddy glanced at the bat and took the nickel-plated pistol out of his pocket and laid it between his feet.

Snake huntin? the old man asked.

These cottonmouth hides ain't worth nothin, Bonedaddy said. Nobody wants a belt made out of em. Too muddy-lookin and no pattern to speak of. I mostly shoot copperheads and rattlesnakes. Once in a while just whatever varmint wanders up to the fire.

Scribner was watching Bonedaddy's right hand. The left clasped a beer bottle but the right never strayed far from the pistol. The hand was big and heavy-knuckled and he couldn't avoid thinking of it slamming into Karen's mouth.

You knocked her around pretty good, he said. You probably ain't more than twice her size.

She ought not called me a son of a bitch. Anybody calls me that needs to have size and all such as that into consideration before they open their mouth.

The old man didn't reply. He hunkered, watching, the stippled water, the farther shore that was just a land in darkness, anybody's guess, a world up for grabs. He listened to the river sucking at the banks like an animal trying to find its way in. He saw that people lived their own lives, went their own way. They grew up and lived lives that did not take him into consideration.

I don't want to argue, Bonedaddy said, patient as a teacher explaining something to a pupil who was a little slow. Matter of fact I come down here to avoid it. But there's catfish in this river six or eight feet long, what they tell me. And if you don't think I'll shoot you and feed you to them then you need to say so right now.

The hand had taken up the pistol. When it started around its arc was interrupted by Scribner swinging the ball bat. He swung from the ground up as hard as he could, like a batter trying desperately for the outfield wall. The pistol fired once and went skittering away. Bonedaddy made some sort of muffled grunt and crumpled in the leaves. The old man looked at the bat in his hands, at Bonedaddy lying on his back. Bonedaddy's hands were flexing. Loosening, clasping. They loosened nor would they clasp again. His head looked like something a truck had run over. Scribner glanced at the bat in mild surprise, then turned and threw it in the river. Somewhere off in the milk-white fog the throaty horn of a barge sounded, lights arced through the murk vague as lights seen in the muddy depths of the river.

He dragged Bonedaddy to the cabin then up the steps and inside. There was a five-gallon can of kerosene and he soaked the floors with it, hurled it at the walls. He lit it with a torch from the campfire. With another he searched for blood in the leaves. Bonedaddy's half-drunk beer was propped against a weathered husk of stump, and for a reason he couldn't name Scribner picked it up and drank it and slung the bottle into the river.

He stayed to see that everything burned. When the roof caught, an enormous cedar lowering onto it burst into flames and burned white-hot as a magnesium flare, sparks rushing skyward in the roaring updraft, like a pillar of fire God had inexplicably set against the wet black bluff.

Hey, he said, trying to shake Rabon awake.

Rabon came awake reluctantly, his hands trying to fend the old man away. Scribner kept shaking him roughly. Get up, he said. Rabon sat up in bed rubbing his eyes. What is it? What's the matter?

I killed a feller, Scribner said.

Rabon was instantly alert. What the hell are you talking about? He was looking all about the room as if he might see some outstretched burglar run afoul of the old man.

A feller named Willard Pulley. Folks called him Bonedaddy. I killed him with Alton's baseball bat and set him afire. Must be twenty years ago. He had a shifty little pistol he kept wavin in my face.

Are you crazy? You had a bad dream, you never killed anybody. Go back to sleep.

I ain't been asleep, Scribner said.

Rabon was looking at his watch. It's two o'clock in the morning, he said, as if it were the deadline for something. The old man was watching Rabon's eyes. Something had flickered there when he had mentioned Willard Pulley but he couldn't put a name to what he had seen: anger, apprehension, fear. Then it all smoothed into irritation, an expression Scribner was so accustomed to seeing that he had no difficulty interpreting it.

You know who I'm talkin about?

Of course I know who you're talking about. You must have had a nightmare about him because we were talking about Karen. He did once live with Karen, but nobody killed him, nobody set him afire, as you put it. He was just a young drunk and now he's an old drunk. It hasn't been a week since I saw him lounging against the front of the City Café, the way he's done for twenty-five years. You were dreaming.

I ain't been asleep, Scribner said, but he had grown uncertain even about this. His mind had gone over to the other side where the enemy camped, truth that had once been hard-edged as stone had turned ephemeral and evasive. Subject to gravity, it ran through the cracks and pooled on the floorboards like quicksilver. He was reduced to studying people's eyes for the reaction to something he had said, trying to mirror truth in other people's faces.

IN THE DAYS FOLLOWING, a dull rage possessed him. Nor would it abate. He felt ravaged, violated. Somewhere along the line his life had been stolen. Some hand furtive as a pickpocket's had taken everything worth taking and he hadn't even missed it. Ellen and his children and a house that was his own had fallen by the wayside. He was left bereft and impotent, dependent upon the whims and machinations of others. Faceless women prodded him with needles, spooned tasteless food into him, continually downloaded an endless supply of pills even horses couldn't swallow. The pills kept coming, as if these women were connected directly to their source, so that no matter how many he ingested there was always a full tray waiting atop the bureau. He pondered upon all this and eventually the pickpocket had a face as well as a hand. The puppeteer controlling all these strings was Rabon.

At noon a nameless woman in a dusty Bronco brought him a foam tray of food. He sat down in Rabon's recliner in the living room and prepared to eat. A mouthful of tasteless mashed potatoes clove to his palate, grew rubbery and enormous so that he could not swallow it. He spat it onto the carpet. This is the last goddamned straw, he said. All his life he'd doubled up on the salt and pepper and now the food everyone brought him was cooked without benefit of grease or seasoning. There was a compartment of poisonous-looking green peas and he began to pick them up one by one and flick them at the television screen. Try not to get this all over everything, he said.

When the peas were gone he carried the tray to the kitchen. He raked the carrots and mashed potatoes into the sink and found a can of peas in a cabinet and opened them with an electric can opener. Standing in the living room doorway he began to fling handfuls of them onto the carpet, scattering them about the room as if he were sowing them.

When the peas were gone he got the tray of pills and went out into the backyard. The tray was compartmentalized, Monday, Tuesday, all the days of the week. He dumped them all together as if time had no further significance, as if all days were one.

Rabon had a motley brood of scraggly-looking chickens that were foraging for insects near a split-rail fence, and Scribner began to throw handfuls of pills at them. They ran excitedly about pecking up the pills and searching for more. Get em while they're hot, the old man called. These high-powered vitamins'll have you sailin like hawks and singin like mockinbirds.

He went in and set the tray in its accustomed place. From the bottom of the closet he took up the plastic box he used for storing his tapes. Wearing the look of a man burning the last of his bridges, he began to unspool them, tugging out the thin tape until a shell was empty, discarding it and taking up another. At length they were all empty. He sat on the bed with his hands on his knees. He did not move for a long time, his eyes black and depthless and empty looking, ankle-deep in dead bluegrass musicians and shredded mandolins and harps and flattop guitars, in old lost songs nobody wanted anymore.

Rabon was standing in the doorway wiping crushed peas off the soles of his socks. The old man lay on the bed with his fingers laced behind his skull watching Rabon through slitted eyes.

What the hell happened in the living room? Where did all those peas come from?

A bunch of boys done it, Scribner said. Broke in here. Four or five of the biggest ones held me down and the little ones throwed peas all over the front room.

Do you think this is funny? Rabon asked.

Hell no. You try bein held down by a bunch of boys and peas throwed all over the place. See if you think it's funny. I tried to run em off but I'm old and weak and they overpowered me.

We'll see how funny it is from the door of the old folks' home, Rabon said. Or the crazy house. Rabon was looking at the medicine tray. What happened to all those pills?

The chickens got em, Scribner said.

THE GOING WAS SLOWER than he had expected and by the time the chert road topped out at the crossroads where the blacktop ran it was ten o'clock and the heat was malefic. The treeline shimmered like something seen through bad glass and the blacktop radiated heat upward as if somewhere beneath it a banked fire smoldered.

He stood for a time in the shade of a pin oak debating his choices. He was uncertain about going on, but then again it was a long way back. When he looked down the road the way he had come, the perspiration burning his eyes made the landscape blur in and out of focus like something with a provisional reality, like something he'd conjured but could not maintain. After a while he heard a car, then saw its towed slipstream of dust, and when it stopped for the sign at the crossroads he was standing on the edge of the road leaning on his stick.

The face of the woman peering out of the car window was familiar but he could call no name in mind. He was wearing an old brown fedora and he tipped the brim of it in a gesture that was almost courtly.

Mr. Scribner, what are you doing out in all this heat?

Sweating a lot, Scribner said. I need me a ride into town if you're going that far.

Why of course, the woman said. Then a note of uncertainty crept into her voice. But aren't you . . . where is Rabon? We heard you were sick. Are you supposed to be going to town?

I need to get me a haircut and a few things. There ain't nothin the matter with me, either. That boy's carried me to doctors all over Tennessee and can't none of em kill me.

If you're sure it's all right, she said, moving her purse off the passenger seat to make room. Get in here where it's air-conditioned before you have a stroke.

He got out at the town square of Ackerman's Field and stood for a moment sizing things up, getting his bearings. He crossed at the traffic light and went on down the street to the City Café by some ingrained habit older than the sense of strangeness the town had acquired.

In midmorning the place was almost deserted, three stools occupied by drunks he vaguely recognized, bleary-eyed sots with nowhere else to be. He sat down at the bar, just breathing in the atmosphere: the ancient residue of beer encoded into the very woodwork, sweat, the intangible smell of old violence. There was something evocative about it, almost nostalgic. The old man had come home.

He laid his hat on the counter and studied the barman across from him. Let me have two tall Budweisers, he said, already fumbling at his wallet. He had it in a shirt pocket and the pocket itself secured with a large safety pin. It surprised him that the beer actually appeared, Skully sliding back the lid of the cooler and turning with two frosty cans of Budweiser and setting them on the Formica bar. The old man regarded them with mild astonishment. Well now, he said. He fought an impulse to look over his shoulder and see was Rabon's rubbery face pressed to the glass watching him.

You got a mouse in your pocket, Mr. Scribner? a grinning Skully asked him.

No, it's just me myself, Scribner said, still struggling clumsily with the safety pin. He had huge hands grown stiff and clumsy and he couldn't get it unlatched. I always used one to chase the other one with.

I ain't seen you in here in a long time.

That boy keeps me on a pretty tight leash. I just caught me a ride this mornin and came to town. I need me a haircut and a few things.

You forget that money, Skully said. I ain't taking it. These are on the house for old time's sake.

Scribner had the wallet out. He extracted a bill and smoothed it carefully on the bar. He picked up one of the cans and drank from it, his Adam's apple convulsively pumping the beer down, the can rattling emptily when he set it atop the bar. He turned and regarded the other three drinkers with a benign magnanimity, his eyes slightly unfocused. Hidy boys, he said.

How you, Mr. Scribner?

He slid the bill across to Skully. I thank you for the beer, he said. Let me buy them highbinders down the bar a couple.

There was a flurry of goodwill from the drunks downbar toward this big spender from the outlands and the old man accepted their thanks with grace and drank down the second can of beer.

We heard you was sick and confined to your son's house, Skully said. You look pretty healthy to me. What supposed to be the matter with you?

I reckon my mind's goin out on me, Scribner said. It fades in and out like a weak TV station. I expect to wake up some morning with no mind at all. There ain't nothin wrong with me, though. He hit himself in the chest with a meaty fist. I could still sweep this place out on a Saturday night. You remember when I used to do that.

Yes I do.

I just can't remember names. What went with folks. All last week I was thinkin about this old boy I used to see around. Name of Willard Pulley. I couldn't remember what become of him. Folks called him Bonedaddy.

Let me see, now, Skully said.

He's dead, one of the men down the bar said.

Scribner turned so abruptly the stool spun with him and he almost fell. What? he asked.

He's dead. He got drunk and burnt hisself up down on the Tennessee River. Must be over twenty years ago.

Wasn't much gone, another said. He ain't no kin to you is he?

No, no, I just wondered what become of him. And say he's dead sure enough?

All they found was ashes and bones. That's as dead as I ever want to be.

I got to get on, the old man said. He rose and put on his hat and shoveled his change into a pocket and took up his stick.

When the door closed behind him with its soft chime, one of the drunks said, There goes what's left of a hell of a man. I've worked settin trusses with him where the foreman would have three men on one end and just him on the other. He never faded nothin.

He wasn't lying about cleaning this place out, either, Skully said. He'd sweep it out on a Saturday night like a long-handled broom but he never started nothin. He'd set and mind his own business. Play them old songs on the jukebox. It didn't pay to fuck with him though.

THE OLD MAN SAT in the barber chair, a towel wound about his shoulders and he couldn't remember what he wanted. I need a, he said, and the word just wasn't there. He thought of words, inserting them into the phrase and trying them silently in his mind to see if they worked. I need a picket fence, a bicycle, a heating stove. The hot blood of anger and humiliation suffused his throat and face.

What kind of haircut you want, Mr. Scribner?

A haircut, the old man said in relief. Why hell yes. That's what I want, a haircut. Take it all off. Let me have my money's worth.

All of it?

Just shear it off.

When Scribner left, his buzz-cut bullet head was hairless as a cue ball and the fedora cocked at a jaunty angle. He drank two more beers at Skully's, then thought he'd amble down to the courthouse lawn and see who was sitting on the benches there. When he stood on the sidewalk, the street suddenly yawned before him as if he were looking down the sides of a chasm onto a stream of dark water pebbled with moonlight. He'd already commenced his step and when he tried to retract it he overbalanced and pitched into the street. He tried to catch himself with his palms, but his head still rapped the asphalt solidly, and lights flickered on and off behind his eyes. He dragged himself up and was sitting groggily on the sidewalk when Skully came out the door.

Skully helped him up and seated him against the wall. I done called the ambulance, he said. He retrieved Scribner's hat and set it carefully in the old man's lap. Scribner sat and watched the blood running off his hands. Somewhere on the outskirts of town a siren began, the approaching whoop whoop whoop like some alarm the old man had inadvertently triggered that was homing in on him.

ALL THIS SILENCE was something the old man was apprehensive about. Rabon hadn't even had much to say when, still in his schoolteaching suit, he had picked Scribner up at the emergency room. Once he had ascertained that the old man wasn't seriously hurt he had studied his new haircut and his bandaged hands and said, I believe this is about it for me.

He hadn't even gone in to teach the next day. He had stayed in his bedroom with the door locked, talking on the telephone. Scribner could hear the rise and fall of the mumbling voice but even with an ear to the door he could distinguish no word. It was his opinion that Rabon was calling one old folks' home after another trying to find one desperate enough to take him, and he had no doubt that sooner or later he would succeed.

The day drew on strange and surreal. His life was a series of instants, each one of which bore no relation to the one preceding, the one following. He was reborn moment to moment. He had long taken refuge in the past, but time had proven laden with deadfalls he himself had laid long ago with land mines that were better not stepped on. So he went further back, to the land of his childhood, where everything lay under a troubled truce. Old voices long si-

lenced by the grave spoke again, their ancient timbres and ca-
dences unchanged by time, by death itself. He was bothered by
the image of the little man in the green checked suit and the derby
hat, rapping the spotted dog with a malacca cane and saying: I
just hate a dog at a funeral, don't you? Who the hell was that?
Scribner wondered, the dust of old lost roads coating his bare feet,
the sun of another constellation warming his back.

He looked out the window and dark had come without his
knowing it. A heavyset man in wire-rimmed glasses brought a tray
of food. Scribner did not even wonder who this might be. The man
was balding, and when he stooped to arrange the tray, Scribner
could see the clean pink expanse of scalp through the combed-over
hair. The man went out of the room. Scribner, looking up from his
food, saw him cross through the hall with a bundle of letters and
magazines. He went into Rabon's room and closed the door.

Scribner finished the plate of food without tasting it.

He might have slept. He came to himself lying on the bed, the
need to urinate so intense it was almost painful. He got up. He
could hear a television in the living room, see the spill of yellow
light from Rabon's bedroom, the bathroom.

His bandaged hands made undoing his clothing even more
complicated and finally he just pulled down his pajama bottoms,
the stream of urine already starting, suddenly angry at Rabon,
why the hell has he got all his plunder in the bathroom, these
shoes, suits, these damned golf clubs?

Goddamn, a voice cried. The old man whirled. Rabon was
standing in the hall with the *TV Guide* in his hand. His eyes were
wide with an almost comical look of disbelief. My golf shoes, he
said, flinging the *TV Guide* at Scribner's bullet head and rushing
toward him. Turning his head, the old man realized that he was
standing before Rabon's closet, urinating on a rack of shoes.

When Rabon's weight struck him he went sidewise and fell heavily against the wall, his penis streaking the carpet with urine. He slid down the wall and struggled to a kneeling position, trying to get his pajama bottoms up, a fierce tide of anger rising behind his eyes.

Rabon was mad too, in fact angrier than the old man had ever seen him. He had jerked up the telephone and punched in a series of numbers, stood with the phone clasped to his ear and a furious impatient look on his face, an expression that did not change until the old man struck him in the side of the head with an enormous fist. The phone flew away and when Rabon hit the floor with the old man atop him, Scribner could hear it gibbering mechanically at him from the carpet.

The hot clammy flesh was distasteful to his naked body but Scribner had never been one to shirk what had to be done. With Rabon's face clasped to his breast and his powerful arms locked in a vise that tightened, they looked like perverse lovers spending themselves on the flowered carpet.

When Rabon was still the old man got up, pushing himself erect against Rabon's slack shoulder. He went out the bedroom door and through a room where a television set flickered, his passage applauded by canned laughter from the soundtrack, and so out into the night.

Night air cool on his sweaty skin. A crescent moon like a sliver of bone cocked above the treeline, whippoorwills calling out of the musky keep of the trees. He stood for a moment sensing directions and then he struck out toward the whippoorwills. He went down into the hollow through the herd of plywood cattle pale as the ghosts of cattle and on toward the voices that called out of the dark. He came onto the spectral roadbed and crossed into deeper woods. The whippoorwills were drawing away from him, urging him deeper into the shadowed timber, and he realized abruptly that the voices were coming from the direction of Brown's Ferry or Deep Elm. Leaning against the bole of a white oak to catch his breath he became aware of a presence in the woods before him, and he saw with no alarm that it was a diminutive man in a green plaid suit, derby hat shoved back rakishly over a broad pale forehead, gesturing him on with a malacca cane.

They're up here, the little man called.

Scribner went on, barefoot, his thin pajama bottoms shredding in the undergrowth of winter huckleberry bushes. Past a stand of stunted cedars the night opened up into an enormous tunnel, as wide and high as he could see, a tunnel of mauveblack gloom where whippoorwills darted and checked like bats feeding on the wing, a thousand, ten thousand, each calling to him out of the dark, and he and the man with the malacca cane paused and sat for a time against a tree trunk to rest themselves before going on.

Crossroads Blues

*D*ID YOU HAVE TO scrub the blood off the walls? Karas asked her. Was the water pink when you squeezed the sponge out? Did you vacuum bits of bloody tissue out of that ugly shag carpet?

In a fever dream that was almost but not quite nightmare Karas asked the Storm Princess those questions, then abruptly realized that he had in actuality asked them this very morning, watching her face intently as he spoke, looking deep into her eyes to see if anything changed in their depths.

What in the world are you doing back here? a voice asked.

Karas thought at first the voice was inside his head. One character in his dream speaking to another, but when the voice came again he judged it behind him and slowly opened his eyes.

He was lying somewhere on his back. The first thing he saw was the tall Ron Rico rum bottle he was clasping erect on his abdomen and from which he had apparently been sipping from time to time. He saw his feet, polished brown loafers, his legs crossed at the ankles and protruding from the passenger-side window of the Grand National. His head was protruding from the opposite window, for he could feel the window frame hard against the back of his neck.

What are you doing?

Beyond his feet Karas could see riotous summer greenery, a sunlit wall of rock, the trunks of trees. A squirrel ran along a shelf of limestone and vanished up the bole of a cypress. A cardinal shot across the emerald undergrowth, abrupt and startling as a spatter of blood. A bobwhite called, and he closed his eyes for a time and listened, amusing himself with explanations he might offer whoever was standing behind him and holding him accountable for driving the pristine Grand National he had restored far into the woods where there had not even been a road to follow. Waiting for deer season to open, he thought. Took a left at that last traffic light and *goddamn,* where is this place? Supposed to meet the devil here around midnight and interview him about Robert Johnson.

I about thought you was dead, the voice said. You ain't are you?

The thought of the Storm Princess, the wife who had fled him, suddenly jolted him clear of all this nonsense. It suddenly occurred to him that he was alive, and he had not expected to be. He raised his left arm and studied the inside of his wrist. A red scratch perhaps an inch and a half long. No more damage than you might do with the end of a paper clip. Either the penknife he had found in the glove box had been duller than expected or he had suffered a severe breakdown in the nerve department. He figured it was some of both, and withdrew his feet from the window and sat up in the driver's seat. He drank from the Ron Rico bottle and lowered it and sat clasping it loosely between his thighs.

There was a little man standing patiently beside his car. Karas glancing his way judged him some sort of woodsprite or gnome or some such nature spirit but when he turned and drank from the bottle then looked back the little man was still there.

What are you doing in here? the man asked.

I'm writing a book about Robert Johnson, Karas said.

The little man wore a peaked green hat with a long trailing cock feather of the sort Alpine mountain climbers might favor and Karas supposed that was why he had taken him for some sort of elf. Beyond the man the sun was slant in the trees with its rays harsh and oblique and Karas could tell that the day was waning and that he had drunk and dozed it practically away.

I don't believe I know any Johnsons in these parts, the man said. Do you always write in the middle of the woods?

Robert Johnson was a blues singer and guitarist who died a long time ago in the Mississippi Delta, Karas said, and fell silent, unable to go on, unable to talk, unable to think about anything save the Storm Princess.

She had been gone for three weeks, and when Karas had knocked on the front door of the trailer she had fled to that morning, not even waiting for decent daylight, he had been just drunk enough to believe that she would climb joyfully into the front seat of the Grand National and ride away with him: it had been a long three weeks, and it should have reduced her to a compliant state of loneliness.

I'm having a little trouble handling this, he told her.

She had a hand on the door, waiting to close it. Well, you're just going to have to handle it, she said. There was a hard-edged quality of finality about her that he was unaccustomed to. There was little evidence of loneliness and none of compliancy, and the phrase Karas had been about to utter, We can pretend this separation never happened, was stuck in his mind like something he had no use for.

I just wanted to talk to you.

There's nothing to talk about, she said. Sublimate it, channel it, write it into one of your books. Isn't that supposed to be good therapy? And why are you drunk? You never drink. Why are you acting like such a fool about this?

Well, I didn't set out to act like a fool about it, he said. It sort of happened to me a little at a time.

He stood for a moment before the door that was barred only by her slender forearm, the bottle slung at his side like a sample case. He felt like a salesman hawking some dread wares no one wanted anything whatever to do with. I want you back, he said, knowing the instant the words left his tongue how inadequate and worthless they were. There was no way to tell her. He had been half of two and now he was one, bloody and illy used, a Siamese twin set upon with a chopping ax.

I never mistreated you, he said.

You mistreated me every day for fifteen years, she said. You only wanted me around when you wanted to go to bed with me. The rest of the time you wanted me out of your way. The mystery is why it took me so long to make this move.

He drank from the bottle and tried another tack. I guess you know the realty company screwed you, he said.

So? You've screwed me a few times yourself. It's not as if I'm unused to it.

I never took your money for it, though. They couldn't move this place. On account of what happened here. Did you have to scrub blood off the walls, vacuum flesh out of the carpet, things like that?

Of course not. They'd hired someone to renovate it. It's been completely recarpeted. She was drinking a cup of early-morning coffee. She hadn't offered him any. She was drinking from a thin blue china cup he recognized as coming from the wreckage of their marriage. Besides, she added, I got a great deal on it.

That's what every sucker's said from day one. I got a great deal on it. How do you sleep here?

I sleep fine, she said. No dreams at all.

Her sleep had always been provisional, what there was of it peopled by demons and faceless shapes and, as she had told him once, by the murderers of children. Once long ago she had cried out no in such a strangled outrage that he had shaken her roughly out of sleep and she had begun to cry. She always awoke in a state of alert apprehension, as if someone had laid a black-edged telegram on her upturned palm, as if the telephone had rung at three in the morning.

She moved her forearm and began to close the door. I have work to do, she said. And God knows I wouldn't want to keep you from your drinking.

MOVE AWAY FROM THE DOOR, Karas told the old man. I want to get out. The little man retreated and sat down on a block of stone and took tobacco from a pocket and began to construct a cigarette. Karas saw that the stone was part of a set of ancient limestone steps laid into the earthen wall of an embankment. He opened the door and climbed carefully out.

The little man had his cigarette going. How'd you get back in here? he asked through a fog of smoke.

I drove, Karas said.

There ain't no road, the man said. Did you wreck?

Karas glanced at the Buick, bright and anomalous midst the brush, like something that had been teleported there, and wondered at the force necessary to wreck a car so far into the woods—some sort of nuclear fission wreck, a chain reaction wreck that kept forcing the car deeper and deeper into the timber.

There is now, Karas said. Of a sort. I made it. I drove around the big trees and it looks like I just drove over the little ones. I was drunk.

How'd you plan to get out? Back where the road is? You did come off a road, didn't you? Or did you just come all the way from wherever you come from through the woods?

Karas had walked around behind the car and he stood urinating with his back turned to the little old man. It was not my intention to get out, Karas said. I came in here to drink and do away with myself. I figured I'd be toted out. I just didn't bring any weapon adequate to the job.

Lord God, the man said. Do away with yourself. What method was you usin, if you don't mind my asking?

Karas came around the Buick zipping his pants. All I could find was a penknife and a jack handle, he said. Do you think a man might beat himself in the head with a jack handle until he died?

I expect it's been tried, the man said. Might near everything has, at one time or another.

Likely you'd just knock yourself out and wake up back at the same old stand with a hell of a headache. It was one of those tire spuds though, I guess a man might fall on it like a disgraced samurai falling on his sword.

I guess, the man said doubtfully. Was you not wearing a belt?

Son of a bitch, Karas said, falling into the spirit of things. Karas was fond of words and suicide seemed to call for a lot of them and he had brought neither pencil nor paper. He had heard of living wills and immediately decided to make of the old man a sort of living suicide note. I don't know why a belt never occurred to me, he said.

Give me a little drink of whatever-it-is. My name's Borum, by the way. He rose from the stone nimbly and took the bottle when

Karas proffered it to him. Borum was wearing strapped across his shoulders a bag that looked like a child's book satchel. On closer examination Karas could see that was just what it was, for there were faded green Ninja Turtles imaged upon it. Borum squatted in what appeared to be a spectral roadway and tilted the bottle and drank, his throat working.

What are you doing in here yourself?

Borum lowered the bottle. He stood up and reached it to Karas. He gestured at the pack he carried. Roots and herbs, he said. I been diggin ginseng, goldenseal. I sell em for medicine. There's a spring right up that holler, he said. Let's go get us a drink. You drink some good cold water, wash your face in it, you'll see things in a different light. First let's see that knife, though. Was that what you was going to do, open a vein?

Karas unpocketed the knife and handed it over, somewhat ashamed of it—the blade was scarcely two inches long and the tip was broken off and it was covered with a scaly orange accretion of rust. It seemed a ludicrous tool for so solemn and daunting a task, and Karas wished he had put more forethought into killing himself.

Borum was looking at the knife and he was shaking his head. I doubt you'd have the stomach for it, he said. It'd be like swallowing a bedspring, or bein eat a mouthful at a time by them little bitin fish. Eatin yourself with a spoon. A gun's quicker and easier.

I don't own a gun, Karas said. I never believed in guns.

Borum had produced a knife of his own from somewhere beneath his clothing, a thin lethal-looking blade with a deep blood groove. He turned back the cuff of his khaki shirt and raked his forearm with the blade—it made a faint, unpleasant sound that Karas felt more than heard. Tufts of crinkly gray hair clotted on the blade and Borum raised the knife to his lips and blew them away. He turned his arm so that the paler underside of the wrist was uppermost and laid the blade across the veins. When he looked up at Karas in the failing light his eyes looked like a cat's watching you through broken jungle greenery. This one'd be like a whisper, he said. Like a woman's fingernail raked real light across it. You want to use this one?

Karas thought his madness must be communicable and the old man had caught it. Then he thought Borum must be something out of one of the Storm Princess's nightmares, demon or child killer made real and malevolently set upon the sleepfast countryside with dire intent.

Then Borum grinned and took from a pocket a flat rectangle of chewing tobacco and sliced a corner off it and tucked it into his jaw. The knife disappeared back into the folds of his clothing. Let's get that drink of water, he said.

Swinging the bottle along, he followed Borum up the stone steps to a smooth slope of land, they crossed through old foundation stones, shards of broken dishes, scattered bricks, past a chimney standing like a sentry with nothing left to guard. An old house place, metal twisted and blackened in some long-lost conflagration. Everything was laden with an enormous silence, and for a bemused moment Karas felt that he used to live here, in a white frame house. The Storm Princess had planted a rose garden, he had tilled the fields. Then some cataclysm of the heart had destroyed it, he had come in from the fields one day and found only rubble. They crossed what had once been a lawn, rhododendron grown rank and feral, and went down the slope on the back side to a small meandering stream. He began to hear the rush of water. They followed the stream up a hollow to its source, where it came boiling out of the fissured limestone rock. The air was cool and astringent and heady with the smell of peppermint.

Long ago someone had hammered a section of iron pipe into

the striated rock and the water that ran from its moss-encrusted end was cold to his fingers. He set the bottle aside and cupped his hands and drank from them and washed his face in the icy water. He dried with the tail of his shirt and when he turned around Borum was studying him.

I expect it's a woman, he said. I've seen it a lot of times. Had it happen to me myself. A woman'll warp your mind worse than whiskey ever thought of doing.

Karas's wife, when she was eighteen, used to wake in the mornings with her black curls so tousled and windswept that he imagined the landscape of her dreams to be beset with perpetual storms. Now years had come and gone and in her dreams ice held dominion. He took up the bottle and drank from it and let it ease him further into despair.

Course you're talking foolishness, Borum said. Doin away with yourself. Let me tell you a story. You notice them stone steps we clumb up? Laid in that bank? I toted that limestone out of this hollow myself. Mixed the mortar in the hood of a forty-seven Studebaker. Laid that rock more years ago than I want to think about. This used to be my place, me and the wife lived here when we was first married. I raised corn and a little cotton, she planted all them flowers. Then later on we had some trouble over one thing and another and she quit me. Went back to her family. Them was hard times. Bitter times. I thought of killin myself, setting the house on fire and just laying down in our bed and letting the ceilin cave in on me. Instead of that I got up my nerve and went and talked to her one last time. Pled my case, so to speak. No politician running for office ever spieled out words the way I did. No lawyer tryin to snatch his client out of the electric chair. Like I had a tongue of gold. Words were sweet as honey in my mouth. So she come back to me.

Karas smiled. So you all lived happily ever after, he said. All your grandkids and great-grandkids turned out for your fiftieth wedding anniversary.

Well, not exactly. Not in my case. I come in early from huntin one day two years later and caught her in bed with my brother. I looked down and I was holdin that shotgun, what else was I goin to do? I shot her where she lay and my brother was up and out the window. I shot a goose down pillow he was lyin on a second before. The air was full of feathers like it was snowin. It was summer and hot like this and they had all the windows up. I sighted down the barrel laid across the windowsill and he was runnin up this spring holler. About where we are. I shot his legs out from under him and went out the window after him.

Jesus Christ, Karas said. I don't want to hear any more of this. These are all things I don't need to know.

You need to know what a man's capable of. You need to know what things cost.

Why would I want to know any of that? Karas asked. What in God's name are you talking about?

Night had almost completely fallen. Darkness was rolling out of the hollow like smoke. Borum was barely visible. He seemed to be fading away.

Because everything has its price, he said out of the dark. And because the two years between talkin her back and shootin my brother's legs out from under him was the two best years of my life. Them was good times. Sweet times. Yet all the same when the bill come it had to be paid.

AT SOME HOUR past all clocking Karas was on the road back to the Storm Princess. It was a road not appreciably better than most of the other roads he had been on this day. Stones sang off the rocker panels and went flying off into the weeds like shot and something, probably the jutting tip of a boulder, slammed the undercarriage and oil pan hard. The engine had taken on a guttural sound as if he'd lost or broken the muffler. He glanced down and saw he was driving too fast. He was going downhill like a stone skittering down the sides of a well and he began to ride the brakes. He parked the car on the shelf of rock where he'd already parked one time too many and got out. He kicked the door closed, one more dent couldn't hurt, the Grand National's sides were streaked with zigzag scars like hesitation marks on the wrists of a would-be suicide.

He leaned against the door and fumbled with his clothing and urinated beside the car, his penis in one hand and the rum bottle in the other, the rum burning his throat. A huge orange harvest moon was just clearing the horizon above the dark field and it looked for all the world like some light enormous and supernatural that was rising out of the black velvet surface of the field itself. He canted the bottle against the starblown heavens as if he'd gauge its contents then turned toward the trailer.

Though by now, he had to admit, it was no longer a trailer. It was the lonely tower where the Storm Princess had fled to escape the attentions of an evil wizard. It was a tall conical tower of white stone, and roses climbed its side, their thorns giving purchase on the almost poreless rock, their blossoms dark as drops of splattered blood on the alabaster stone. Slits of window climbed the tower in an ascending spiral, he knew that inside a staircase wound toward a bower at the top where the Storm Princess had sequestered herself to make her stand, all the furniture in the room hastily skidded across the floor to barricade the door against the weight of his shoulder.

The evil wizard fell twice on plates of slick shale rock, once rapping the bottle smartly but not breaking it. He rose and went on, the bottle held aloft like a beacon that was lighting his way or yet like a child held one-handed out of harm's way by someone fording deep swift waters.

The trailer was dark, not even a porch light. Long and low and tacky, it no longer bore any resemblance to a white stone tower, no more resemblance than the woman who finally answered his knock bore to the Storm Princess of so long ago. Her face was scrubbed clean of makeup and by the bare-bulb glare of the porch light she clicked on he could see the fine wrinkles at the corners of her eyes, a few gray strands of hair swept back from her temples.

Are you alone? he asked, knowing that tonight she was still alone. Yet he was weary with the knowledge that flesh can be no more than flesh and he knew of time's implacable attrition on all good resolve. He knew that a time would come when his fist would pound the flimsy door and a man in his wife's bed would stir and sit up. This faceless man would grasp the Storm Princess by the shoulder and shake her gently awake, asking, Who in the world can that be at two o'clock in the morning?

Of course I'm alone, who did you expect to be here? What do you want? She wore a blue bathrobe unbuttoned but clasped loosely at the throat with one hand and at the waist by the other. She did not seem particularly surprised to see him, nor pleased that he could still number himself among the living.

You of all people should know what I want.

Well, she said, it's—she turned and glanced over her shoulder to a wall clock, a round white clock that was garlanded with fake roses that reminded him of the roses climbing the tower—two o'clock in the morning. You're going to have to be more specific than that. I have to work tomorrow.

I'm drunk but not so drunk I don't know what day it is, Karas said. Tomorrow is Sunday. Is it all right if I come in?

I suppose so, she said. You seem determined to run through all the definitions there are for a fool. What's the matter with you?

Not exactly knowing, he did not reply. When she stepped aside to allow him passage he entered the small claustrophobic living room, stood for a moment in its center breathing in the caustic smell of imitation wood paneling, old violence, his own violent despair. He crossed the room, a bare few paces, and seated himself on a vinyl sofa. He held the bottle across his lap the way a commuter awaiting a train clutches his briefcase.

This place feels wrong, he said. Distinctly bad vibrations. You can feel it in the air, double murder, love gone wrong. This place has been cleaned up but I'll bet if I look I can find blood on the walls, bits of tissue in the nap of the carpet.

Just shut up, she said. I don't want to hear your drunken nonsense. A man killed his wife and his brother, the man wasn't even killed in here, it was the backyard. We saw it on the TV, both of us saw it on the news. It didn't affect this place one bit.

He unscrewed the cap and raised the bottle and drank. The face of his wife, the room itself, darkened like a world abruptly cut to half power. He imagined holding a cigarette lighter to the cheap paneling until it caught in a thin blue spreading flame, holding her away one-handed while fire climbed the walls like roses. If suicide was feasible, was murder beyond conjecture? But when he glanced at the inside of his left wrist the blood still kept its appointed rounds through the dimly visible veins, its slow blue pulse as regular as the ticking of the clock. He screwed the cap on and set the bottle on the carpet between his feet.

Do you want a cup of coffee? It occurs to me that you could use one.

I suppose I could drink one, he said agreeably, and leaned his head against the cool vinyl of the couch. When she raised an arm to open a cabinet door her robe fell open and he could see her rounded breast, the dark smudge of her pubic hair. Then she turned her back to him and held the bowl of the coffeemaker to the sink. He closed his eyes.

When he opened them she was crossing the room carrying two cups of coffee. She set one on the table before his knees. There was a swivel rocker beside the television set and she seated herself there and turned the rocker slightly toward him, adjusting the robe closer about her knees. She sipped her coffee and watched him with a look almost of speculation.

Karas had not yet taken up his cup. He took up the Ron Rico and drank from the bottle. He had felt the first uncomfortable intimations of reality, as if you really could drink yourself sober, as if he'd been on some dark journey and the first harbingers of his destination had reared up starkly against the horizon, and it was a hostile and barren place he did not want to go to. He felt as if this day had used up all the emotions he possessed save a bleak and bitter despair.

Well, she said after a time. What are your plans?

I thought I might sleep here on the couch tonight.

That's what I expected you might think.

Is it all right?

I suppose it is. I don't want to live with you anymore, but I don't want you killing yourself in a car wreck. Or killing a carload of innocent people.

Just on the couch, he said. I won't bother you and I'll be on my way first thing in the morning.

She smiled at him, not a particularly pleasant smile, a smile that said she knew him better than he knew himself and that he was continuing to live down to the expectations she had for him. You're so facile, she said.

You don't have to use words like facile, he said. We both know you went to college.

All right then, how's this? You're such a bullshit artist. You're so manipulative. Words are all you care about and you think you can do anything with them. Don't you think I know what's wrong with you? It's sex. You're used to it every night or two and it's been what, three weeks? You want to spend the night with me. You'll lie down on the couch when I go to bed, then you'll get up. Then you'll stand in my bedroom door and ask if you can lie down beside me. Just for the company, you won't touch me. Then you'll put your arm around me.

Karas wondered if any of this might be true. He suspected that just such a thought might have been nibbling at the corner of his mind, like a cautious but persistent mouse.

Do you have any money with you?

What? Karas asked. He had been thinking that spending the night in her bed might be just the ticket; it was possible that he might persuade her to come back to him, and failing that perhaps she was right, it was just sex, something might collapse in him like a dam breaking and all the images of despair and blood and suicide might vanish in a clean orgasmic rush and he would be himself again, a sensible and literate middle-aged man writing a book about Robert Johnson. But the sudden shift in the conversation from sex to money threw him off balance.

When I moved in here the electricity didn't work. The meter base or something was broken. It cost me three hundred dollars to hire an electrician and the realty company hasn't reimbursed me. When I left I said I didn't want anything from you, but I do. The repairs left me three hundred short of what I need this month, and that's what it's going to cost you. If you want me half as badly as you say you do then that ought to be the bargain of a lifetime.

Hellfire, he said in a kind of appalled despair. That isn't what I wanted. Why didn't you just ask me for the money? Why didn't you just screw the electrician and cut out the middleman?

That isn't what you wanted? You didn't want sex?

Well. I don't know. Of course I did, but not like this. I wanted us to make up, to get back together. Then go to bed, and everything would be the way it used to be.

It will never be the way it used to be, she said. And I thank God for that when I wake up every morning.

Karas was silent a time. That seems a reasonable figure, he finally said.

IN THE BEDROOM moonlight fell through the gauzy curtains. She slipped off the robe and lay atop the covers. She lay on her back, hands folded placidly across her stomach. He kissed her and gently stroked her breasts. Her lips were pliable, rubbery and unresponsive, and after a while he just sat on the bed beside her, elbows on his knees, his hands clasping the bottle.

What's the matter? Can't you do anything?

Why hell yes, I can do whatever needs to be done. It's just this place, I keep wondering if it's the same bed . . . let's go to a motel.

What?

If you won't go home with me then let's go to a motel.

Don't be so ridiculous. There's nothing wrong with this bed.

There's just something about this place. Something . . . unhealthy about it.

You're just too sensitive, she said in a sleepy ironic voice. At any rate I'm not going to a motel. I like it here.

Karas sat in silence, listening to the various nighttime hummings and whirrings of the trailer. They began to sound like voices, sourceless and disembodied, replaying old accusations and recriminations, words he could almost but not quite decipher. The very atmosphere had turned oppressive and claustrophobic, the perfect setting for the story Borum had told him, and he wondered if any of it was real, if he was real. When he glanced at his wife her eyes were closed and her mouth slightly open. He saw to his surprise that she had fallen asleep.

The exact nature of his malady perplexed him. You could stand on a street corner waiting for a traffic light to change and see a dozen women who were prettier, more smartly dressed, more confident in their congress with the world. There had always been something tentative about her, a look that said, All right, here I am. I hope you won't hurt me, but if you have to, go ahead. Only a thin silver cord still bound him to her. He watched the measured rise and fall of her breasts and wished that she would do something so appalling the cord would snap like a kite string, as he had been unable to snap it with the penknife.

He saw that they had, hand in hand, come to a crossroads. They had been walking one of Robert Johnson's fabled red backroads and they had come to a crossroads. The Storm Princess had scarcely glanced to the right or the left, without a falter or a stitch in her pace she had made her decision and gone on without a backwards look. But a crossroads presented Karas with too many options. Confounded, he had sat down on his suitcase to smoke a cigarette and think about things.

He rose from the side of the bed so abruptly the bottle rapped the edge of the dresser and she stirred but did not awaken. She turned over on her left side and pillowed her head on a folded arm and drew her knees up, her naked body in the filigreed moonlight at once real yet as remote and lost as a dusty nude study stacked in a museum's forgotten corner.

He set the bottle on the corner of the bureau and took out his wallet. The movement of his reflection in the mirror was furtive, that of a prowler, a midnight rambler. Like a burglar returning something he has stolen. He withdrew three bills from the wallet and tilted them toward the moonlit window to ascertain their denomination. He folded them once and slid them under the edge of the bottle. The room seemed close and more claustrophobic than ever, decadent and diseased, perhaps there really was blood on the walls and baseboards, shreds of rotting brain tissue in the nap of the carpet. Voices from darkened corners of the room muttered secrets he wanted no part of. Holding his breath he crossed through the doorway into the living room, went out the front door for the last time. He pulled the door to behind him then as an afterthought opened it and reached in and turned the lock and pulled it closed until it clicked. He went down the steps from the deck.

It was almost as bright as day. The moon was well up now and the world as pristine as if no one had yet torn the cellophane off it, left a footprint on it. The slabs of limestone reared out of the dark white as snowbanks. He went to the car and climbed in.

He had his hand on the ignition when something his eyes had seen but his brain had not immediately registered struck him and he opened the door and got out.

Well I'm a son of a bitch, he said.

Oil had pooled beneath the engine and trickled down the rock in streams that in the moonlight looked like blood, dark heart's blood coagulating on white leather seat covers. There was an enormous quantity of it, and he guessed the crankcase was empty, the engine bled white.

Well, it's only an oil pan, he told himself. An oil pan could be fixed. He opened the door of his wife's Taurus. He did not expect the keys to be in the ignition and they were not. He could go in for the keys, but it might be better to send a wrecker for the Buick. She would lend him the car, but in order to get the keys he would have to knock on the door and he did not want to knock on that door again. He had a superstitious fear that something dread might answer his knock, who knew what.

Like a crossroads, the night itself had confounded him, possibilities he'd never considered swirled like smoke—he might borrow the keys and be on his way, he might seek value received for his three hundred dollars, like Borum he might sweet-talk her into giving him one more chance, he might strangle her where she lay.

Of course a man might walk away. The yellow moon lay low in the southern sky and that would be enough light to walk by. Just walk off toward it, give up cigarettes and Ron Rico and thoughts of suicide and bloody violence. Take up Zen, needlepoint, the salvation of heathen souls. Find a southern star and use it as a sextant as mariners were told to do and set a course for the Mississippi Delta so absolutely undeviating he would clamber over things instead of walking off course around them, crossing interstates and freeways and clotheslines and barbed-wire fences until he was deep in the Delta, sitting in some smoky club drinking Wild Turkey and listening to the blues. Then farther still until there was no longer any question of going back, you couldn't go back. Until the turnpikes and the Burger Kings and the Taco Bells and acres of smashed cars that looked like the broken and discarded cartons death had come in vanished and time itself distorted like light through warped glass and he was in some yellow-lit shack that smelled of coal oil and bootleg whiskey and where the ghost of Robert Johnson scowled at him and turned his body away so that Karas could not see the chords his fingers were making on the guitar.

Then finally into the warm night until the Delta itself, smooth as velvet and sweet as honeysuckle, took him as absolutely as if he had walked into dark and bottomless waters that had closed over his head remorseless as time, implacable as fate, seamless as the heavens.

Closure and Roadkill on the Life's Highway

RAYMER HAD BEEN working at the housing project for more than a month, and during this time the little old man had consistently moved with the sun. Raymer had begun work during the chill days of a blackberry winter, and the man had shuttled his chair as each day progressed, claiming the thin, watery light as if he drew sustenance from it. Now it was well into June, and at some point the man had shifted into reverse, moving counterclockwise for the shade but always positioning his lawn chair where he could watch Raymer work.

Raymer hardly noticed him, for he was in more pain than he had thought possible. He could scarcely get through the day. He was amazed that hearts could actually ache, actually break. Secretly he suspected that his had been defective, already faulted, a secondhand or rebuilt heart, for it had certainly not held up as well as he had expected it to. Corrie, who had been his childhood sweetheart before she became his wife, had inserted the point of a chisel into the fault line and tapped it once lightly with a hammer, and that was the end of that.

By trade he was a painter, and some days he was conscious only of the aluminum extension ladder through his tennis shoes and the brush at the end of his extended arm, which leaned out, and out, as if gravity were just a bothersome rumor, as if he were leaning to paint the very void that yawned to engulf him. When Raymer came down to move the ladder, the old man was waiting for him at the foot of it holding a glass of iced tea in his hand. He was a wizened little man who did not even come to Raymer's shoulder. He had washed-out eyes of the palest blue, and the tip of his nose looked as if, sometime long ago, it had been sliced off neatly with a pocketknife. He was wearing a canvas porkpie hat that had half a dozen trout flies hooked through the band, and he was dressed in flip-flops, faded blue jeans, and an old Twisted Sister T-shirt.

My name's Mayfield. Drink this tea before you get too hot.

Raymer took the glass of tea as you'd take a pill a doctor ordered you to, and stood holding it as if he did not know what to do with it.

Drink it up before that ice melts. You don't talk much, do you?

What?

You don't have much to say.

Well, I work by myself. Folks might think me peculiar if I was having long conversations.

I mean you ain't very friendly. You don't exactly invite conversation.

I just have all this work to do.

Who do you work for?

Raymer sipped the tea. It was sweet and strong, and the glass was full of shaved ice. A sprig of mint floated on top, and he crushed it between his teeth. I work for myself, he said.

I been watchin you ever since you come out here. You're right agile on that ladder. Move around like you was on solid ground. How old a feller are you?

I'm twenty-four, Raymer said, chewing the mint, its taste as evocative as a hallucinogenic drug, reminding him of something but he could not have said what. Where'd you get that T-shirt?

It was in some stuff that my daughter left when she married, Mayfield said. You ever do any bluff-climbin?

Any what?

Bluff-climbin: Climbin around over these limestone bluffs down by the Tennessee River.

No.

I bet you could, though. I used to do it when I was a hell of a lot older than twenty-four. I can't do it now, though—my joints has got stiff, and my bones are as brittle as glass. .

I'm sorry, Raymer said, feeling an obscure need to apologize for infirmities of age he hadn't caused. He was thinking of Corrie the last time he'd seen her, thinking of her hands pushing against his chest.

It ain't your fault. Listen, I got somethin I need a coat of paint on. You stop by when you knock off work this evenin, and I'll show it to you.

Well, I don't know. I push myself pretty hard. I'm usually about worn out by the end of the day.

It ain't much, and I ain't lookin' to get it done for nothin. I'll pay you.

If I'm not too tired.

The main thing is I want to talk to you. I've got a business proposition for you.

Raymer drained the glass and handed it to the old man. He began repositioning the ladder. I'll see at quitting time, he said.

He made it through the day, and when he was behind the apartment building, washing his brushes, he thought he might make it to his truck and escape without painting whatever it was the old man wanted painted. He wanted to go home to the empty house and sit in the dark and think about Corrie. But Mayfield was a wily old man and had anticipated him. He was leaning against the front of Raymer's truck when Raymer came around the building with his brushes in his hand. He had one flip-flop cocked on the bumper and was leaning against the grille with an elbow propped on the hood. He wasn't much taller than the hood of the truck. I'll show you that thing now, he said. It's over on the porch of my apartment.

Raymer didn't even know what it was. It appeared to be a sort of flattened-out concrete lion. Its paws were outstretched, and its eyes looked crossed or rolled back in its head. It looked like an animal on which something had fallen from an enormous height, flattening its back and leaving a rectangular cavity.

What the hell is it?

It's a homemade planter, of course. It was my wife's. It's all I've got left after fifty years of marriage, all I have to remember her by.

Raymer gazed at the sorry-looking thing. It seemed precious little to have salvaged from fifty years of marriage, but he guessed it was more than he had.

What color you want it? Paint won't stay on that concrete anyway, not out here in the weather.

I ain't worried about the weather—that thing'll be on this porch longer than I will. Paint it red, brighten things up around here.

While Raymer painted it red, the old man told him a tale.

I was watchin the way you get around on that ladder, he began. You ain't got no fear of heights. That ladder must run out forty foot, and you never make a misstep. Course it wouldn't take but one, and that'd be all of you. I was thinkin about them bluffs down on the Tennessee River. Down there below Clifton. I bet a young man like you wouldn't have no trouble climbin up to some caves I know of on them bluffs.

Raymer was barely listening. While he was painting the lion, he was replaying a loop of tape in his head of Corrie telling him about the emptiness in her life. What's the matter? he had asked, but whatever was the matter was so evasive and intangible that it couldn't be pinned down with a word. No word was precise or subtle enough to explain it. We never have enough money, but it's not really about money, she had said. He had dropped out of college so that Corrie could finish nursing school. She had dropped out of his life, and the bottom had dropped out of everything. My life is empty, she said, before she packed her bags and rented an apartment in Maury County. He didn't know what kind of emptiness, or what had been removed to cause it, but the space must have been sizable, because she had found a six-foot-four guitarist in a country band to fill it. The guitarist's name was Robbie, and he had a wild mane of curly red hair and a predatory, foxlike face.

Hell, he's not even good-looking, Raymer had told her. He looks like a goddamned fox.

Like a what?

Like a fox. A red fox. That sharp nose, all that red fur. Hair. Hell, I'm better-looking than he is.

You're very good-looking, Buddy. You're a lot better-looking than he is—but life's not always about looks, is it?

You a married man? Mayfield asked.

She quit me, Raymer said, putting the finishing touches on the lion.

I bet ten thousand dollars would put things in a whole other light, Mayfield said.

It wasn't really about money.

It's never about money, but still, a few thousand dollars would fix a lot of things right up. Smooth things over, round off a lot of sharp corners. She got another man?

Raymer was growing uncomfortable talking about it. Thinking about it. Not until after she left, he said carefully.

I bet she had him picked out beforehand, though.

Raymer laid the brush aside. You do? What the hell do you know about it? What is it to you anyway?

I know I'm seventy-five years old, and I ain't went through life blindfolded. I know you're pretty down in the mouth, and I know there's nearly twenty thousand dollars in that cave I was tellin you about. I put it there myself, a long time ago. You can't even get to it from the top, from the bluff side. You got to get up to it from the river. A little over nineteen thousand dollars, to be exact.

A little over nineteen thousand is not exact, Raymer said.

Nineteen thousand seven hundred something, then, Mayfield said. At that time Alabama was dry for beer. Dry as a chip. I lived right across the state line then. I had two coolers on my back porch and didn't sell nothin but tallboy Bud. Sunday afternoons in the summertime you could stand in my front yard and look up the highway and the line of cars windin around my house looked like it went on forever. You'd wonder where all them cars come from. Where they went. I had a beer truck comin from Tennessee twice a week. I was payin off everybody from county judges to dogcatchers, and still I was hooked up to a money machine. I didn't drink, like most bootleggers. I didn't gamble. What was I goin to do with all that money? Put it in the bank? Mail it to the IRS? I was makin money faster than I could spend it, and I was never a slacker when it come to spendin money. We had a daughter in a finishin school in Atlanta, Georgia, and we was drivin matchin

Lincoln Continentals. I was accumulatin it in fruit jars, paper sacks. The money kept growin all the time.

Why didn't you just bury it? Raymer asked, as if he believed any of this.

I did, but folks was always slippin around and tryin to dig it up. They took to watchin me in shifts. They knew I had money. I had to get it somewheres nobody prowled around. I was thinkin in terms of a sort of retirement fund. Then I come in this part of the country and found that cave. You can barely see it from the river, much less get into it. Nobody had been in there in a hell of a time. Some skeletons were in there, and old guns. Swords. I've got one of them I'll show you. It was a old Civil War cave.

Let's see it, Raymer said, interested in spite of himself.

The sword was wrapped in what looked like an old tablecloth. The old man unfolded the oilcloth and held up the sword for Raymer to see. Raymer was expecting something polished and lethal, but the steel had a dull patina of time, and it seemed to draw light into itself instead of reflecting it.

It's one of them old CSA officer's swords, ain't it? the man said.

I really wouldn't know one from a meat cleaver, but I guess it is if you say it is. It's certainly some kind of sword. What else was in there?

Belt buckles. Rusty guns. Bones, like I said. Further back there was different kinds of bones, arrowheads, and clay pots. That place was old. I ain't no zoologist or nothin, but them was Indian bones.

Hellfire, Raymer said. I thought you needed someplace nobody knew about. It sounds like folks were just tripping over each other to get into your cave. It must have been the Grand Central Station of caves.

The old man took the sword back and folded its shroud around it. Nobody's interested in that kind of stuff anymore, he said.

Everybody's forgot about it. When I was in there, I guess I was the first in seventy-five years. Nobody's been there since—I'd bet on it.

If you left nineteen thousand dollars in there, you bet pretty high, Raymer observed. I thought you said you didn't gamble.

Mayfield had not yet turned on the lights in his living room, and behind him the door loomed dark and silent. Raymer thought of his own still house, where he must go.

I've got to get on, he said. What happened to your nose?

I had plastic surgery. I wanted it this way. I picked this nose out of a book.

Were you in an accident?

No, he did it on purpose. I was in a beer joint over on the Wayne County line. Goblin's Knob. This big farmer off of Beech Creek set on me and held me down and cut the end off of it with a pocketknife.

Jesus Christ.

No, he was a Pulley. He disappeared right after that. Nobody ever knew what became of him. I believe he's in a dry cistern with his throat cut and rocks piled down on him. What do you think?

I think I can feel you pulling on my leg again.

Maybe. Maybe not.

SIX WEEKS AFTER she left, he had seen her in a mall, coming out of a JCPenney. She had had her hair shorn away and what was left dyed a glossy black. She was slim and graceful, and she looked like the willowy child he had grown up with. He walked along beside her. Standing by a wishing pool where coins gleamed from the depths, and with a brick wall hard against her back, he kissed her mouth until she twisted her face away. Let me alone, she said. What are you trying to do?

He was still holding her. He could feel the delicate framework of bones beneath her flesh. Like a rabbit, a fawn, like something small. I'm trying to save our marriage, he said.

She shook her head. This marriage is shot, she said quietly. A team of paramedics couldn't save it. This marriage wound up roadkill on the life's highway.

On the life's highway, Raymer repeated in wonder. You've been helping Robbie with his country lyrics, haven't you?

She was pushing harder against him, but he was still holding her. His arms wouldn't release. When they finally did, they hung limply at his sides, like appendages he hadn't learned the use of. She was looking into his eyes. Was she about to cry? Maybe. Maybe not. She turned away, and he didn't follow.

Corrie lived in an apartment complex near the college where she was learning to be a nurse. He had been there a time or two before she took up with the country musician. Tonight her light was out. Early to bed, early to rise. Robbie owned an old green Camaro, and Raymer drove around the parking lot until he found it. Then he got back on the interstate and drove toward home.

IT'S IN A FIVE-GALLON VINEGAR JAR, Mayfield said.

What in the world would a person ever do with five gallons of vinegar? Raymer said.

They'd make a lot of pickles. Anyway, that's where it's at. I started out with fruit jars, but they were too hard to keep up with. I figured, keep all my eggs in one basket. If the weather clears up, we might do it this weekend. I believe it'd do you good to get your mind off that girl that quit you. We might fish a little. You get down on that river, you'll be all right.

I never said I believed any of this tale. And I damn sure never said I'd do it.

You never said you wouldn't. We'll split right down the middle, half and half. I'd even give you the even ten.

Raymer was sitting on Mayfield's porch, a porch stanchion against his back, drinking from a warming bottle of beer and watching rain string off the roof. A sudden squall had blown in from the southwest, and Mayfield had been standing there in the rain waiting for him before he had his ladders and tools stored away. Now Mayfield was rocking in the porch swing, and for some time he studied Raymer in silence.

What you're doin is draggin this out way too far, he said. You're a likely young feller. Not too bad-lookin. You need to get over it. Get on to the next thing. You need some kind of closure.

Closure? Raymer was grinning. Where did you hear that? Was relationship therapy part of the bootlegging trade when you followed it?

I heard it on TV. I got no way of gettin out anywhere. I watch a lot of TV. Them talk shows—them shrinks and social workers are always talkin about closure. Closure this, closure that. I figure you need some. You need somethin for sure. You got a look about you like you don't care whether you live or die, and maybe you'd a little rather die. I've seen that look on folks before, and I don't care for it. It ain't healthy.

Raymer was thinking that maybe the old man was right. He did need something, and closure was as good a word for it as anything else. Everything had just been so damned polite. She had not even raised her voice. Just I'm going, goodbye, don't leave the light on for me. If only she had done something irrevocable, something he couldn't forget, something so bad she couldn't take it back. Something that would cauterize the wound like a red-hot iron.

Did it have a metal lid, this famous jug?

What?

If it did, after twenty years in a wet cave the lid's rusted away and the money's just a mildewed mess of rotten goop. A biological stew of all the germs that came off all the people who ever handled it. Fermenting all these years.

I never heard such rubbish. Anyway, I'm way ahead of you. The money's wrapped in plastic, and I melted paraffin in a cooker and sealed it with a couple of inches of that. Like women used to seal jelly.

This silenced Raymer, and he took a sip of beer and sat watching Mayfield bemusedly. After a while he set his bottle aside. He seemed to have made up his mind about something.

Do you believe in God? he asked.

Do what? Of course I do. Don't you?

Do you own a Bible?

I believe there's one in there somewhere.

Go get it.

Mayfield was in the house for some time. Raymer watched staccato lightning flicker in the west out of tumorous storm clouds. Thunder rumbled like something heavy and ungainly rolling down an endless corridor, faint and fainter. When Mayfield came out, he had a worn Bible covered in black leather. He held it out to Raymer.

Did you want to read a psalm or two? he asked.

Raymer didn't take the Bible. Do you swear you're telling me the truth about that money? he asked.

The old man looked amused, as if he'd won some obscure point of honor. He laid the Bible in the seat of the lawn chair and placed his palm on it. I swear I hid a vinegar jar with nineteen thousand seven hundred dollars in it in a cave down on the Tennessee River.

Raymer figured he might as well cover all the contingencies. And as far as I know, it's still there, he said.

And as far as I know, it's still there, Mayfield repeated.

IT WAS NEVER ABOUT MONEY, Corrie had said, but Raymer thought perhaps it had been about money after all. Corrie had been happiest when they had money to spend, and she fell into long silences when it grew tight. The happiest he had seen her was when they bought an old farmhouse to remodel. But everything ate up money: mortgage payments, building materials. Anyway, what Corrie seemed to enjoy was the act of spending, not what she bought.

He had given her a $300 leather jacket for her twenty-second birthday, and she had left it in a Taco Bell and not even checked on it for a week. Naturally, it was gone. They probably made a lot of others just like it, she said. Somewhere someone Raymer didn't know was wearing his $300.

HE CUT THE MOTOR and let the boat drift the last few feet toward shore, rocking slightly on the choppy water. He took a line up from the stern and tossed it over a sweet-gum branch. He drew it around and tied it off and just stood for a moment, staring up the face of the bluff. The cliff rose in a sheer vertical that he judged to be almost two hundred feet. The opening he was looking at was perhaps thirty feet from the top.

You went up that thing?

I damn sure did. With a five-gallon vinegar jug of money.

The hell you did.

The hell I didn't. It's not as steep as it looks.

It better not be. If it is, Spiderman couldn't get up it with suction cups on his hands and feet. Are you sure it's the right one?

I'm almost positive, Mayfield said. He had opened a tackle box and sat with an air of concentration, inspecting its contents. At length he selected a fly and began to tie it to the nylon line on the fishing rod he was holding.

It was ten o'clock on a balmy Saturday morning. They had already been inside several inlets where the river backwatered and had inspected the bluffs for caves. They had seen two openings that could have been caves, but the openings had not looked right to the old man. Mayfield had brought a cooler of beer and Coca-Colas, a picnic basket filled with sandwiches, his tackle box, a creel, and two fly rods. Raymer had brought only a heavy-duty flashlight and a two-hundred-foot coil of nylon rope, and he was disgusted. If we had one of those striped umbrellas, we could lollygag on the beach, he said. If we had a beach.

He began a winding course up the bluff. It was cut with ledges that narrowed as the bluff ascended, and sometimes he was forced to progress from ledge to ledge by wedging his boots in vertical crevices and pushing himself laboriously upward. From time to time he came upon stunted cedars growing out of the fissured rock, but he didn't trust them to hold his weight.

Halfway up, the ledges ceased to be anything more than sloping footholds on the rock face, and he could go no farther. He stood on a narrow ledge not much wider than his shoe soles, hugging the bluff and glancing up. The rest of the bluff looked as sheer and smooth as an enormous section of window glass. The hell with this, he said. He worked himself down to a wider outcropping and hunkered there with his back against the limestone and his eyes closed. He could feel the hot sun on his eyelids. When he opened them, the world was spread out in a panorama of such magnitude that his head reeled, and for a moment he did not think of Corrie at all.

Everything below him was diminished—a tiny boat with a tiny man casting a line, the inlet joining the rolling river where it gleamed like metal in the sun. Far upstream, toward the ferry, a barge drifted with a load of new cars, their glass and chrome flashing in the sun like a heliograph. Mayfield glanced up to check his progress and waved an encouraging hand. Raymer was seized with an intense loathing, a maniacal urge to throttle the old man and wedge his body under a rock somewhere.

When he reached the base of the cliff, he was wringing wet with sweat. He waded out into the shallow water and got the coil of rope. Mayfield was unhooking a small channel cat and dropping it into his creel.

What's the trouble? he said.

Raymer shook his head and did not reply. He lined up the mouth of the cave with a lightning-struck cypress on the white dome of the bluff and went up the riverbank looking for easier climbing. He entered a hollow, topped out on a ridge, and then angled back toward the river looking for the cypress. Finding it seemed to take forever. When he did find it, he tied the end of the rope around its base and dropped the coil over the bluff. Then he hauled thirty or forty feet of rope back up and began to fashion a rough safety line. The idea of swinging back and forth, pendulumlike, across the face of the bluff, dependent on an old man with a fishing pole to rescue him, did not appeal to him, but he tied the rope off anyway. He felt like a fool to the tenth power, and in his heart of hearts he knew he wouldn't find any money.

His feet reached the opening first, and for a dizzy moment they were climbing on nothingness, pedaling desperately for purchase until the bottom of the opening connected with his shoes. When he was sure he was safe on solid rock, he unclipped the flashlight from his belt and shone it into the opening. This could not be it. Here was no huge room like the one the old man had described, no dead soldiers or guns, no money. It was not even a proper cave—just cannular limestone walls thick with bat guano, sloping inward toward the dead end of a rock wall. He rested for a time and then clicked off the light and went hand over hand back up the face of the bluff.

When Raymer waded out to the boat and tossed in the rope and the light, Mayfield did not seem concerned. Likely it's another bluff, he said. All these sloughs get to lookin' the same, and it's been upwards of twenty years since I was here. I used to fish all these backwaters when I first come up from Alabama. Now I think on it, it seems the mouth of that cave was just about hid by a cedar. That's why I picked it to begin with. I never would have found it if I hadn't been watchin' a hawk through some field glasses.

Then you just deposited your twenty thousand and sat back waiting for the interest to add up.

I told you, I didn't need it. I'd tip a waitress a dollar for a fifty-cent hamburger. I never cared for money.

I guess you were just in the bootlegging trade for the service you could render humanity.

Right.

I wish I had sense like other folks, Raymer said. Why does everybody think I just fell off the hay truck?

You've got that red neck and that slack-jawed country look, Mayfield said placidly. And a fool is such a hard thing to resist.

✦ ✦ ✦

HE HAD SENT HER three dozen American Beauty roses, and the apartment was saturated with their smell. Raymer sat on the couch with his legs crossed and a cup of coffee balanced on his knee and had the closest thing to a conversation he had had with Corrie since the day she left.

This is so unlike you, she said. All these flowers. How much did they cost?

They were day-old roses, half off. I told you it didn't matter.

And climbing around in caves looking for hidden treasure. It's so unpredictable. Who would have thought it of you? Are you having some sort of a crisis?

Raymer kept glancing around the apartment. He had neither seen Robbie nor heard mention of his name, but the place made him nervous anyway. It was fancier and more expensive-looking than he remembered, and he wondered how she could afford it. Everything looked like a sleek and dynamic symbol for a life he could not aspire to. The furniture was low and curvilinear, as if aerodynamically designed for life in the fast lane.

He's almost certainly senile, she said. What makes you think he's telling you the truth?

I know he's telling the truth. He's religious, and he laid his hand on the Bible, and . . . wait a minute—quit that. It may be funny to you, but he took it seriously.

Religious and bootlegger just sort of seem contradictory terms to me.

I'm not going to argue semantics. The point is, he's telling the truth. I even drove down below the state line and talked to some folks who used to know him. He was a bootlegger, and he was successful enough at it to have socked away twenty thousand dollars without missing it. That's ten thousand for me. Us, if I can talk you into it. We could just spend it, just piss it away. Buy things. Go on a cruise. I'm making money for us to live on, and I've got more work to do.

She gave him a sharp took of curiosity. What's in it for you?

You. If you'll give me a chance, I'll win you back. By the time we spend ten thousand dollars, I can persuade you to give it another shot.

We gave it a four-year shot. It wasn't working.

I'll try harder.

Oh, Buddy. If you tried any harder, you'd break something. Rupture all your little springs or something. It wasn't you. It was just a bad idea—although you did make it worse. You're such an innocent about things. You get a picture of things in your head and your picture is all you see. You don't know me. You don't even know yourself. All you know is your little picture of how things ought to be, and that's the way you think they are.

Well, whatever. Ten thousand dollars is still a lot of money.

She didn't argue with that. Wouldn't it be fun to go down to the Bahamas? I'm on summer break. We could lie on the beach. All that white sand. We could just lie in the sun and drink those tall drinks they have with tropical fruit in them.

Then you'll do it?

I'll think about it. Like you said, it's a lot of money. She paused, and was silent for a time. There's just one thing, she said.

Where's the fox at?

Robbie? He's playing a string of club dates in Nashville, trying to get a record deal. By the way, you shouldn't call him that—it just shows how petty you are. I told him about it, and he wasn't amused.

Piss on him. I never set out to be a comedian.

Back to what I was saying. The way you tell it, you're doing all the work. Swinging around on those bluffs—that's dangerous.

You could get killed. I'm only twenty-three, and I could be a widow. I think you deserve the entire twenty thousand.

Hellfire, Corrie, it's Mayfield's money, not mine.

You said yourself he doesn't care about it. Besides, it would take twice as long to spend it. If you're really trying to, as you put it, win me back, this would give you twice as long to do it.

Raymer was put off balance by what she'd suggested, and he felt a little dizzy. He thought the smell of the roses might be getting to him. The room was filled with a sickening sweet reek that seemed to have soaked into the draperies and the carpet. It smelled like a wedding, a funeral. You may be right, he said.

Of course I'm right. You could take six months off from work. We could spend it remodeling the house. Maybe you're learning, Buddy. You did right to tell me this.

I could tell you about it all night long, Raymer said. He'd heard that money was an aphrodisiac, but he suspected this was more likely to be true of actual as opposed to conjectural money, and Corrie's reply bore this out.

I've got to think all this through, she said. I've got to decide what I'm going to tell Robbie.

At the door she kissed him hard and opened her mouth under his and rounded her sharp breasts against his chest, but her mouth did not taste the same as it had that day by the wishing pool, and the odor of the roses had even saturated her hair. An enormous sadness settled over him.

Going back, he was five miles across the county line when a small red fox darted up out of the weedy ditch and streaked into his headlights. He cut the wheel hard to miss it, but a rear wheel passed over the fox, and he felt a lurch in the pit of his stomach. Goddamn it, he said. He put the truck in reverse and backed up until he could see the fox. It wasn't moving. He got out. The fox's eyes were open, but they were blind and dull; its sharp little teeth were bared, and blood was running out of its mouth. Its eyes had been as bright as emeralds in the headlights, and they had gleamed as if they emitted light instead of reflecting it. I don't believe this, Raymer said. This is just too goddamned much.

He rose and took a drop cloth from the bed of the truck and wrapped the fox in it. He stowed it in the back of the pickup and drove on toward home.

RAYMER WAS SHAKING HIS HEAD. Why don't you just admit it? he asked. You wanted to go fishing. You wanted to get away from the project and picnic on the river. So you fed me all this bullshit, and here you are, with your little basket and your little fishing pole.

Mayfield regarded him placidly. It don't matter what you think, he said. The money's not there because you think it is. It's there because I put it in a jar and poured paraffin over it and packed it up the side of that bluff. If you think it's not there, that don't change nothin. It'd be there even if you didn't exist.

Because you packed it up the side of that bluff.

Right.

Raymer sat in the stern of the boat looking at his hands. He had slipped twenty scary feet down the face of a bluff before he could stop himself, and the nylon line had left a deep rope burn across each palm, as if he'd grabbed a red-hot welding rod with both hands.

Truth to tell, though, exploring the caves was interesting. He had not found any dead Confederates, but he had been in a cave in whose winding depths Indians had left flint chippings, pottery shards, all that remained of themselves.

As always, Mayfield seemed to know what he was thinking. Why won't you admit it yourself? You know you're gettin a kick out of it. I bet you ain't thought of your wife all mornin.

Raymer shook his head again. He grinned. You're just too many for me, he said.

THURSDAY HE WAS RAINED OUT in midafternoon, and he drove to the bank and checked the balance in his account. It was a lot higher than he had expected. He was amazed at how little he had spent. Like the old man, he seemed to be accumulating it in paper sacks, fruit jars. It was growing all the time.

He asked to withdraw $500 in ones and fives. The teller gave him a peculiar look as she began to count out the money.

It's for a ransom note, Raymer said, and for a moment she stopped counting. She was careful to keep any look at all from her face. Then she resumed, laying one bill atop another.

He drank the rest of the day away in a bar near the bypass. The place was named Octoberfest and had a mock-Germanic decor, and the waitresses were tricked out in what looked like milk-maids' costumes. He drank dark lager and kept waiting for the ghost of Hitler to sidle in and take the stool across from him. A dull malaise had seized him. A sense of doom. A suspicion that someone close to him had died. He had not yet received the telegram, but the Reaper was walking up and down the block looking for his house number.

You've sure got a good tan, the barmaid told him. It looks great with that blond hair. What are you, a lifeguard or something?

Something, Raymer said. I'm a necrozoologist.

A what? Necrowhat?

A necrozoologist. I analyze roadkill on the highways. On the life's highway. I look for patterns, migratory habits. Compile statistics. So many foxes, so many skunks. Possums. Try to determine where the animal was bound for when it was struck.

There's no such thing as that.

Sure there is. We're funded by the government. We get grants.

She laid a palm on his forearm. I think you're drunk, she said. But you're cute anyway. Stop by and see me one day when you're sober.

When he went to use the pay phone, he was surprised to see that dark had fallen. He could see the interstate from there, and the headlights of cars streaking past looked straight and intent, like falling stars rifling down the night.

The phone rang for a long time before she answered.

Where were you?

I was asleep on the couch. Where are you? Why are you calling?

I've got it, he said.

Jesus. Buddy. You found it? All of it?

All of it.

You sound funny. Why do you sound like that? Are you drunk?

I might have had a few celibatory—celebratory—beers.

If you were going to celebrate, you could have waited for me.

I'm waiting for you now, he said, and hung up the phone.

A CHEST FREEZER STOOD on the back porch of the farmhouse they had bought to renovate. Raymer raised the lid and took out the frozen fox, still wrapped in its canvas shroud. He folded away the canvas, but part of it was seized in the bloody ice, and he refolded it. He slid the bundle into a clean five-gallon paint bucket. A vinegar jar would have been nice, but he guessed they didn't make them that big anymore. The money was in a sack, and he dumped it into the bucket, shaking the bag out, the ones and fives drifting like dry leaves in a listless wind. He glanced at his watch and then picked up the loose bills from the floor and packed them around the fox. He stretched a piece of plastic taut across the top of the bucket and sealed it with duct tape. He replaced the plastic lid and hammered it home with a fist. Then he went into the kitchen and filled up the coffeemaker.

When headlights washed the walls of the house, he was sitting at the kitchen table drinking a cup of coffee. By the time he had crossed to the front room and turned on the porch light, Corrie was standing at the front door with an overnight bag in her hand.

She came in looking around the room, the high, unfinished ceiling. Looks like you quit on it, she said.

I guess I sort of drifted into the doldrums after you left, he said. Is that bag all you brought?

I figured we could buy some new stuff in the morning. Where is it? I want to see it.

He'd expected that. He pried off the lid and showed her. He'd been working on the wiring in the living room, and the light was poor here. She was looking intently, but all it looked like was a bucket full of money.

Can we dump it out and count it? I thought it was in some kind of glass jar.

The jar was broken. I think a rock slid on it. If he hadn't had the whole mess airtight in plastic, it would probably have been worthless. I've already counted it, and we're not going to roll around in it or do anything crazy. I still don't feel right about this, and we're leaving for Key West early in the morning, before I change my mind. I can see that old man's face every time I close my eyes.

Whatever you say, Buddy. Five gallons of money sure has made you decisive and take-charge. It looks good on you.

Later he lay on his back in bed and watched her disrobe. You don't have to do this, he said. We don't have to rush things.

I want to rush things, she said, reaching behind to unclasp her brassiere.

Raymer's mind was in turmoil. There was just too much to understand. He wondered if he would ever drive confidently down what Corrie had called the life's highway, piloting a sleek car five miles over the limit instead of standing by the road with his collar turned up and his thumb in the air. There were too many variables—the rates of chance and exchange were out of balance. The removal of Corrie's clothing was to her a casual act, all out of proportion to the torrent of feelings it caused in him. Her apartment was less than forty miles away, but it was no-man's-land, off-limits. She had laid stones in the pathway that had driven him to a despair that not even the sweet length of her body laid against his would counterbalance.

An hour or so after he should have been asleep, he heard her call him. Buddy? When he didn't answer, she rose, slowly so that the bed would not creak. She crossed the floor to the bathroom. He could hear the furtive sounds of her dressing, the whisper of fabric on fabric. Then nothing, and though his eyes were still closed, he knew that she was standing in the bathroom door watching him. He lay breathing in, breathing out. He heard her take up the bucket and turn with it. The bucket banged the door-jamb. Goddamn, she breathed. Then he heard the soft sounds of bare feet and nothing further, not even the opening and closing of the front door, before her car cranked.

It was hot and stale in the room. It smelled like attar of roses, like climate-controlled money from the depths of a cave, like a rotting fox in the high white noon.

He got up and raised a window. Night rushed in like balm to his sweating skin. She hadn't even closed the front door. The yard lay empty, and still and so awash with moonlight that it appeared almost theatrical, like the setting arranged for a dream that was over, or one on which the curtain had not yet risen.

When he crawled back into bed, he lay in the damp spot where they had made love, but he felt nothing. No pleasure, no pain. It was just a wet spot on a bed, and he moved over and thought about getting up and changing the sheets. But he didn't. He was weary and, despite all the coffee, still a little drunk. He tried to think of Corrie's lips against his throat, but all his mind would hold on to was the hiss in her voice when the bucket banged the door. Then even that slid away, and on the edge of sleep a boat was rocking on sun-dappled water, an old man was changing the fly on his line, and Raymer was feeling the sun hot on his back and wondering, Would you really lay your hand on the Bible and swear a lie? The old man's face was inscrutable, as always, but somehow Raymer didn't think he would, and when he slipped into sleep, it was dreamless and untroubled.

Sugarbaby

WHEN FOLKS TALKED about divorce statistics or the disintegration of the American family they would hold Finis and Doneita Beasley up as the example of the perfect marriage. They had been married thirty years. They worked their place side by side. Raised their kids and now they've got each other. You couldn't blow them apart with a stick of dynamite.

In the months before their thirty-first anniversary Doneita bought a dog. Their two daughters were grown and married with concerns of their own. Finis was much to himself, and he was not easily given to conversation. He was a hard worker yet and had always made them a good living but in all truth he was not very good company. Finis knew a dog would be company for Doneita. A dog would be almost like another child. A dog could not talk to her but she could talk to it. Doneita had told him that bonds form between dogs and their owners and she looked forward to the formation of these bonds.

It was a small dog of some indeterminate breed and Finis just called it a lapdog. A kind of terrier perhaps. It was an ugly dog with black, bulbous eyes and an improbable number of sharp little teeth. There was an atavistic look about it as if millennia had passed and left it unchanged, as if evolution had deemed it not worth bothering with.

Finis did not like the dog. It didn't seem to like him either. It growled at him when he came into the room. He'd turn to look at it and it would be watching him with something akin to speculation in its protuberant little eyes. Once it bit the back of his ankle where the tendons are, leaving his sock bloody and the prints of its little teeth like claw marks.

Doneita had Finis build it a small plywood house. Black shingles on the roof. She bought jars of paint and lacquered the house a glossy blue and wrote the dog's name above the door: Sugarbaby. She painted delicate roses ascending the front corners of the house, the briars hunter green, the blossoms dusky rose.

Sugarbaby did not take to living in the small house. Every night about ten o'clock just as Finis would be drifting off to sleep, it would turn up on the porch scratching at the screen. Yip yip yip, it would say. Its claws dragging down the screen were like fingernails scraping across a blackboard that went on and on forever.

That goddamned yip yip yip is driving me crazy, Beasley said. Get up and make it shut up.

Just ignore it and go to sleep, Doneita said. It doesn't bother me anyway. It doesn't keep me awake.

This went on for over a week and one night something seemed to break inside him and he got up and blew the dog off the porch with a .44 magnum. The concussion in the small parlor was enormous. Pictures fell from the walls, window glass rattled in its sashes. There was a ringing in his ears. An appalled silence rolled on him wave on wave like the waters of an ocean.

He couldn't hear her footsteps for the ringing but abruptly Doneita was standing in the doorway of the bedroom. She was looking at him in a way that he had never seen before.

What on earth are you doing? Was somebody breaking in on us?

I shot at that dog, he said.

You did what?

I can't stand that racket anymore. I shot at Sugarbaby.

Good God. You didn't hit him did you?

I don't think so, Finis said. I was trying to scare him into shutting up. Go back to bed.

There is something the matter with you, she said.

IN THE MORNING he was about early. He gathered up the remnants of the dog and buried them below the barn lot. He had been very impressed with what a .44 magnum was capable of. It had virtually disintegrated Sugarbaby and torn out a deep groove in the floorboards then knocked loose a four-by-four porch column so that it dangled out of plumb from the porch beam.

When he came up from burying the dog Doneita was leaving. She had a small station wagon and she was loading possessions into it. Clothing, knickknacks, pictures. I'll send Clarence after the rest, she told him.

He nodded. Take whatever you want, he said.

In days to come his life went on as usual. He farmed, he fed the horses. His life seemed largely unchanged. He knew how to run a washing machine, he knew how to cook. In truth he preferred his own cooking. He had always believed that Doneita used too much grease, too little salt, though he had been too polite to say so.

WHEN BEASLEY CUT the chainsaw off and turned around his daughter Berneice was standing there watching him.

Hellfire, he said. Why didn't you speak up? I could have cut a tree on you.

I did but you can't hear anything for that saw. I don't believe you can half hear anyway.

I hear fine, Beasley said.

Berneice had had to leave her car and climb the fence and cross the pasture to the edge of the timber where Beasley was sawing firewood. She didn't look happy. Beasley thought she looked torn between raking him over the coals and crying on his shoulder. He hoped it wouldn't be crying, but there was a tremulous look to her mouth and a slick wet gleam to her eyes.

What's all this about Mama? she asked.

Beasley set the saw down and knelt beside it and unscrewed the gas cap. He poured fuel into it from a milk jug he was using as a gas container.

What you see, I guess, he said. Me living out here and her living wherever she's living.

She's living out there in one of those housing authority apartments, Berneice said. Out on Walnut where the old people live. Most of them widows, old women waiting to die. One of them had to die before she could even get in there. She stayed with me and Clarence for a few days.

I guess you got an earful, he said.

Well. How come you shot Sugarbaby?

Beasley thought about it a time. He had unpocketed a file and begun to sharpen the saw. I don't know, he finally said. I expect it was that yip yip yip every night.

Mama said you told her you meant to just shoot at it. Did you mean to hit it?

I don't know. I just shot, and there it was.

She don't need to be out there with nothing but old folks. Mama's not anywhere near ready to give up and die.

Does she like it out there?

She claims she does but she don't. She's trying to fit in. She plays bridge with those old ladies. She's planted a bed of petunias. They sit around talking about quilts and their dead husbands.

If she says she likes it then she probably does. Doneita was never one to hold her tongue when something needed saying.

What makes you the way you are, Daddy? Everything's gone, it's just such a waste. Thirty years of memories. You've just thrown it away.

You can't throw away a memory, Beasley said. Anyway she can always come back. Nobody ever said she couldn't come back.

She's too stubborn. Both of you. All our Christmases gone, all the birthdays. Now she was crying silently, tears tracking down her cheeks. Beasley was growing more uncomfortable by the second.

Go out there and talk it over with her, Berneice said. Try and work it out.

Beasley was silent. He didn't know why people were always trying to change things, to get back to where they were. People were who they were, and the things they did were just the things they did. He could not call back the bullet, silence the enormous concussion of the pistol.

And you might take her a little dog of some kind.

Beasley watched her cross back through the pasture.

In due course Beasley received a certified letter from a lawyer's office in Ackerman's Field. He read it through three times. He studied it in a sort of bemused wonder. He was being sued for divorce. He had been mentally cruel, there were irreconcilable differences. Doneita wanted support, a division of their mutual properties. A date was shown for a hearing where these particulars might be discussed.

Beasley saw no need for that. If she wanted a divorce she was entitled to one. He personally did not believe in divorce. He decided to have no part of whatever happened. He would do nothing to prevent it but he would not abet it.

As the year drew on more letters came. They grew more insistent, the legalese the message was couched in more strident: His presence was requested in court. His lack of cooperation was making things more difficult for everyone. The letters began to anger Beasley. Who are the sons of bitches? he wondered. Why are they aggravating the hell out of me? Why is everybody nosing around in my business?

WHAT YOU SHOULD HAVE DONE at the beginning was go talk to her and get her to come back home, Clarence said.

I guess, Beasley told his son-in-law.

And since you didn't do that, what you should have done was go talk to her when the court served you with those papers. Work something out. That's what she wanted. But you didn't do that either. You just let it roll.

I just let it roll, Beasley agreed.

It was the first cold day of winter and he had the rocking chair dragged before the fireplace and his feet propped on the brick hearth. He had been cutting and hauling firewood all day and he was tired and cold. He liked Clarence but he did not want to discuss this with him. At the very bottom of things he did not consider it any of Clarence's business. It was not even any of his business. It was the business of Doneita and the lawyer she had hired.

Clarence was a schoolteacher and the word he always used to

describe Beasley was stoic. He's tougher than a cut of sweet gum, he told Berneice once when Beasley was still within earshot. You can't break him or split him, the grain runs every which way. He's a vanishing breed. An anachronism.

This stoic anachronism sat regarding Clarence from the rocking chair. I appreciate your advice, Clarence, he said. But I decided a while back to just not have anything to do with all this mess. To just let it roll over me and get on out of sight.

It'll roll over you, all right, Clarence said. You need a lawyer. It's not any of my business, but this place has been in your family for generations. Now a bunch of lawyers are going to be fighting over it like dogs over a garbage can. They won't leave you a pot to piss in. Nor a place to set it down if you had a pot.

I've always minded my own business, Beasley said. Kept my own counsel. I've always believed if a man minded his own business everybody would leave him alone.

You don't understand, Clarence said.

Maybe not. But I haven't bothered anybody. I pay my debts, I don't owe a dime in this world. If they think they can do anything to me let them bring it on.

Well they'll damn sure bring it. They'll bring it in wholesale lots. She's pissed about that dog. That Sugarbaby, and from what I hear the judge she went before is pissed too. They're going to take you out.

Clarence, Beasley said, wanting to explain but unable to articulate what he meant. It was just that it wasn't his kind of deal. He was not going to explain his business to a bunch of people in neckties and suits.

What was the use of having principles if you abandoned them when the going got rough? If you said, Well, maybe I'll do this but I won't do that. If you said, Well, I'll move the lines back to here, but no farther? Beasley wasn't moving any lines. The lines stayed where they were.

This has all gotten out of hand, Clarence said in frustration, rising to go, resting his hand a moment in passing on Beasley's shoulder. You were together thirty years. What's this all about?

I just couldn't stand that goddamned yip yip yip, Beasley finally said.

BEASLEY HAD ON clean overalls. He had on a clean chambray shirt so faded by repeated launderings that its collar had gone soft and shapeless. He was freshly shaven and there was a streak of talcum on his throat.

Well, the elusive Mr. Beasley, the lawyer said. Take a seat there, Mr. Beasley.

Beasley seated himself in a wooden chair with rollers on it. It creaked when he adjusted his weight. He sat studying the lawyer. The lawyer's name was Townsley. He was a thin young man given to the wearing of loud sport coats. Today he wore a coat of some woolly fabric in blue and green checks whose clash was almost audible. The coat had plastic buttons as big as golf balls. He had smooth oily hair, smooth oily skin, a smooth oily voice.

I'm only here because my son-in-law said I ought to be, Beasley said. I thought there might be some misunderstanding and I aim to clear it up. It's never been my intention to beat her out of anything. I want that understood. The farm's half hers and always has been. I thought she knew that. If you want it in writing then that's what I'm here for.

I'm afraid it's not that simple, the lawyer said. The time for arbitration has come and gone. What we're asking for is an accounting of assets. Then an equal division of them.

Half the farm? That's fine with me. Half of two hundred acres is one hundred acres. That's fine with me.

It's not that simple, Townsley said again. We're asking half the value of your total assets in cash. Your wife no longer has an interest in the farm. There'll be an appraisal of your properties to determine their value. Which you will pay for, by the way, it'll be itemized on the bill for expenses. The court has already sent you a demand for an accounting of assets by certified mail. Ignore it at your peril. Ignore it and you'll be in contempt of court.

I don't have that kind of money, Beasley said after a time.

The lawyer shrugged. We're not asking for more than you've got, he said. Simply half of it.

BEASLEY ALREADY HAD his glasses on when the deputy brought the warrant and so did not have to get up to go get them. He had been sitting before the fire reading a seed catalog that had come that day and he laid it in a magazine rack and took the warrant and unfolded it and read it. Then he handed it back to the deputy.

The deputy looked outsize and strange in Beasley's small parlor. His pressed khakis, the black garrison belt. The holstered pistol and all that it conveyed.

I have to arrest you, the deputy said. But it don't amount to that much. We'll go to city hall and post bond. They'll let you sign for yourself, hell, everybody knows you. Or Clarence could sign for you.

I don't want anybody signing for me, Beasley said.

What?

I don't want to tie Clarence up. He might be out some money.

How's that?

I might just head out. All this is getting too heavy to carry around. Hellfire, a man's not rooted to the ground the way a god-damned tree is.

All they want you to do is comply with the court, the deputy said. I heard the judge say so himself. Talking to Townsley. He said you were an arrogant son of a bitch and he was going to teach you a lesson.

Then let's be for learning it, Beasley said.

BEASLEY WAS TURNED into the bullpen with other nightshade denizens who'd run afoul of the law. It was a weekend and business had been brisk and here were miscreants of every stripe. Dread-locked black men and ponytailed white drug dealers, luckless drunks and wifebeaters and child molesters of every taste and in-clination. Beasley judged he could keep himself entertained for a day or two just reading the tattoos.

A huge black man stood regarding this clean-cut and well-barbered man of advancing years with some interest.

What'd they get you for? he asked.

Contempt of court, Beasley said.

Shit. And I thought I was a judge of character. I had you fig-ured for a murderer at the very least.

Later they locked him into a cell with a heavyset man named Brenner. Brenner was a soft sluglike man who was awaiting trial for murdering his mother. He had lived in a house trailer with her for years out on Metal Ford Road, supported by her government money. Then one day she met a widower from Jack's Branch and began to have a social life. One night Brenner watched through the window as she and the widower made love. When the man left Brenner went inside to confront her. He'd had in mind a heart-to-heart talk, tears of repentance. But things had gotten out of hand and he was caught in the act of burning her body.

Brenner wanted Beasley to understand why he had killed her. My mother was a great lady, he said. A saint. I revered my mother. I wouldn't have harmed a hair on her old gray head. She changed. Something happened to her morals. I believe it's these times we live in.

Beasley just looked at him and didn't say anything.

What are you doing in here? Brenner asked him.

When Beasley told him contempt of court Brenner just shook his head in disbelief. That's a bullshit charge, he said. That's just paperwork. You must be crazy.

At least I never burned my mama in a goddamned brush pile, Beasley told him.

NO ONE EVEN KNEW he was in jail for a week and then Clarence came to get him. Berneice is just jumping up and down, he said. She said get you out and no mistake about it. Why didn't you call somebody?

I didn't see much sense in it, Beasley said.

They were standing in a concrete courtyard. It was enclosed by a chain-link fence. The day was coldlooking and bleak. A few flakes of snow fell. You could see the street from here and Beasley stood watching the cars pass as if he had some interest in where they were going, some investment in what they were up to.

Clarence lit a cigarette. His hands shook. He was wearing a heavy overcoat and he put the burned match into a side pocket. I don't understand you, he said through the smoke. This has gone way too far. Way too far. It's gotten out of hand and we need to get our act together here.

Telephone poles ran along the street and small sparrows had aligned themselves on the wire. Beasley watched them. They all flew away, as if they'd simultaneously received the same urgent message.

Will you not come, or what?

I may as well lay it out and get it over with.

God*damn,* Clarence said. I don't know about you, Finis. I think I'm beginning to not know about you.

Beasley had his hands in his pockets and he was hunched against the weight of the cold. He smiled. I'm beginning to not know about myself, he said.

Later he lay on his cot with his fingers laced behind his skull and thought about things. Things had gotten out of hand, Clarence had said, and Clarence was undoubtedly right. He couldn't fathom what had happened to him. Some core of stubbornness he hadn't even known about had set up inside him like concrete. There had been some curious juxtaposition of lives. He'd been switched around somehow and he was living out the balance of someone else's chaotic life. Somebody somewhere had burnt out and they'd handed it to him to finish up. Somewhere somebody was placidly living out the balance of his.

JUDGE MORRIS made her tell that part about you shooting her terrier dog twice, a deputy named Harris told him. He couldn't believe it. He's going to give you a minimum of thirty days, or I'll kiss your ass right here in front of the courthouse.

They were sitting facing the courthouse in a police cruiser. Harris kept glancing at his watch. It was not quite time to enter the courtroom and Harris sat in the cruiser smoking cigarettes.

They were in the front seat. Harris had not considered it neces-

sary to confine Beasley to the rear seat where there were no door han-
dles and there was a steel mesh barrier between front and rear.
Beasley was not a common criminal. Harris's baton lay on the seat
between them. Beasley had noticed that the end of it was pegged and
he figured Harris had drilled it out and poured melted lead into it.

Harris had once been sheriff. He had been sheriff until he had
beaten a teenager to death with perhaps this very baton and now
he was only a deputy. There had been some controversy about the
beating and it had ultimately been decided that the teenager had
had to be confined in a straitjacket and had choked to death on his
own vomit. But Beasley knew that the county had quietly come
up with twenty thousand dollars for the boy's family and that all
it had cost Harris was the next sheriff's election.

Time to go in, Harris said. He got out and shoved the baton in
his belt. I'll come around, he said.

Harris opened the door and Beasley got out. They had turned
to go when Harris said, turning, Oh shit. I forgot the cuffs.

What? You forgot what?

Morris wanted you brought in in handcuffs. He wants to make
an example of you.

Hellfire, Beasley said. What kind of example?

To tell the truth I was a little foggy on that myself, Harris said.
But he's the judge. To other dog shooters maybe, I don't know.

He had turned back to the cruiser and opened the door and
was leaned fumbling in the console. When he started to straighten
and turn with the cuffs in his hand Beasley slipped the baton from
Harris's garrison belt and with a continuation of that single swift
motion slammed him with all his might just above the right ear
and Harris dropped as if he'd been depending from suddenly cut
strings.

Beasley was dragging him back onto the grass when a station

wagon pulled into a parking space and a woman got out. The wind was getting up and the woman got out into it holding her hat on with both hands and gaping at Beasley.

He's had some kind of attack, Beasley said. I believe it's his heart. Would you run across to the General and call the ambulance while I get him over here?

Of course, the woman said, and hurried off. Beasley watched her. She'd forgotten her hat and the wind blew it off but she went on anyway.

Beasley got behind the wheel of the cruiser. When the woman went into the General Care he cranked the engine and sat a moment just listening to the rock-steady lick the cam was hitting. Then he put the cruiser in gear and drove away.

The first place he went was home. Clarence had sent him from the Navy PX a Winchester .32 Special he wouldn't have traded for an emerging nation and looking about the small front room he saw little else he could not do without. Then he went into the bedroom and came out with a heavier coat and a blanket. When he left he didn't even pull the door closed behind him or turn the lights out and glancing once over his shoulder the house looked as temporary and impersonal as a motel room.

He drove toward Riverside. He knew already that he was going into the Harrikin, a wild stretch of land that had once been mined for iron ore. It was all company land, dangerous mine shafts, abandoned machinery. No one lived there, and there were miles of unbroken timber you couldn't work your way through with a road map in one hand and a compass in the other. He felt he knew the country well enough to struggle through into Wayne County and strike out for Alabama. He didn't envision posses. How many bounty hunters could be on your ass for contempt of court? And coldcocking an overweight deputy sheriff.

He stopped at a country store and bought pork and beans and tinned Vienna sausages and crackers. He bought a quart of milk and a pound of coffee. The storekeep was totting up these purchases on a ticket book with a stub of pencil and he kept glancing out at the cruiser idling before a rusting gas pump that did not work and that advertised a brand of gasoline that no longer existed.

Finis, I can't help but notice that you've swapped vehicles, he finally said.

No, the county hired me to try her out, Beasley said. It's one of these new thirty-two-valve jobs and the county itself don't know how fast she'll go. None of them deputies got the balls to wind her out. They hired me to take her out to Riverside and straighten out a few of them curves.

The storekeep was regarding him with a benign skepticism. Long as you pay before you wind her out I don't care how many lies you tell me.

Beasley was counting out ones, laying coins atop. That was my intention, he said.

Beasley left and drove to where the terrain began its steep descent toward the river. He stopped on a sharp switchback curve and parked on the shoulder of the road and got out. The day was blue-looking and windy and the horizon looked as hard as iron and it was very cold. The cruiser sat idling puffing little bursts of exhaust. He looked around. A high-tension power line crossed the road here and following it with his eyes he could see where the towers faded into the blurred multiple horizons of the Harrikin.

He cocked the front wheels of the cruiser toward the hollow and with the stock of the Winchester tapped the gearshift into drive and stepped away. The cruiser bumped off the shoulder of macadam and eased over waist-high scrub blackjack and gaining momentum sped down the hillside toward the hollow. The car started around the side of the steep incline like a daredevil motorcycle in a wheel of death but it wasn't going fast enough and grew top-heavy and rolled over again and again and fetched up at the bottom of the hollow upside down against an enormous beech. It ran for a while and then it quit.

He had started down the opposite side of the embankment where the power line wound toward the Harrikin but then he turned and came back across the road and stood looking down at the cruiser. It was almost hidden by brush. He stood with the rifle across his shoulders and both arms hung from the barrel and stock. He just stood for a time thinking. He was thinking about the weighted baton. He could see Harris making it. Harris had it clamped in a vise, he was drilling a hole in the end, pouring melted lead into it.

After a while he went down the embankment, the hillside so steep in places he was sliding tree to tree. When he'd reached the door-sprung cruiser he leaned the Winchester against the trunk of a tree and began to gather up windfall branches and lengths of dead wood and a stump weathered thin and silver and almost weightless and to fill the cruiser with them. He piled on leaves and set them afire and then he went back the way he'd come with the fire popping and snapping like something alive coming up the hillside after him.

He was a mile and better along the power line before he looked back. The black smoke was rolling against the sky and he felt he'd drawn a line forever between the world that yawned before him and everything that had gone before. When he looked forward the way he was headed the long endless line of marching towers looked like angular giants skeletoned up out of steel.

Goddamn you, Sugarbaby, Beasley said.

✦ ✦ ✦

HE CAME UP THROUGH a long blue dusk that lay like smoke between the cedars, wending his way through a sage field to where
the house sat almost hidden by trees. The wind had shifted around
to the north and grown more chill yet and he could hear it sough-
ing through the cedars and rattling a loose section of tin and bang-
ing a shutter against the wall in random percussion.

The house was abandoned. A cedar had grown up through the
rotted porch and was slowly dismantling the roof. The stone
chimney had tilted away from the house or the house away from
it. At his step over the threshold something unseen scrambled up
and went with near-liquid grace through an unglazed window
sash and gone.

He leaned the rifle carefully against a wall, set the paper bag of
food by the fireplace hearth, and looked about for something to
burn. He broke up rotting floorboards from the porch and stacked
the fireplace with them and with the bag for tinder set them
alight. He could hear a heavy swift beating of wings up the flue
and a rain of soot fell. After a while the area immediately before
the hearth warmed but the wind came looping across the windowsill and he wrapped the blanket about his shoulders and sat
crouched before the fire with his hands extended like a supplicant.

When he was warm he opened a can of the beans and a tin of
the sausages and set them near the coals to heat. He ate crackers
while they warmed and when they did he ate with his pocketknife, chewing slowly and staring abstractedly into the fire.

He was warm and dry and almost content. He figured at least
he wasn't in jail. Nobody was telling him about burning their
mother's body or crying out in their sleep and if the notion struck
him to just walk out the door into the night there were no bars.
All around him was the Harrikin, miles of uninhabited woods

smothered in rain and darkness and he drew a small bitter comfort from it.

After a while he dozed crouched before the fire but awoke cold and disoriented and for a moment he couldn't fathom where he'd got to. The dead wood had burned away to the faintest glow in the depths of a feathery caul of ash. It was still raining and the wind was still blowing in a cold mist through the broken windows so that the blanket felt damp across his shoulders. He got up and went through the house striking matches looking for something to burn. Beneath a collapsed shelf he found a motley of books and he stacked an arm-load and carried them back to the fireplace. He ripped out pages and piled them on the quaking ash until they flared up and then he laid on the volumes. Finally they caught and he sat before them watching little blue flames flicker over the leather bindings.

He noticed with some amusement that they comprised a set of State of Tennessee law books and it occurred to him how all-encompassing the law was: he and Doneita had both appealed to it each in their own way and both had drawn a modicum of comfort from it each according to their natures.

WITH THE BLANKET mantled about him and the rifle slung under it he watched from beneath the wet ruin of his hat four police cruisers creep up the road far below him. From his aerie the red chert road wound like a capillary of road on a map. The road widened where fifty years before the post office and commissary had stood and here the cruisers pulled over side by side and stopped. Across the folds of rain-blurred horizons the cars looked tiny and insignificant. Men got out of the cars into the rain and stood in a loose group. He wished he'd had the foresight to bring binoculars. He'd have liked to know was Harris along.

In truth he was a little surprised. He'd have thought they'd have waited for better weather but he guessed burning a squad car raised the ante considerably and he was truly a wanted man.

He was not alarmed. The men moved into the sodden woods with a reluctance that was almost visible to the naked eye. The deputies he had seen around the jail looked soft and out of shape. They looked as if they drank too much beer, smoked too many cigarettes, ate too many doughnuts. Beasley did not drink and had not smoked a cigarette for twenty-five years and he could take a doughnut or leave it alone and scrambling up the bluff toward deeper timber he was not even breathing hard.

As the day progressed the weather did not warm as he'd expected nor did the rain abate and if there was sun at all behind the leaden weeping sky he saw no sign of it. By noon he was far back in the Harrikin, following the spine of a ridge that kept breaking off into deep blue hollows. He could hear the rain in the trees and by midafternoon it had begun to be mixed with sleet and it was freezing on the leaves and branches and the leaves he brushed had the tinny half-musical sound of a carillon.

He passed by an ancient graveyard, the tilting slabs leached thin and fragile, transient as whatever souls they'd marked. Sheltered beneath a cedar he ate the last of the Viennas and crackers and listened to the sleet rattle in the leaves. Graveyard cleanin, dinner on the ground, he thought sardonically.

The day wore on gray and cold and darkened so incrementally you couldn't have told the exact moment night fell but after a while he was walking in darkness.

He knew he had to stop. Only a fool would continue on here. He knew this country as well as anyone but there were core-sample holes deep as wells, their bottoms drifted with leaves covering the bones of luckless animals or perhaps worse that

stumbled into them. And if he became lost he would in all proba-
bility wander for miles in the wrong direction.

By the time he had a fire going he was half frozen. He finally
found tinder beneath a rotten husk of log and when he had it
going he piled on whatever he could find, branches and fallen
saplings and finally the log itself was burning and he had an enormous bonfire going he figured you could see for miles. Snow had
begun falling with the sleet and huge flakes drifted into the toiling smoky glare and vanished. The wet earth began to steam and
standing before the fire with the blanket cowled about him
Beasley looked like some cautionary symbol set up to warn of such
depths of misery as the human race can sink to.

Beasley thought of his other life but already it was lost to him.
It had been a mere prelude to this. He seemed to have been born
the moment he shot Sugarbaby through the screen. He stood back
to the fire with the rifle at port arms scanning the darkness. There
was nothing beyond the limits of the fire, where the light tended
away the world simply ceased to exist. Come on you sons of
bitches, Beasley called. If you're out there come up and warm.

For the first time in his life he realized that sometimes in life
you go through doors that only open one way. You can stand before them and think about whether you want to go through them
or not. But when you do and the door closes behind you there is no
way to go back. The door is featureless and unknobbed and
smooth as a sheet of glass. You can pound on it and claw till your
fingers are bleeding, scream until your throat is raw, but no one
will open the door, no one will even hear you.

HE WAS LOST and he had been lost for some time, the drifting
snow obscuring landmarks and giving the landscape a curious

sameness, the snow already ankle-deep and falling so fast and hard he could scarcely see where he was going.

He was following a sound, a hollow clang of metal on metal that he seemed to have heard subliminally for hours, maybe longer, maybe since the moment something had wound too tight inside him and finally broken and he'd blown Sugarbaby off the porch. The sound seemed all there was left in the world, all there was of reality beyond the curtain of shifting white. It was a random and infrequent noise, and sometimes he'd have to stand still in the hushed woods waiting for it to come again so that he could get a fix on it, waiting and hearing nothing but the sound of his breathing and the soft hiss of the woods filling up with snow. Then finally the clang would come again and he would go on.

At length he stood beneath the source of the sound. Four legs of structural steel rose high into the air. A tiny house set atop them, what he judged was sixty or seventy feet up. He didn't know what it was. An abandoned fire lookout station perhaps, or maybe something that had been built by the mining company so long ago its very purpose was lost.

He hunkered for a moment against the trunk of a tree and stared upward at the house. A steel ladder began a few feet off the ground and ascended to heights that made his head swim. The metal sign that said CLIMB AT YOUR OWN RISK was rusted and pocked by ancient rifle fire. As he watched a steel door slammed against the wall, the wind whipped the sound away. The higher he'd climbed the thinner the timber had gotten and here the wind came whipping down out of the north and howled through the steel tower like a banshee's warning.

He knew he should have been out of the Harrikin by now and across the county line into what passed in these provinces for civilization but he was not. Somehow the snow had turned him around, and he was someplace he'd never been. His hands ached but he was more worried about his feet for he couldn't feel them anymore and he was afraid they might be frozen. He thought of hot breathless July nights, dryflies crying from a velvet wall of sweet mimosa. The bottled matches in his coat pocket, steel walls impervious to the winds. He rose and kicking through the snow began to gather dead branches and break them and stuff them into the pockets of the overcoat. When he had all he could carry he went over to the ladder and stood looking at it for a time. He took off his belt. He put it back on over the coat and shoved the rifle under it and worked the rifle around to his back and tightened the belt a notch. It was snowing harder. He took a deep breath and began to climb the ladder.

BEASLEY DREAMED brokenly but when he woke the dream was lost to him no matter how hard he tried to call it back. All he could remember was that Doneita was in it.

He guessed the cold had wakened him but then he heard someone yelling. Beasley, Beasley, the voice called.

Company out here in the middle of the goddamned woods, he thought. Where do you have to go to get a little privacy around here?

When he stepped onto the platform and looked down and saw Harris staring up at him down the barrel of a rifle. Beasley wasn't even surprised. He just felt strange, as if everything had been imbued with inevitability—everything had been taken from his hands, events had become steel balls rolling unfrictioned down grooved boards and there was no stopping anything.

See you don't fall, Harris called. It's so goddamned cold you'd break like a china cup. But the first thing you need to do is throw that rifle over the side.

Beasley guessed the clanging door had drawn Harris up out of the woods and he wished he'd tied it back somehow. He turned and leaned the Winchester against the wall of the tower.

I don't want this busted, he called down. My son-in-law give it to me.

I been lost all night, Harris said. How the hell do you get out of here?

You don't, Beasley said.

What's that supposed to mean?

This is the end of the road.

You crazy son of a bitch.

What? Step up close, I can't hear you.

Harris approached the steel legs of the tower. He had his mouth open to say something when Beasley abruptly pulled his coat aside and unzipped his trousers and hauled himself out to urinate over the edge of the platform. Harris backpedaled frantically away from the arc of urine and fell with his feet crumpled beneath him. He immediately slapped the stock of his rifle into his shoulder and Beasley felt in the pit of his stomach the muzzle lock onto him.

You know what that was, Harris? he called. That was contempt of court.

I'm going to blow your sorry ass off there.

Your balls are too small, Beasley said. I expect you'll have to come up and get me.

We'll just see if I can't manage to knock you down here.

Beasley stared down the gun barrel for what seemed an interminable time. It looked like a hole into nothingness, or a tunnel that might wind its way out of these woods.

After a time Harris lowered the gun. He approached the ladder and stared at it as if it were something he couldn't make up his mind about. Beasley judged he was envisioning himself halfway up and Beasley suddenly blowing him off the ladder with the Winchester. After a time he began to climb anyway. He was ascending the ladder left-handedly, the rifle clutched in his right.

Beasley looked out across the world. Everything was snow and trees, an unmapped landscape black and white. Everything looked reduced to its essence, all that was left at the end of time. He thought inexplicably of Doneita, endearments that she had said, sweet nights that were as lost as anything that ever was. Above the treeline a hawk hung motionless against the frozen void.

When Harris was almost three-quarters of the way up the ladder, Beasley stepped off the platform. The landscape reeled away and upward. Snowflakes drifted heavenward. It seem to take forever for him to tilt and slam against the ice-locked earth.

Standing by Peaceful Waters

IN BENDER'S DREAM the stag came full tilt out of a thin stand of scrub blackjack and leapt the chain-link fence. Its hooves barely cleared the top strand of wire. There was yet a thin skift of snow on the ground melted and re-frozen and when the stag's hooves struck they slid and it went momentarily to its knees. It was up instantly but the wolf was already there, morphing yellow-eyed and immediate out of the tall broom sedge and moving close and swift along the ground like winter smoke. Muscles bunched to bolt the stag quartered but the wolf was there before it. The stag's eyes were huge and its breath steamed bluely in the cold moonlight.

The moon cleared the raft of clouds it had shuttled before it and everything in Bender's vision went varying shades of black and silver. The stag lowered its head as the wolf bore in as if it would disembowel it with its antlers but the wolf feinted sidewise and leapt and opened a gash in the stag's side and coiled back on itself to leap again and when the stag quartered this time its hooves splayed out on the ice and out of balance it took the full weight of the leaping wolf with its chest. When the wolf's snout burrowed into the stag's throat the spray of blood was black in the moonlight and was as stark on the snow as bas-relief shadows.

Feeding the wolf looked up at the moon. Its face and ruff were dark with blood and the moon was no moon Bender was familiar with, so close he could have tiptoed and touched it, as if whatever laws governing the distance it kept no longer applied so that it was settling slowly toward the surface of the earth.

BENDER HAD BEGUN to think he lived in a countryside so be-leaguered and desolate even the dead were fleeing it. The last truck went out at dusk and he was there by the fence to see it go, hands in his hip pockets and no expression at all on his face. The flatbed truck pulled a lowboy carrying a backhoe secured by chains and the backhoe shifted in its moorings when the truck started down the grade toward the main road, the dead or what-ever dust remained of them hidden decorously under tarpaulins lashed to the truck through eyelets in the canvas, and under the taut canvas oblong shapes like archetypes out of some primal memory.

There were men holding shovels and picks squatted about the lowboy and some studied Bender as they went out but one or two raised their hands in greeting or dismissal and one young man with shoulder-length blond hair beneath a yellow hardhat grinned and gave him a thumbs-up signal. Bender raised an arm in an oddly formal gesture and watched them go.

He stood by the fence the length of time it took him to smoke a cigarette and by the time he was finished with it he could hear the truck far off on the highway, gearing down for the hills ring-ing the town.

It was scarcely a foot from Bender's garden fence to the government's chain-link fence and contrasted with it Bender's looked like a child's mock-up of a fence, something Jesse might have built. Chain-link wire was stretched taut on steel posts and the sign affixed to it had an authoritative look and seemed to have been positioned for Bender's eyes alone. KEEP OUT, the sign said. PROPERTY OF THE US GOVERNMENT. TRESPASSING IS PROHIB-ITED AND VIOLATORS WILL BE PROSECUTED.

Bender climbed the woven-wire fence and stepped onto a lo-cust post and grasped the top of the government's fence and swung one leg over it. The other. He balanced momentarily then dropped onto the other side.

He felt the sensation he always felt when he crossed the prop-erty line, as if he had swung from one dimension to another. Here the earth lay in ruins. Scraped raw and bloody by the blades of bulldozers, trees dozed into long curving windrows and burned. They burned for days, for weeks, and smoke still rose in columns like council fires and hot ash drifted in the unwinded twilight.

He followed the roadway back the way the truck had come. The road steadily descended and as far as he could see the world was laid to waste. To his left hand lay the Indian mounds the ar-chaeologists from Knoxville had disinterred and on his right he could see the concrete pylons of the dam rising out of the earth and he judged it near completion. Time was getting away from him and he suspected that the government's patience was well-nigh exhausted.

All day the trucks hauled stone for the riprap and all day the earthmovers took on earth here and disgorged it there and packers wore the earth hard as stone. Enormous armies of machinery toiled over the earth like insects and somewhere out there in the mauve dusk the river, not yet tamed, its course not yet altered, rolled on toward the sea the way it had always done.

Here Bender stood. His grandfather had long ago deeded this land to the church but it did not belong to the church now. The cemetery lay on a rise not yet leveled and his feet remembered the path and he walked a path not even here anymore, that had been hauled away for backfill. He wandered this vacant cemetery like a visitor come to call and there's no one home.

Crude oblong holes dug deeply into the earth. Rectangles of dark leaking upward from some ultimate dark. Bits of worm-scored wood, shards of bones, nameless dross. The stones still stood amidst the savaged sassafras trunks, leaning weather-thinned tablets and carved marble angels with folded wings and graven names and dates. Some of the names said Bender.

He sat there for a time smoking while the dusk deepened and nightbirds began to call to him out of the purple dusk. When he rose he looked instinctively to where the church had stood as if to see if it had been miraculously restored but of course there was no church nor anything at all that he recognized anymore.

I EXPECT WE NEED TO TALK, Lynn told him.

I expect we do, Bender said. He'd been watching her and he always knew when she thought they needed to talk.

Did you know old man Liverett took their offer?

No.

I guess you're the last one left now.

I've always been the last one left, Bender said.

They ate supper in silence and Bender gathered up the dishes and washed them while Lynn played with Jesse. He washed the dishes as if this simple act might placate her, might be so far-reaching as to placate the very government that was stirring itself to move against him.

They sat on the porch in the swing awhile. The weathered wood seemed somehow to draw out what coolness the dusk held. Everything about the house was wood from the sills to the shingles, cypress and chestnut Bender's grandfather had cut and hauled to the sawmill in a mule-drawn wagon. He had built the house himself and time had settled it and silvered the wood until the house seemed something organic that had just grown out of the earth, something that had always been there and that man had had nothing to do with. Honeysuckle grew all around the house and its vines climbed nigh to the roof itself. Full dark was falling and was intensifying the scent of the blossoms until the air felt drugged, some sweet narcotic that had sung in Bender's blood all his days.

His three-year-old son Jesse was dozing on his lap with his blond curls against Bender's chest and Bender's arms loosely clasped about his waist. The boy was a wonder to Bender. Even the small things about him, the way his face looked subtly different when the light falling on it altered, as if here was an entirely different Jesse. Bender loved him so it scared him sometimes, and not because Jesse was some scaled-down and newly minted edition of Bender but a new and separate individual, innocent and unmarked as yet by the world.

He must have tightened his grip more than he thought for the child awoke and slid down Bender's legs to the porch floor. Go shoot some wolves, he said sleepily.

Well all right, Bender said. Let's waste some of them suckers. He figured the game would last awhile, perhaps even until Lynn was asleep, postponing the need to talk.

He did not even suspect where Jesse had come up with the game but it might have been from something he had seen on television or something he had heard someone say. They had been playing it two or three months and lately it had become every night's ritual.

All the game required was two black plastic popguns and Bender and his son crouched peering through the sliding glass door into the backyard. Past the flagstone patio and where the porch light tended away into darkness the woods began and this was where the wolves came from. Jesse would point one out and Bender would pretend to see it and shoot it and then Jesse would kill one. There, he'd say, raising the rifle and sighting down its barrel: bang. Sometimes they would kill wolves for upwards of half an hour before Jesse wearied of the game, sometimes only one or two each would suffice. One of the rules seemed to be that they both had to kill the same number of wolves.

Tonight he was sleepy and grew bored with the game early. When he was asleep in his room and Lynn was undressing for bed she said:

What are we going to do?

Wait it out a few more days.

We can't wait it out. We've gone as far as we can go. Something has got to be done.

Bender was standing by the window with an outspread palm on the frame and he was just looking out into the darkness. The EPA is going to shut the goddamned thing down and you know it.

I don't know any such thing. Nothing is going to shut it down. Nothing. All this is going to be underwater and I don't know why you can't see that.

Bender watched the dark and thought about that awhile. He thought about the slow seep of water rising, first his shoe soles dampening and the summer dust going to mud and the water cascading over the lips of the barren graves and rising more until the mimosa fronds trailed in the deep like seaweed. The dam looked to be at least eighty feet in the air and Bender guessed the water would rise for days, for weeks, who knew.

That goddamned fish, Bender said.

What?

I was thinking about that goddamned fish.

Just come on to bed, David.

Bender got into bed with all his clothes on and then noticed his shoes and got back up and pulled off his shoes and socks and lay back down with his hands clasped behind his head. She touched his face, let her arm rest across his chest. David, she said, baby, I know what all this means to you, but—

Bender lay there not listening. Nobody knew what all this meant. He felt an enormous sorrow for the inadequacy of everything. For everything that was said, for everything that was done. There in the dark Lynn kissed his throat and tried to draw him to her. She was trying to comfort him in the only way she knew but dread lay in him heavy as a stone and Bender would not be comforted.

SOMETIME IN THE NIGHT Bender awoke and lay staring at the ceiling above him and thought about the fish. There for a while he had had high hopes for the fish.

He had first heard of it months ago. He had been keeping his eyes open and he had known something was up when he had seen a news crew from a Nashville television station interviewing folks wearing hardhats over by the main gate. Then a night or two later he had seen the fish itself on the evening news being discussed by an earnest-looking young man in a pith helmet. The fish was about as ugly a thing as Bender had ever seen, angular and goggle-eyed and atavistic as something which had simply decided not to evolve. It was called a snail darter and the interesting thing about it was that it seemed to thrive nowhere in the known universe save in the riverbed not three miles from Bender's farm.

Bender was exultant. Salvation was at hand. It did not even strike him as ironic that all his efforts had been impotent but that a fish as ugly and apparently useless as the snail darter had a branch of the federal government working night and day to save its home. He was more than willing to just go along for the ride. The man in the pith helmet said that the snail darter was an endangered species. Endangered himself Bender felt more than a passing empathy with it.

AT MIDMORNING a sheriff's department car from the town of Ackerman's Field pulled up Bender's driveway towing a wake of dust fine as talcum. Bender went out to see. He'd come to dread cop cars, mailmen, ringing telephones.

It was the sheriff himself. Bellwether stood smoothing the wrinkles out of his khaki trousers and adjusting the pistol on his hip.

We're all peaceable here, Bender said. You won't need that.

I was just driving out to see what was going on out here, Bellwether said. I ain't been out in this neighborhood in no telling when.

You can hear what's going on, Bender said. He realized that he'd lived with noise so long he'd become accustomed to it. It was like the low hum of a swarm of distant bees.

Bellwether stood in an attitude of listening. The dull drone of who knew how many kinds of heavy machinery; to the south they could see the dust they stirred hanging in a shifting cloud.

They do make a hell of a racket, don't they? Busy as little beavers.

All day long.

I figured you to be gone. Thought I'd see.

Well. I'm not.

I see you ain't. You hear about old man Liverett coming to terms with them?

Everybody keeps telling me about it.

The sheriff squatted in the earth yard. He tipped out a Camel and put it in his mouth and lit it and took a drag off it. He exhaled and took the cigarette out of his mouth and looked at it in mild surprise. He crushed the fire out under a polished shoe and tossed the butt away. I'm trying to quit, he said, but I keep doing that out of habit.

Bender waited. He watched. The high sheriff took up a twig and began to draw meaningless hieroglyphs in the dust. Bender let me talk to you a minute, he said.

All right.

I've known your people all my life. You've known me all yours. Your mama and daddy was fine people, both of them. Paid their debts and minded their own business. The way you are your ownself. And I know this piece of land goes way back but don't you think you've done about all you can do?

You're telling it.

You've hired lawyers and fired lawyers and hired more lawyers. You've tried to get injunctions and court orders and exemptions and about every kind of legal paper they make. I don't know how much money you've spent and I don't give a damn. It's nothing to me. But I know you ain't a rich man, and for what value you've got you might as well have stuck that money up a wild pig's ass and hollered sooey. They're going to build that dam. It's for flood control and the government holds that the common good is more important than what one individual, you for example, has to say about it.

They're going to shut the goddamned thing down, Bender exploded. That fish. That snail darter. It's on the endangered species list and the EPA is not going to let it be destroyed.

Bellwether was shaking his head. There is just no way in hell, he said. Not in this lifetime. They're going to finish it and cut the channel for the river and all this is going to be under a hundred feet of water. Are you by any chance building a boat in your backyard?

Bender didn't say anything,

Now listen. You've got a wife and a kid and a good job teaching English out at the high school. Them boys of mine had you, they thought the world of you. You've got it made. Why do you want to piss it all away? Your wife and kid still here?

Yes.

You know they've offered you market value for this farm. Take it. There's plenty of land. Buy some more.

Bender felt awkward and inarticulate the way he did every time this happened. He was continually called upon to explain himself and day by day it had grown harder so that by now there didn't seem to be any words, the right phrases hadn't been coined yet. It was easy to say buy more land but hard to explain this was all the land there was. This was all the land he had been born on and that had absorbed the lives of his ancestors. His dead parents' voices rose and fell in measured cadence just out of hearing and their shades stood almost invisible in dark corners.

Bellwether stood up. Now his face looked curiously remote,

and Bender divined that he was distancing himself from him. Bender's folks were good folks and all that but the law was the law and the federal government was where the buck stopped.

I'd like to talk sense to you, Bellwether said. Sometimes a man in my position is called on to do things he might not want to do, but he's got to do them anyway.

He climbed back into the cruiser and pulled the door to. I'll see you, Bender, he said. But I hope for both our sakes it's some-place else.

BENDER IN HIS OLD FORD truck drove through a countryside almost surreal in the degree of its devastation. As if some great war had been won or lost here. No soul seemed to have survived. He drove past shotgun shack and mansion alike, all empty, houses canted on their foundations by dozers, shells of houses gutted by fire, old tall chimneys standing solitary and regal like sentries left to guard something that wasn't even there anymore.

The old man was sitting amidst the motley of plunder on his front porch like some gaunt-eyed dust bowl survivor. Ninety-five years old and he lived alone and did his own cooking and mowed the yard himself and until recently he had driven an old pickup truck homemade from a '47 Studebaker. Liverett had outlived the '47 Studebaker and all his children and a number of wives and all this outliving had begun to turn him bitter against things in general.

Come up, Bender, the old man said.

Bender sat on the doorstep. He hadn't seen the old man for a while and age seemed finally to be catching up with him. His face seemed caved as if it were decaying internally and the skin stretched over the cheekbones looked nearly transparent. He went inside to fetch Bender a cup of coffee and now he seemed to move as carefully as if he conveyed something of incalculable value and marvelous fragility.

When Bender had taken a sip of his coffee he figured to work the conversation around to the government. Those home health people still bothering you? he asked. The old man was fiercely independent and for years he had waged a running battle with various agencies determined to take care of him.

I reckon they about give up on me, Liverett said. They send em out once and I run em off and next time it'll be somebody else. They sent this little snip of a girl out here a week or two ago. Said she was new on the job. Purty little thing, big blue eyes, fine little titties. Said she was supposed to check my blood pressure and give me a bath. A bath? I said. Why I never heard of such a thing. A little snip of a girl givin a grown man a bath and him a stranger at that. Well Missy, I told her, I'll tell you what. You let me give you one first and we might work up some kind of a deal.

Bender grinned weakly. In his later years the old man's mind seemed to have turned to sex and in some manner locked there. Bender judged that were he stronger and more agile he might have turned into some kind of sex maniac.

I hear you let them beat you, Bender said. You finally knuckled under.

Is that what you hear? You heard wrong. What I heard was that I asked em a certain price and they finally met it.

You already sold?

Damn right. Wait here a minute. He got up and opened the screen door and went inside. Bender could hear him rummaging around inside the house. When the old man came back out he was carrying a paper bag, a grocery sack with the top folded down. He unfolded it and held it for Bender to peer into. Looky here, he said. Bender looked. Great God, he said. The sack was full of money. Neat stacks of bills as square and crisp as if some kind of machine had bundled them. They paid you in cash?

No. They wouldn't. I had to carry the check to the bank and cash it. They raised Cain but I didn't give em no selection. I wanted it with me. All of it. The notion might strike me to roll around in it.

What are you aiming to do with it?

I been studyin some on that. I'm goin out to Las Vegas, Nevada. I'm goin into one of them gamblin places they got and pick out the purtiest girl in the place. I'm goin to pay her just whatever it takes to dance naked on the table I'm sittin at.

Bender looked at the money again. I expect that would do it, he said.

I may get two of em dancin.

I meant really. What are you really going to do, Mr. Liverett?

The old man looked sharply at Bender and for a moment his eyes looked confused and disoriented. I'm damned if I know, he said, and Bender wished he'd left him his casinos and dancing girls.

What do you plan on doin, Bender?

Hang on as long as I can. I believe that fish is going to shut it down.

Not anymore it ain't. Don't you never watch the news? They found a bunch of them little son of a bitches down around Muscle Shoals, Alabama. In the Tennessee River. Then they found some more somers else. Seems they ain't near as scarce as they thought they was. I look for em to find em in mudholes and everywhere else before they're through. They may have to cut the river channel just to thin em out some.

Bender drained his coffee cup and set it carefully on the porch railing. He stood up and dusted off the seat of his pants. I got to get on, he said. You be careful with that money, Mr. Liverett.

I aim to. The old man arose as well. He stuck out a hand in a curiously formal gesture. I expect I won't ever see you again, Bender.

I guess not. Bender took the hand. It was dry and papery and the bones felt light and hollow as bird's bones.

I don't know what you're going to do out there in Nevada. You won't know a soul.

I don't know a soul anymore anyway, the old man said. That's all folks are good for. To die off on you.

GAUNT-EYED AND INTENSE Bender stepped out of the thick woods to see why the government truck had stopped in his driveway. The motor of the pickup was idling and the door was open and a young man in a white hardhat already had the sign in his left hand and a claw hammer in his right hand. He was holding tacks in his mouth.

I believe you've wandered onto private property here, Bender said.

The young man said something around the tacks Bender didn't get.

Spit them out, Bender said. You won't be using them on my property anyway.

The man palmed the tacks and stood holding them. I don't believe I'm on private property. I was told this was government land, part of the dam project.

You were told wrong then.

They sent me up here to post all this property. I just do what I'm told.

If you do what you're told then I'm telling you to get the hell off my land.

Interfering with the United States government can put a world of hurt on you. Have they not served you with eviction papers?

No.

Well they're fixing to.

The man had the sign affixed against a utility pole and was positioning a tack when Bender closed on him. They struggled for a moment in the roadside ditch like drunken dancers. The government man's hardhat fell off. Bender had him in a headlock and when he released him he crumpled. Bender wrenched the claw hammer out of his right hand and threw it as far as he could into the woods. The man's left hand had made a fist over the tacks and he was pulling them out of the flesh of his palm.

Hellfire, the man said. His lip was bleeding and he was looking around for his hardhat. When he had found it and had it on he got into the truck and slammed the door. He rolled down the glass. I heard them talking about you, he said. You don't watch it mighty close you'll be in a place where the rooms got rubber walls.

Get off my property, Bender said.

THE WOLF HAD SLEPT out the day in a hazelnut thicket near the river and it was full dark before it came out and when it did it crept unbidden into Bender's dreams. It came delicately down the tiers of limestone shelving to the riverbank and drank and angled across a cleared area toward the dam. This area was laid out with wooden stakes tied with garlands of red plastic but the wolf went on. Far across the manmade basin low thunder rumbled and on the western horizon lightning flickering a fierce staccato rose. By its photoelectric glare the scraped treeless world was as barren and alien as a moonscape.

The wolf paused and raised its head toward where the moon would be were it not overcast and when the horizon quaked and trembled again it increased its pace and by the time the first drops of rain came it was moving at a slow lope. It went down the limestone riprap with surefooted steps and crossed the concrete floor weaving between the rebar without diminishing its speed. It had a brief yellow-eyed glance for all these works of man but seemed to have no interest for it.

The wolf's shaggy coat was wet now and the stag's blood coagulated and matted began to melt in his ruff and his front was stained with spreading pink as if he were some jaunty tie-dyed wolf a child might create.

He went past the desecrated Indian mound where long ago men had laid their dead with solemnity and later other men had with like solemnity disinterred them and when it reached the chain-link fence it did not falter but turned at a right angle and ran along the fence until it came to a bulldozed pile of charred trees and scorched topsoil. It ran up the jumble of logs until it was almost at a level with the top of the fence and then it jumped. It landed in thick honeysuckle it had in past times wallowed into a lair and slowed its pace cautiously and followed its path through the sweet smell of honeysuckle into the wild nightshade that had taken Bender's fallow garden.

From where it stood chest-deep in the tangle of nightshade it could see through the falling rain the yellow squares of light from the house and after a while it took shelter beneath the riot of honeysuckle and lay with its chin on its paws and watched the house.

✦ ✦ ✦

LYNN WAS TALKING but Bender had his eyes closed and he was not listening. His mind was occupied with thinking about the days before the dam project was even rumored and he realized that he and Lynn and Jesse had been living an idyllic life without even knowing it and that this life was as remote to him now as his childhood.

. . . taking him to my sister's for a few days, were the first words he heard clearly.

He raised onto his elbows. What? he asked. He noticed with mild surprise that she had been crying.

Just until this is all settled one way or another. We can't go on like this, this is like living in a motel. We can't live in a motel the rest of our lives.

I don't know as I like the sound of any of this, Bender said.

I don't know as we have a choice, she said. You won't even talk about leaving. About taking the money and finding another place. It's like we're just sitting here waiting until the police pick us up and carry us across the property line. I don't know what you plan to do. If you plan to do anything at all. You won't talk anymore.

We're a family, Bender said. Me and you and Jesse. Together we can do whatever we have to do. Split up and scattered we're nothing, just three separate people.

A family talks about things and makes decisions for the good of the family. Not like this . . . this craziness. Your whole life depends on what they decide to do about some stupid fish.

Bender decided not to tell her what Liverett had said about the snail darter. If you want to go a few days I can't stop you. But you're not taking Jesse. He's as much my son as he is yours. What makes you think you can pick him up like a suitcase and just go away with him?

Bender was sitting on the side of the bed with his hands cupping his knees. He watched her get out of bed and pace away from him—her white nightgown drifting behind her.

In fact, I don't think you should go at all. We'll figure something out.

She paced back to him. I've already called Ruthie and told her we were coming. I've got to get away from here a few days. If you come over tomorrow we can talk about it.

He grasped her arm but perhaps harder than he meant to for she cried out and twisted away and her eyes were panicky and wild-looking. She was backpedaling away from him. When he was almost upon her with arms outspread to grasp her she jerked the lamp off the end table and swung it at him. God*damn,* Bender said. Only the shade caught him a glancing painless blow but he was so shocked at her striking him that he shoved outward both-handed as hard as he could. The lamp swung away and slammed the wall and the bulb broke. He heard her fall somewhere off in the dark. She didn't even cry out. He picked up the lamp and righted it and plugged it in. The room stayed dark. He crossed the room, almost running, and clicked on the ceiling light.

Oh Jesus, Bender said. Oh Jesus.

She was lying with her head on the edge of the raised brick hearth and her neck cocked sideways at a crazy-looking angle. Blood like shadows was already seeping onto the brick from the back of her head and with her eyes open and lying there on her back with arms and legs outflung she looked as if she had fallen from some unreckonable height and slammed onto Bender's carpet.

With his face close to hers he tried to ascertain was she breathing or not. He couldn't tell for sure but he didn't think she was. Her pulse was either faint or absent at her throat and his own heart beat too loud and too fast to be sure.

He ran out of the room and down the hall to the open door of Jesse's room. Jesse lay with his face toward Bender and the sheet rising and falling in measured respiration.

He went back to the bedroom and squatted in the middle of the floor and watched Lynn. After a while he put his face in his hands and sat there swaying soundlessly and trying to think. What to do. It had grown very quiet. He could hear the rain soft and suspirant on the roof and far off beyond the dam the rumble of thunder like something heavy and out of control rolling downhill toward him. He didn't care if it was. He couldn't fathom how or why this had happened. Someone he loved lay still and bloody pillowed on the hearth and no hands but his had touched her. He felt strange in his skin, it was light and uncomfortable, like some ill-fitting costume he had struggled into, and he did not know how to get out of it. He divined that he was somewhere he'd had no intention of going, that he was someone he did not want to be.

He got up and stripped the sheet off the bed and laid it spread out on the carpet and lifting Lynn by the arms he dragged her to the center of it. He lowered her gently onto it. Her head kept lolling back loosely as if it would fold beneath her and he had to adjust her head with a foot while he positioned her. He folded the sheet about her like a shroud and straightened and just stood for a moment staring down at her. He stooped and picked her up and cradled her in his arms and turned her so that she was draped over his left shoulder. He went cautiously past Jesse's door and out of the house and into the rain.

He'd decided that somehow he had to get her across the garden fence and across the chain-link fence and back to the graveyard. Then he could place her in one of the empty graves and maybe cave the sides in on her. Only one body to a grave, who'd look in an empty grave? He'd tell Ruthie they had had an argument and Lynn had driven off and left him. Nobody was going to buy that story long but maybe it would give him enough time to think of something.

He was halfway across the garden staggering in the mud and vines when he stopped dead-still. He stood in an attitude of listening. Well I'm a son of a bitch, he said. He could hear a car engine toiling up the hill. He turned with her. He stared in disbelief. A slow wash of headlights coming up the hill like the very embodiment of ill luck. His face had an angry, put-upon look as if the world would not leave him alone long enough for him to get on with the things he had to do. Then all at once he came to himself and half ran, half fell, into the nightshade and honeysuckle with her. He pulled vines over her as best he could and struggled up and ran into the shadows keeping the house between himself and the headlights. When he came around the corner of the house the car was sitting parked in his driveway with the door sprung open and a dark silhouette getting out. Rain was falling slant in the headlights and he could hear the disjointed crackling of a police scanner.

What is it? Bender asked. His voice sounded like a harsh rasp and he felt he could not bear just one more thing. Not one more thing. He felt some enormous dark weight settling over him and smothering him. He wondered that he could place left foot in front of right, string one word in a coherent sequence after another.

Of course it was Bellwether. He saw Bender as he closed the door of the cruiser. Bender?

What is it?

Do you not know enough to get in out of the rain?

Bender raked his wet hair out of his eyes. Water coursed down his face. He grinned weakly.

What the hell are you doing out in this mess?

Bender took a deep breath. He forced himself to think. I thought lightning struck something. It came a hell of a clap of thunder and the power went off a second then came back on. I thought it might have hit my pump but I reckon not. A tree over there I guess.

Listen, Bender, I'm sorry as hell to come out here this late, but they want those papers served. I've got them right here. You want to go in the house where it's light and I'll read them to you?

I think not, Bender said. Leave them and I'll read the god-damned things myself.

I told you all this before. Sometimes I have to do things I don't want to do, and this is one of the times. You know I got to read them to you. Now get in the car.

Bender did as he was told. He pulled the door closed and sat clasping the door handle loosely with his right hand. Bellwether turned on the dome light and read the papers. They might have been Sanskrit, Latin, so little did Bender comprehend. He sat staring at Lynn's face so pale in the wet black honeysuckle and not one coherent word did he hear.

That's about it. This is where it stops. You are ordered off this property by ten o'clock tomorrow morning or suffer whatever consequences failure to comply entails.

Like getting my ass carried off it?

Like getting your ass carried off if need be. When you roughed that feller up or whatever you done you pissed them off.

Bender opened the door and started to get out. All right, he said.

All right what?

Just all right. I'll be gone.

They'll give you sufficient time to get your property and personal effects moved. Listen, Bender, you fought and you lost. Let it go. For what it's worth I'm sorry.

Bender was standing by the car. Sorry is not worth a damn to me, he said. He shoved the door but Bellwether leaned across the seat fast and caught it and pushed it open hard. The edge of the door caught Bender on the hip and he staggered back.

Let me tell you this straight out, Bellwether said. I'll be here myself to see about your wife and kid. You do what you want. A man wants carried out can damn sure find somebody to carry him. But I'm escortin your family away from any trouble myself. Are we right clear on that?

Bender stood rubbing his hip. He didn't say anything.

Are we right clear on that?

Yes.

All right then. Bellwether eased the car in gear and pulled the door closed. He had scarcely begun to turn in the drive before Bender was moving rapidly toward the corner of the house. Out of the lights he stood leaning for a minute against the side of the house with the rain from the eaves falling on him until he heard the car going down the hill and then he struck out for the garden.

When he reached both-handed into the honeysuckle and felt nothing he gave a sort of grunt of dismay or disbelief and felt all about the dark vines. He was looking around wildly when lightning bloomed and she was standing by the fence in the rain specterlike in her funeral windings and her hair plastered to her skull and her eyes closed just swaying slightly then gone in abrupt dark and Bender raised his face to the heavens and gave a cry scarcely human, a hoarse unarticulated scream of outrage and horror and such utter despair as should have stitched a caesura in the wheeling of the earth on its axis.

He whirled and ran back toward the house and fell once and

got up and went on. When he came to himself he was sitting on the couch in the living room with water dripping out of the cuffs of his jeans and pooling on the floor.

He got up and methodically began to search the kitchen. Cabinet drawer to cabinet drawer leaving each standing open in its turn as he went on to the next and finally the cabinets themselves. In the cabinet over the oven he found a pint of peach brandy three-quarters full and went with it back to the couch and sat down. He drank the brandy while the night drew on and rain blew against the windows and lightning wrought the mimosa in stark relief until finally the storm passed over and the thunder dimmed away. All this time by an act of sheer will he had not thought of Lynn at all.

He was weary and after a while the brandy bottle slipped from his fingers and tilted and spilled on the floor and he laid his head on the arm of the couch and fell asleep.

At some point he began to dream. In his dream all this tumult and disorder had fallen away and his life stood in marvelous symmetry. He and Lynn and Jesse had survived. The world had done its best to unhinge them but they had come through unscathed. The world had tried them with fire and water but the water had cleansed and soothed them and the fire had tempered them so that they were the stronger for it, and they were together, hand in hand, standing by peaceful waters.

When he awoke there was a sour taste in his mouth and a weight in his chest and his face was wet with tears. He got up and shambled into the kitchen to the sink and halted abruptly when he saw Jesse standing by the sliding glass door looking out at the patio.

Jesse saw Bender's reflection in the glass and he turned. There was a curious look on his face, almost a sly complicity as he looked at Bender in silence and pointed at the glass.

They crouched before the plate glass like conspirators. The rain-wet flagstones, the dripping trees. Then in silent wonder he saw the wolf. It came at a lope out of the trailing honeysuckle, ragged and ill kept like some wolf cobbled up out of the leftover parts of other wolves and resurrected and set upon him by some dark alchemy. It bounded onto the flagstones and sprang at the glass. It slammed against it and for a microsecond the glass bulged inward with a marvelous elasticity and glass and wolf alike were frozen in midair as if time had skidded to a halt. Then the glass exploded inward and all Bender's senses were so assailed by stimuli he could scarcely comprehend everything: the smell of the rainy night blown in and the sweet nostalgic reek of flowers and the feral charnel smell of the wolf. The air was full of pebbled glass. It rattled off the walls like hail and sang along the Formica countertop like grapeshot. He could hear the wolf's claws snicking along the tile floor and clawing for purchase and he had only time to enfold the child and turn Jesse's face into the hollow of his throat before the wolf was upon them.

Good 'Til Now

VANGIE THOUGHT this day would
never end, and what got her through it was thinking about the
time her husband had been fired for having sex with a woman in a
cardboard carton. Vangie had always been more interested in the
carton than in the woman. The woman was just a faceless coworker
who had crawled—how else would you get in there?—into a cardboard box and had sex with Charles. But the box was something
else. How big was it? Was it lying horizontally? Who crawled in
first? Was there protocol involved here, etiquette? What did you
say to someone in a cardboard box? They had been caught not by
one person, who might just conceivably have kept his mouth shut,
but by four or five workers who'd come into the storeroom to sneak
cigarettes and been treated to an impromptu floor show.

It was about the size of a goddamned refrigerator box, Charles
had said sullenly. Charles had been contrite and humiliated for
about fifteen minutes, and then the Hemingway implications of
the whole thing had struck him. It seemed in some manner tied to
the level of his testosterone. It proved beyond all conjecture the
appeal he had to women. It was an ego thing, and since Charles

240

was a hunter who mounted the heads of his victims on wooden plaques, Vangie thought it was a shame he hadn't managed to get some sort of trophy out of the whole affair.

This had been five years ago, and it had crossed her mind a few times that she and Charles might not be as made for each other as they had once thought; but by then their son, Stephen, was a year old, and Stephen was such an enormity in her life that he dwarfed even so tacky a thing as adultery committed inside a cardboard box.

All day she had been thinking that she and Stephen and Robert might just pile everything into the car and flee. *Flee* had been Robert's word. Just flee west 'til the wheels run off and burn, the upholstery cracks and the paint fades and the moccasins die. She was wondering if adultery had an expiration date like something you'd pick up from a supermarket shelf. A statute of limitations. If she left and Charles tried to win custody of Stephen, maybe she could hit him with that. Perhaps hit him first. He had even beaten her once, in a halfhearted way, but he had been drinking a lot then, and he had cried and promised that it would never happen again, and it had not.

Even this Robert Vandaveer business could be laid at Charles's door, if you wanted to carry things back far enough.

Charles had been deer hunting with a band of his friends down on the river, and he came back talking about Vandaveer. We met this weird fellow down on Buffalo, Charles said. Some kind of writer, songwriter or something. Weird, but all right. He gave us permission to camp on his place. Hair down to his ass, but he's all right. He even drank a beer with us.

For a while all Charles could talk about was Robert Vandaveer. Vangie figured he'd taken Vandaveer for some proponent of the cult of machismo, some writer of the Hemingway–Jim Harrison school. Robert had done this, Robert had done that. Robert had constructed his lodge with his bare hands. Robert had even cut the timber with which he bare-handedly constructed his lodge. Then Charles had abruptly stopped talking about Robert Vandaveer.

What happened to Robert Vandaveer? she asked him.

We're not hunting down there anymore, Charles said.

Yet that night a year ago the name had stirred some lost memory, and before bedtime she went through her record collection. She'd always loved music, had written songs herself, and she owned an enormous number of tapes, CDs, records. She found what she was looking for with absurd ease. As if they had been stored, all stacked in sequence and lying in wait for her. The subtle machinations of fate, Robert would have said in an ironic tone, if she had ever told him. Emmylou Harris had covered two of Robert Vandaveer's songs. Johnny Cash had recorded a Dylanesque song that Vandaveer had written. There was even a recording by Vandaveer himself, one of his own songs, on a Rhino collection called *Folk Troubadours of the Seventies*.

Later she wondered why she had searched for the songs. Why she hadn't just let it lie. Maybe we are all the authors of our own doom, she thought. Maybe we lay by the cobwebbed artifacts we'll need for our future undoing. At some unknown point we'll rummage through them for the cord that fits the throat just so, the knife with the perfect edge.

VANGIE WAS A TEACHER'S AIDE and a counselor. Stephen was in the second grade, and she had taken the job when he started kindergarten. The days had been long then, too. They had been long, but they hadn't cut the way this one did.

At noon she went to the teachers' lounge and used the phone to dial Robert's number. The phone rang and rang. She held it so tightly against her ear that it hurt, but she just let it ring. She could see the room the phone was in. The scarred pine table it sat on. She wondered if he was drinking. She wondered if he was passed out on the couch with an empty Wild Turkey bottle cradled against his chest as you'd cradle a child. She didn't think so. She figured he was laying rock on the chimney he was building. He'd completed the fireplace, but the lodge was an A-frame and high roofed, and the chimney would have to be enormously tall to clear it. He kept building scaffolding higher and higher. She kidded him about the thin air, about nesting eagles. He wrestled the stones from one level of the scaffold to the next. Five-gallon buckets of mortar. He was stronger than he appeared.

He had called her Sunday to see if she would come out. She was still off balance, disoriented; she could not. His voice didn't sound quite right, but she couldn't put her finger on why. There was a feeling of distance in it, distance you couldn't measure in miles. You're not drinking are you? she asked him. There'd been a pause, as if he'd looked to see was he drinking or not. No, no, he said. I'm not drinking. I thought I might mix up some mortar, lay a few rocks.

A teacher came in and stood watching her. Waiting perhaps for the phone. She hung it up. She wondered how long she had let it ring, but she really didn't want to know. She didn't look at her watch. She wondered what she was going to do.

YOUR BUDDY Robert Vandaveer's going to be at the school, she told Charles. This had been almost exactly a year ago.

Say he is? What in the world for?

He's supposed to address one of the English classes on creativity. On poetry, the process of converting experience into a poem.

My question remains unanswered, Charles said.

Well, he is a songwriter. A poet. A long time ago he was almost famous, in a fifteen-minute kind of way. The superintendent heard there was a poet living in the wilds of Buffalo River and figured the English class might benefit from hearing him talk and asking him questions.

I have a question of my own, Charles said. How much money is the county pissing away on this?

They're not paying him, she said.

She had a free period that day, and she thought she might just see this semifamous Vandaveer. When the lecture was over and the students had filed out of the classroom, she was standing in the hallway. She'd stood aside to let them pass, and when Vandaveer went by he nodded to her. She nodded in return, and that should have been that, except she heard herself say: My husband, Charles, told me about meeting you.

He paused and turned to study her. I knew you the moment I saw you, he said.

You what? How could you do that?

Your husband showed me your photograph.

She wondered why Charles was going around showing strange men her picture. She wondered if he'd had a leer on his face to show them what hot stuff she was.

How did he come to show you my photograph?

It was my fault, Vandaveer said. I led him into it. I just had a feeling he had a photograph I wanted to see. I thought it might be you, and as it turned out I was right.

Then why did you nod and just walk on past me without

speaking? She figured to let him know she could play word games as well as he could.

He smiled. Because I was sure you'd speak to me.

Vangie was trying to relate the aging hippie before her to the young man whose photograph was on the back of the album sleeve. A young man with anarchic hair, firebrand eyes, an impatient look of arrogance on his face. Vandaveer looked about fifty, like a man salvaged weatherworn but intact from the '60s. He had a gray-brown ponytail, and he was wearing an old black sport coat over a white shirt. His jeans were faded, and his shoes were spotted with what looked like dried brick mortar. There seemed little of the revolutionary left in Vandaveer's face, and his eyes were the most changed feature of all: There was an enormous stillness to them. There were depths, blank spaces, burnt landscapes. They seemed to say that they had seen all the world had to show them and there was nothing they could do about it.

I have a recording you made, she said. Some of your own songs. She knew he was going to ask her which songs, and she had the titles ready, even the lines that she had liked best. He didn't, though.

Do you like music? he asked.

I like it very much.

There's a thing, a folk music part of the arts and crafts fair. Some pretty good guitar players and songwriters are going to be there. Would you like to go?

She was confused. You mean with you?

That's what I mean.

Well, you know my husband. Charles. If I have a husband, it follows I'm married.

It was just to listen to music, he said. Bring the boy. He was in the picture, too. Bring Charles, it's just a family thing. Folks show up from all over, campers full of families.

Charles doesn't even like music, she said. He hates crowds, too.

Then I wouldn't bring him. This pretty much consists of crowds listening to music.

I'd have to tell him.

I would imagine so.

It really might be fun. There's a lot of questions I'd like to ask you about music, anyway.

He had unpocketed a cigarette. He lit it with a thin gold lighter. There was engraving on the side, but she couldn't read what it said.

You can't smoke in here.

He didn't seem to hear. Oh hell, he said. I forgot. I'm sorry I even brought it up. The transmission's out of my truck, and it might not be ready.

That was another place when that should have been that, but she said: Stephen and I will pick you up if you'll give me directions.

He told her where the road turned off and which fork to follow to the river. Just drive 'til you run out of road, he said.

When he'd turned to go, she said: I really am happily married.

He looked surprised she'd bring it up. That's cool, he said. I've been there a few times myself.

IF THEY HAD NOT LOST Stephen that night, she would not have gone to bed with him. That was what she told herself later, but she did not believe it. If they had not lost Stephen, they would have lost something else. It was fated, Robert had said, and she believed

him. *Fated* was a word Robert was fond of. Fated and flee. We are
fated to flee.

Though before that happened, a year had passed and they had
fallen into the habit of going places together. First to the music
festival, then to a music store Robert knew about in Nashville
that sold hard-to-find records on obscure labels. To art galleries,
musty-smelling bookstores. To other places beyond reproach.
Once, he took her and Stephen to a Mexican restaurant in
Franklin. Stephen was always along, nothing was going to happen with Stephen along. Stephen seemed to have fallen in love
with Vandaveer. Robert talked to him the way he might talk
with another adult. When he took Stephen fishing, Vangie
sipped a Corona and watched but would only let Stephen fish
from the riverbank. She would not allow Robert to take him out
in the boat.

Of course she knew this was crazy. Each time when the days
ended—they ended too fast, like events rushing in fast-forward—
she told herself how crazy it was. They were just comfortable together, they had grown too fond of each other. They seemed to fit.
Something about him affected her the way medicine might. She
thought she affected him the same way, but she didn't ask. They
didn't talk about it. Maybe comfort was just another kind of medicine. She'd be all right a week or two, and then the need for the
comfort would tighten her nerves, tighten his nerves, and one of
them would call.

Partly it was the music, but it was not entirely the music.
When she pestered him hard enough, he'd laugh and tell stories
about people who were just names on record labels, names in the
pages of *Rolling Stone.* Once in the early '70s he'd been playing the
Fifth Peg in Chicago's Old Town with John Prine and they had

gotten drunk and stolen shopping carts from a supermarket parking lot and raced them in the streets, and he told her about getting in a fight with Townes Van Zandt in a Texas honky-tonk so rough the stage was chicken-wired to deflect the beer bottles and Van Zandt had hit him in the corner of the eye with a metal wastebasket. He showed her the scar.

These stories with their names familiar to her did not seem to be told to impress her. The names he dropped were just names, and he did not tell stories that made him look good. They were just things that had happened to him, and in time the most sordid of them became very dear to her.

For there were times when the stories darkened. Once when he'd backslid and was drinking Wild Turkey, his mind sidestepped past the harmless pranks to a point where the high, wild times were lost past all reclaiming, and he and Van Zandt were shooting heroin in the bathroom of a honky-tonk with vomit on the floor and a drunk sleeping sprawled in a stall and a hole in the roof where you could see the constellations turning slowly on themselves like carousels of unreckonable magnitude, and the night itself seemed to be settling over him like the folds of a shroud.

Or maybe he just knows which buttons to push, she told herself in a moment when her mind was clear. He's been at this all his life; by now he knows what works, what doesn't.

There were silences when he seemed to be hearing something she couldn't hear, or maybe just listening for it to begin. Silences that gave her the eerie impression that he was not there, maybe not even alive, as if all his life had been used up. As if his life had consisted of a finite number of events and the time to do them, but everything had become unphased, and the things had all been done, and he was left with dead space he did not know how to fill.

✦ ✦ ✦

WHAT IS THIS Robert Vandaveer bullshit about? Charles wanted to know.

Charles wants to know what this Robert Vandaveer bullshit is about, she told Robert.

What did you tell him it was about?

I told him I enjoyed your company, that nothing was going on. I told him I didn't complain about the time he spent with his friends, and that Stephen was always with us.

What did he say to that?

He said his friends weren't old enough to be his father and they didn't have hair down to their ass.

By now they'd passed some subtle point. It wasn't marked, but they knew they'd passed it anyway. They weren't exactly flirting, but they weren't exactly anything else, either.

Tell him I'm gay.

What? she was laughing. Are you?

No, but I don't mind if Charles thinks so. In fact I want him to think so. Tell him I'm using you to get to him. Tell Charles I have designs on him.

Charles, when told a slightly modified version of this, was surprised. I knew the son of a bitch was queer when he wouldn't let us kill deer off that place, he said.

SHE WAS WATCHING a music documentary on public television and reading a book when a heavyset young man with a wing of blond hair falling over his left eye was being interviewed and mentioned Robert's name. The volume seemed to grow louder just for the length of time it took to say Robert Vandaveer. She closed the book and laid it aside.

He was the daddy of us all, the young man, whose name was Steve Valle, said. Without him we'd never have been, it's as simple as that. He kicked open a lot of doors, and the rest of us slipped through. He could have been the biggest of us all. He could have been another Dylan. But booze and sex and drugs, maybe in that order, brought him down. Brought him down hard.

How well did you know him?

Vangie suddenly realized they sounded as if they were discussing a dead man.

I knew him as well as one man can know another. He took me under his wing. He showed me the ropes.

Vangie thought the young man sounded pompous and arrogant. He'd only recorded one album.

Robert was working on his interminable chimney when she told him about Valle. She wondered what he'd do with his time when he finished the chimney. Perhaps commence another right beside it.

He made you sound important, she said. He said you were the daddy of them all.

I believe I remember him, Vandaveer said. But not like that. But God knows I don't remember a lot of things. I've got whole years with long stretches erased out of them. The way I remember it, he was just another hustler. Trying to steal songs, lines out of songs. There were a thousand of him. Kids who'd slit your throat for a killer line.

You took him under your wing.

Grinning, he laid the trowel down and extended his arms out from his side. Then he was obviously lying, he said. As you can see, I possess not a wing to my name.

You could have been the biggest of us all, but booze and sex and drugs brought you down hard, she told him, grinning back. You never showed me the ropes.

WHEN THEY LOST STEPHEN they were watching the night-hawks. They lost him that quick. He was there, he was gone. They were at a music fair in a Nashville park. The Parthenon was lit by a battery of floodlights, and the stage bled strobic, pastel neon into the August night. They were sprawled on their backs before the stage where a funk band was playing, and where the light merged seamlessly with the ebony heavens, thousands of nighthawks darted and checked on the updrafts like bats, and they seemed to be feeding on the light itself.

Stephen? she said.

She was up instantly, looking wildly about. There were so many people sprawled around them. Did you see my little boy leave? she demanded of the man next to them on the grass. The man was apologetic; he seemed to feel this was something he'd be held accountable for. I'm sorry, the man said, I wasn't even look-ing, I was watching the stage. Stephen's Coke and a CD Robert had bought him still lay on the grass. She snatched them up. Let's go, she said.

They searched in widening circles through the crowd. Every-one looked alike, a faceless mass. Hundreds of children, none of whom were Stephen. Everyone else seemed to have kept up with their children. She was scared, and then she was more scared. We've got to get his name over the public-address system, Robert said. She looked once at Robert's face for comfort, but he looked as frightened as she felt. Stephen was hopelessly lost, kidnapped, and already jammed roughly into the trunk of a car, riding away, easing into a night of horror that would climax with his naked body flung in a ditch and a piece of dirty plastic thrown over it.

When Robert saw him, Stephen was coming out of a yellow portable toilet fastening his jeans. He was almost on the other side of the park, but he didn't look as if he knew he was lost. Robert picked him up, held him tightly in his arms. There was a bandstand nearby where no one was performing, and they went and sat down on folding chairs. By now Vangie was crying. She was crying, and she couldn't stop. She kept shaking her head and trying, but she couldn't stop. Finally Robert put his arm around her. It was the first time he'd touched her. She twisted away. We can't, we can't, she said, don't touch me. He released her, lowered the arm. Robert had only seen him coming out the door of a portable toilet, but she felt he'd snatched Stephen from the arms of a madman, from the path of a drunken driver. It felt like a miracle. As if the rest of her life had been torn from her to show her what loss would be like, then handed carelessly back.

Let's go home, she said.

Charles is on that week-long fishing trip. He won't be back tonight.

No, all the fun's gone out of this, I'm leaving.

I'll get the blanket.

No, leave it, I don't care about the blanket, let's just go.

The ride back was mostly silent. Usually, they talked all the way, and there was never enough time to get everything said, but tonight she drove and Robert smoked and watched the night roll by, lights of distant hillside towns rolling up and subsiding like St. Elmo's fire in the wake of a ship.

This was a bad idea, she finally said.

No, it was a good idea. I loved it. You know me, I'd go with you anywhere. A rattlesnake hunt. A Baptist foot washing.

That's not what I meant, and you know it. I meant it's crazy, this whole thing's crazy.

A public stoning. A hanging. Well, maybe not a hanging.

Crazy, she said, smiling in spite of herself.

When she stopped the station wagon in front of Robert's lodge, he opened the door to get out, then paused and turned toward her. You want to come in awhile?

No, she said, but her hand was on the door latch, then the door was open and she was standing beside the car. Robert got out. He opened the rear door and unbelted a sleeping Stephen and took him up in his arms. He started up the flagstone walk. Vangie followed. Her feet seemed to be taking steps on their own; they needed no instruction from her. The lodge, all rough-hewn timbers and glass, was built on a bluff, and below it you could see the river rolling dark as tarnished brass through the cedars.

They went from the deck through French doors into the living room, and Robert made a bed for Stephen on the couch and tucked a blanket around him.

You want a drink?

No, she said. Her voice sounded strange to her, as if she had never heard it before, or heard just that precise tone in it.

Then she didn't say anything. She didn't move. When he looked in her eyes, he stepped toward her and laid a hand on her shoulder. She moved against him. They embraced. She felt as if their flesh had flowed together, merged in some manner, as if they'd fallen from some enormous height and struck the earth clasped in this fashion. He felt so thin, but his arms almost crushed her. God, he said against her face. God. For a moment he just held her. As if after so long a time the embrace itself was enough. Then he lowered his mouth to hers, and she drew him tighter and opened her mouth under his.

In the bathroom she washed her face, but she didn't look in the mirror. She felt that Charles might be staring back. She felt that after all a cardboard box is simply a matter of geography.

THE ROOM WAS DARK, and a woman was singing out of it in a smoky listless languor: *Balled out, wasted, and I feel I'm goin' down. . . .*

I love this record, Robert said.

It doesn't seem very apt, Vangie said. I'm not going to get wasted on half a glass of wine, and I seem not to be balled out. I can't keep my hands off you.

Just indulge yourself, Robert said.

Hard to find a place I won't get cut on, you're all angles and bones. Don't you ever eat?

Goodbye, darl'n', I've been good 'til now. . . .

Well, it seems apt to me, Robert said. You've probably been as pure as milk, or at least good 'til now, and I'm for damn sure going down.

She glanced sharply at him as if she'd read the context of his words, but he made no move toward her, and he wasn't even looking at her. He was just lying there staring at the ceiling.

What are we going to do? he finally asked.

I don't know. I don't know. She was sipping from a glass of wine he'd brought her. She was half reclining on pillows stacked against the headboard of the bed. Robert still wasn't drinking. He was smoking, and in the dark she could see the orange pulse of his cigarette when he drew on it.

What we ought to do is just flee, Robert said. Just get the hell out of Dodge. I was reading this book by Robert Penn Warren, and this guy Jack Burden found out the woman he'd loved all his life was sleeping with his boss. His boss was supposed to be Huey Long. Burden drove all the way to California and checked into a motel. He drank a pint of whiskey, and in the morning he just started driving back. He said *Flee is what you do when the telegram says all is discovered.* It's what you do when you look down and see the bloody knife in your hand.

She didn't say anything. The wine was strawberry, and she could smell summer in it, hot green leaves, berries warm in the sun. She was thinking how little time it took to alter things forever. To arrive at a place you can't get back from. She realized the mental picture of herself she'd carried all these years didn't favor her much anymore.

We ought to just go and not look back. Like that Dylan song. Go all the way, 'til the wheels run off and burn, the upholstery cracks and the paint fades and the moccasins die. Something like that.

She wondered how much of him was real. How much was Robert Vandaveer and how much was cobbled up out of lines from songs, words from books, wisdom that fell ponderous as stones from the dust-dry tongues of dead philosophers.

I've got to go, she said.

She got up naked and set the wineglass on the nightstand. She began to search for her clothes. They seemed to be everywhere. She started putting them on.

What are we going to do?

I don't know, she said. We'll just sort it out. We can't do this.

If you go, you'll just come back. I told you a year ago it was fated, and I wasn't lying. I knew it the moment I saw you. Before I saw you, when a man showed me a picture of his wife. We're like the two halves of something—what, I don't know—but together we're a whole. Apart we're just cripples, half a set of twins.

She was buttoning her blouse. You can't do this to me, she said. You can't put a lien on my life, some sort of attachment. On me, on my child. With your lines about fate and talking to Charles because he had a picture of me in his wallet. I admit I fell in love with you, but that talk's all bullshit. I can't lose my son, that's what's real to me.

By now he was up and putting on his clothes. I'll get Stephen for you, he said.

Don't start drinking. Don't you start drinking.

She didn't think he ever used drugs anymore, but she thought he might have a stash laid by for hard times. These were hard times. She knew he kept an unopened fifth of Wild Turkey sitting on the table where he could see it. She'd asked him about drugs once and never forgotten what he'd said. Everybody's on drugs, he said. The world's on drugs. Heroin, sex, booze, money. Television. Comfort. What I get from you, that's a drug. Calmness. Any kind of crutch you can hobble through the goddamned day on is a drug. Darkness. They say when you get old enough, you look forward to dying. That's the drug you reach for when the other crap doesn't work anymore.

It was hard to leave. Harder than anything she'd ever done. She kept going back, leaving in stages, on the steps of the lodge, in the yard, leaning across Stephen's sleeping body to kiss Robert. She clung to him when he snapped Stephen in and closed the door. She was half crying. Go in the house and shut the door, she said. I can't leave like this, I can't drive off looking at you standing in the yard.

He went.

She felt like a thief who'd stolen something it was impossible to return, she felt like Jagger the Midnight Rambler, Joan Osborne with her panties stuffed in the bottom of her purse, the girl in the song, balled out, wasted, feeling she was going down. There in the moonlight with her shoes in her hand and dew on her feet, with Stephen in the backseat looking not like her child but some waif she'd snatched at random from a Wal-Mart parking lot and shuttled far from his home, there wiping condensation from the windshield with Charles's wadded shirt and the moon a yellow blur through the glass, even then she knew—she knew she was going down.

SHE PICKED UP STEPHEN at three o'clock, and by then she had decided to leave Charles. She hadn't thought much past that. Just take Stephen and a change of clothing and head out for Robert's lodge. Just flee.

The first thing she did was run a stop sign behind the school, and a beat-up yellow Econoline van slammed into her right rear quarter panel. Her head struck the window frame hard, and she bit her lip, but Stephen was strapped in, and he wasn't hurt.

Stephen was outraged. Are you crazy? he asked. That was a stop sign, are you crazy?

A fat man wearing a Red Man baseball cap was at the window. Jesus, lady, he said, then he saw Stephen. Are you both all right?

We're fine, she said. She'd found a paper napkin in a crumpled Hardee's bag and was wiping the blood off her mouth.

Lady, that was a stop sign.

I know. I know it was my fault.

I got no insurance. The damn cops'll pull my license because I don't have liability. Even with you running the stop sign and all, it'll still be my fault.

There didn't seem to be any cops around. Even any onlookers. It might have been a midnight collision in trackless desert.

She got out, and they looked at the damage. The van didn't have a mark on it, but the fender of her station wagon was folded against the wheel.

Never mind the police, she said. We won't call them. Your van's not hurt, and I have insurance. I'll think of something to tell them.

He got a galvanized pipe out of the back of the van. ATKINS PLUMBING, she read from the van's side. He inserted the pipe into the fender well and, grunting, pried the crumpled fender away from the tire.

I really am sorry, she said.

Forget it, the plumber said. He tossed the pipe into the van and climbed behind the wheel.

She got in the station wagon and put it in gear and drove cautiously away.

If Daddy's there, don't run in telling him about the accident the first thing, she said. I'll tell him after supper.

Can I tell him?

You can even tell him you were driving if you want to, she said.

She was hoping it wouldn't be, but Charles's pickup was in the driveway loaded down with tents and camp stoves and fishing gear. He was in the living room drinking a beer and reading through the daily copies of the *Tennessean* she had saved for him. He laid the papers aside and grasped Stephen and tossed him into the air and caught him. Stephen came down laughing and yelling to be thrown again.

Don't do that, Charles. I'm always afraid you'll hurt him.

You're next, Charles said. He set down Stephen and grinned at her. While you're getting supper, I aim to take a bath, he said.

Haven't seen you in a week, and you might appreciate me more tonight if I smelled a little better.

She sat on the couch and closed her eyes. He hadn't said anything about her mouth. But the cut was inside her lip, and he hadn't kissed her. Her head hurt. Maybe she'd slammed it harder than she'd thought. She could hear Charles clattering around in the bathroom. Stephen turned the TV on and put a cartridge into his video game console. She could hear the music from his Mario Brothers game.

For a moment terrible in its intensity, she thought of leaving them both. Just for an instant. Slipping into the night and leaving them sleeping, shoes in her hand like that midnight rambler, just another hard traveler down the line and gone. She knew it was going to be a long night, and she didn't know if she could take it: shouting, cursing, crying, perhaps he'd beat her, she hoped he'd beat her, that might make going easier. All she knew for certain was that she and Stephen were leaving.

You could save me, Robert had said a long time ago, if you could call five months a long time. By then she was attuned to nuances in his voice, and he'd said it in the self-mocking tone he used when he wanted you to think he didn't mean it. He had been drinking whiskey then, but he was not drunk.

It seemed a terribly presumptuous thing to say, laid out like that. You can save me, you can let me slide. Having someone lay their life in your hands was oddly embarrassing, like accidentally walking in on someone naked. She did not want this weight on her, and she brushed all these implications lightly aside.

I can't even save myself, she smiled.

You could save two birds with one stone, Robert said and smiled at that to show her it had all been a jest to see what her response would be. And that it hadn't been the one he wanted to hear, but he'd have to settle for it.

She rested her head against the upholstery, and after a few moments she dozed. She must have slept for only a moment, but the dream she had seemed to encompass an enormous amount of time.

In the dream she was swinging somehow far above the earth, so high she could see the hazy ellipse of its curvature, the azure blue of the oceans. She was descending, arcing back and forth, the distance of the arc controlled by whatever suspended her by the left ankle. She looked up. A thin silver strand led up and up, tended away to nothingness in the high, cold air. When she looked down again, the earth was closer. The countryside was covered with snow, detail was rushing at her, fences, a pasture, a tarnished brass river snaking through cedar and cypress.

She was still swinging out, and she felt the moment of pause when her body strained against its tether. Then the pull of momentum back. She had no control over it. She was just arcing on the silver strand of cord. There was a snow-covered beech tree on the side of a wet black bluff, its branches reaching earthward as a beech's will. It was in her path. She was going to slam into it hard, it was physics, it was gravity, it was fate. At the speed she was moving the impact would kill her, impale her on broken branches.

When she struck the tree, she felt only a rush of cold air, but the tree exploded into broken crystal glass that went glittering away in the light of a sun she couldn't see and dimpled the snowy earth for miles when they fell.

Are you going to get that or not? Charles yelled.

The phone was in the kitchen. She answered it leaning against the counter. She turned on the tap and began to fill a glass with cold water. It was someone from the sheriff's department, she didn't get the name. Someone wanted to know her name, and she told them. There seemed to be too much noise. Water was running in the bathroom, water was running in the sink, Mario and Luigi were bouncing around the living room.

Do you know a man named Robert Vandaveer?

Yes.

Why is there no soap in here? Charles yelled from the bathroom. How about bringing me a bar of soap?

. . . Meter reader found him. Of course, it could be an accident, but it's under investigation. The thing of it is, there was a sealed letter with your name on it in his pocket. I don't actually have to have your permission, considering the circumstances, but I thought as a courtesy . . .

Cold water was running in the glass, running out of the glass.

No, she said viciously into the phone. If it's sealed and it has my name on it, it's mine. It's mine, and you leave it alone.

She slammed the phone down. Stephen had come into the room, and he was staring at her. He seemed to be rising into the air, floating, growing as tall as she was. Then she felt the cold linoleum against the calves of her legs, the handle of a cabinet door against her back, and realized she was sitting on the floor. The phone began to ring.

Are you getting the goddamned soap or not? Charles had come into the room. She looked up. Charles looked ludicrous with water streaming off him and a towel clutched in front of his loins. She saw that Charles was getting fat.

I leave for a week and this place just . . . Charles's face was altering, anger that had been rushing toward rage shifted to uncertainty, confusion, finally to consternation.

She folded Stephen into her arms so hard he cried out and tried to twist away. He couldn't, she was holding him so tightly. She thrust her face against the hollow of his throat. She could smell him, feel his hair, the poreless texture of his skin.

I'm getting your goddamned soap, she cried against the coarse fabric of Stephen's sweater. *I'm looking for it, I'm looking for it, I'm looking for it.*

The Lightpainter

JENNY'S MOTHER once shot her husband in the thigh with a small-caliber pistol. She had been aiming higher but she was angry and the target was in desperate motion so she missed. She told it about the town with a kind of grim humor. If it had been anything like normal size I would have brought it down with one shot, she said. Who could hit a teensy old thing like that?

Tidewater heard this story or its myriad variations in disparate places. In the barbershop, in the county courthouse waiting in line to renew his license plates, in a Mexican restaurant on South Maple. He even heard a truncated version from Jenny herself. Mama tried to shoot Daddy in his thing but she got him in the leg, she said, laying the phrase out for their inspection as emotionlessly as a dealer turning up a card and awaiting betting or folding. Tidewater did not know which to believe but there was an irrevocability about the remark that seemed to call for one or the other.

Tidewater had studied her face. Jenny was a child then and her face had not yet assumed the impassivity of still waters that masked it in adolescence but still he could not read it. What response did she expect from the remark? Humor, honor, compassion? Tidewater was touched in varying degrees by all these things but he wanted to know her intent. Beneath the dark fringe of lashes her violet eyes told him nothing. Her pale heart-shaped face held only the promise of beauty and its customary vulnerability. It said what it always said: Well, here it is. Help me or hurt me, it's all the same to me.

Jenny in those early years lived an ambivalent existence. She was part of the time with Tidewater and his wife Claire and his daughter Lisa and part of the time with her mother and whatever live-in boyfriend she was involved with at the time. Jenny's father had wisely moved on in search of an environment where his drunken abuse would be dealt with more tolerantly. She seemed to move effortlessly from chaos to the order that Tidewater insisted upon, that in fact he had created by an act of sheer will.

Once there was a showdown of sorts in Tidewater's front yard. Tidewater and his wife and daughter aligned on the porch with Jenny, the mother and her boyfriend standing on the brick sidewalk before the porch.

Are you Jenny's father? Tidewater asked.

Hell no, the man said. He wore Ray-Ban sunglasses and Tidewater couldn't see his eyes.

What is it to you?

The woman stood before the doorstep looking up at them. Like some show she was watching from the first row.

If you think you can come between me and my daughter, the woman began, listing slightly to the northeast as if she stood in the force of a strong southwesterly wind that nobody else felt, if you think you can just step in and take my child away from me then you're living in a goddamned dream world.

Nobody's trying to take anybody, Tidewater said. She's Lisa's friend and she likes staying over here. Nobody tries to persuade her one way or the other, but I'm not about to refuse to let her stay. She does what she wants to.

Well right now she's doing what I want her to, the woman said. She's going home. Come on, Jenny.

Jenny glanced at Tidewater then started toward the steps.

Tidewater said: Wait a minute.

The man in the yard laughed and spun his cigarette away. He wore a white shirt with the cuffs folded two careful turns over his forearms. His forearms were thick and the right bore a tattoo of the Marine Corps insignia. The tattoo was blurred as if the ink had run in the rain or as if the man was drawing sustenance from it, using it up, assimilating it into his bloodstream.

She's not getting in that car with you, Tidewater said.

Charles, Tidewater's wife said. She had never particularly cared for Jenny, as if she sensed something about her that Tidewater did not. I think you may be getting in over your head here.

I'll drive her home myself, Tidewater said. You two go ahead. I'll follow you.

I'd like to know why she's not going to get in my car, the mother said.

Because you're drunk, Tidewater told her.

On the way to the Harrikin the car Tidewater followed drifted across the centerline, whipped back, slipped onto the shoulder with gravel singing off the fenders. Tidewater gave them plenty of room. The car sometimes drifted into the path of oncoming traffic as if it were driverless, controlled by some deathwish volition of its own.

I don't know if they're going to make it or not, Tidewater said.

Jenny sat small and shrunken against the passenger-side door of the van. Her face was turned toward the sliding autumn scenery and he could see only the dark straight fall of her hair.

If they don't I guess we could always go back to your house, she said.

TIDEWATER SAT in a hard-backed wooden chair across a littered desk from a soft-looking woman with hair the color of flax.

It's an unpleasant situation, the woman said.

It's a dangerous situation. She could be killed in a drunken car wreck. She could be abused sexually by a boyfriend. They could burn the house down over their heads while they sleep.

The woman shuffled the papers. Applications for help, field reports, evaluations. As if after false starts and side roads and dead ends lives had come down to this, all the identity there was contained in these neatly typed government reports.

I'm not sure precisely what you expect us to do.

I'm just reporting it. I don't expect you to do anything. I've never done this before, interfered in people's lives. I have a daughter of my own.

What he wanted done was something to eliminate the inequity in people's lives. A balancing out of things. Jenny's life did not seem fair. It seemed to bear little relation to Lisa's life or the lives of other young girls who came and went in Tidewater's house. Their lives seemed controlled, assured, as if they possessed some sort of celestial insurance policy. Jenny's life seemed random, open-ended, unstable as quicksilver.

The flaxen-haired woman had no control over the inequity of lives. Tidewater was sorry that he had come, that he had even interfered. People's lives went the way they went. They conformed to some law no physicist had yet devised a formula to explain.

The woman took up a form and a pen. Do you know of a specific incident of abuse? she asked.

Her life is an incident of abuse, Tidewater said.

THE LIFE THAT JENNY aspired to had been created solely by Tidewater. It was order pressed on chaos. Tidewater had fallen out of love with the world. The world no longer wanted to do his bidding. The world was going to hell in a handbasket and Tidewater wanted no part of it.

He was sick of violence. He was sick of wars, and politicians' rationalizations for wars, of politicians themselves. Beyond Tidewater's fences the world was falling apart. Chaos swirled like the smoke off a battlefield. Bloody insurrection stirred in the rubble of great industrial cities. In the mountains of Montana grim-faced men caressed their hoarded weapons and waited for Armageddon the way a teenager awaits a phone call. Strangers crossed in the night and gave each other AIDS as casually as handshakes. Mothers basted their children in ovens and burned them with cigarettes because there was nothing good to watch on television, drove them into deep cold waters with their safety belts thoughtfully secured.

In his youth Tidewater had courted violence like a lover but these years he wanted it out of his life, scalpeled cleanly out of his body and the clean living flesh cauterized by fire. He owned sixty-five acres and a lot of fences and a century-old farmhouse. He renovated the farmhouse and converted a screened-in porch to a studio where he painted and these years he hardly left it. His hair grew long, the ends turned up loosely on his shoulders. The soft blond beard that covered his cheeks made him look ascetic and intense as a devout young monk, photographs taken of him during this period in Tidewater's life looked like photographs of Jesus, if Jesus had ever taken the time to have his picture made.

Yet if the farm was an island of calm, disorder flourished beyond its borders, chaos lapped constantly at its shores.

He had once been far back in the woods, carrying a sketchpad and pencil, headed for a grove of beeches he wanted to paint. Halfway across a barbed-wire fence a voice out of the trees hailed him.

Hey.

Hey, Tidewater said. He climbed down the fence.

A man came out of the bracken with an unbreeched shotgun in the crook of his arm and a brace of squirrels strung on his belt.

Did you not see that sign? the man asked.

What sign?

That sign that said, trespassers will be shot, survivors will be prosecuted. Did you not see that?

No. No such sign existed but Tidewater did not say so. He waited.

What are you? Some kind of goddamned hippie, livin off the government?

I don't live off anybody. I work.

You work? You look like a wild man to me, like you run wild in the woods for a livin.

I'm a painter, Tidewater said.

The man was half a head shorter than Tidewater and fully twenty-five pounds lighter but there was an outsized belligerence about him, as if he perpetually needed more space than he had been allotted, as if he'd suck a room dry of oxygen just by entering it. He hit Tidewater on the muscle of the arm, not lightly, a solid blow. He struck again, in measured insistence, like someone knocking at a door that just won't open.

Suddenly he dropped the shotgun and shoved Tidewater hard and hit him while he was off balance. Tidewater slung the sketch-pad and went backpedaling away and fell on his back in the dry leaves with the man astride him. He was trying to cover his face and the man kept slapping him, not hard, just contemptuously flicking his face.

Say I'm sorry I trespassed on posted land, the man said out of clenched teeth.

Tidewater had a crazy urge to laugh. What?

Say it goddamn you, or I'll pound your head into the ground.

All right, Tidewater said, not lying, I'm sorry I trespassed on posted land.

The man seemed dissatisfied, perhaps with Tidewater's inflec-tion. His grip tightened. Say I'm sorry I trespassed on posted land and I promise never to do it again, he said.

Oh for Christ's sake, Tidewater said. You don't know when to quit, do you?

He began to strain against the man's weight, the arms pinning him seemed banded by iron but little by little he began to rise, the man pushing as hard as he could and his arms trembling and cords standing out in his throat but being lifted inexorably upright, his face congested and his eyes going crossed and peculiar.

Tidewater threw him aside and grasped up a windfall tree branch and began to whip the man with it. The man cursed and flailed both-handed at the branch then tried to crawl out of its reach, Tidewater following beating him until the man was crazed with sweat and leaves and squirrel blood.

Tidewater threw the branch across him. The man was cringing away in something akin to horror. Who the hell are you? he cried.

Tidewater was sick at heart at what he'd done. He'd fire-bombed his good intentions back to ground zero and so had to begin again. He took up the fallen shotgun by the barrel and slammed it against a tree trunk. The stock shattered.

I'm The Lightpainter, you son of a bitch, he wanted to scream, needing some trademark with which to mark the folks he beat up like the Z of Zorro's rapier. Perhaps he'd have cards printed up and leave them stapled to the foreheads of the victims of his wrath.

IN TRUTH HE WAS the light painter. In the years when Lisa and Jenny had been children he had painted while Claire worked. She was an accountant and the money she earned balancing folks' books and preparing their income tax returns made their living while Tidewater painted. He painted one picture after another that no one wanted. He'd paint and frame all year then in the fall load up the van to its ceiling with paintings and make a circuit of the craft shows and art fairs throughout rural Tennessee.

Then one year he'd painted a picture so perfect he felt he could not have done it. Perhaps he'd dozed and elves had completed it while he slept. It was a picture of a hay cart loaded with straw in the hall of a barn. A pitchfork, rude farm implements, leaned against it. But what was perfect was the light. He had caught the quality of indirect light perfectly, soft diffuse dust-moted light that fell through a high gable window, the harsher sunlight falling on the earth past the hall of the barn, each blade of straw on the cart imbued with soft gold light.

He was drunk on the power to re-create light on canvas. He painted one picture after another in an orgy of creativity. Bucolic pictures that existed nowhere save in the geography of his imagination. He painted firelight flickering warmly on the walls of a room, soft yellow lamplight falling through a window, lantern-light from a sleigh on reefs of drifted snow, moonlight on snowy mountains, the light from bonfires on the faces of homecoming game revelers. They were pictures of a time that was irrevocably gone and perhaps had never truly been.

After he had put up a small show in Huntsville a newspaper called him the light painter and the appellation had stuck. Soon the light painter was in great demand. The more sophisticates sneered at his paintings' sentimentality the more folks embraced them. The paint would scarcely be dry on a canvas before someone was pressing money upon him. Then a lithograph company signed him to a contract. They made prints of his paintings and advertised them in magazines and sold them for more money than the light painter himself had been able to get for the original canvases.

Tidewater began to think of The Lightpainter as a sort of alter ego and he sometimes referred to himself in the third person in a self-deprecating way as The Lightpainter. He thought this was mildly funny, though no one else did.

I'm The Lightpainter, he had told Lisa and Jenny when they were small. He had taken them to the creek, they were in scarcely to their knees and afraid to wade deeper.

I'm watching you, Tidewater told them, I'm always watching you. If anything goes wrong I'll zip into a phone booth and leap out of my clothes and I'm in my Lightpainter superhero uniform, cape and all.

We'd drown before you found a phone booth on this old creek, Lisa giggled.

Let's see, Jenny shrieked. Take off your clothes and let's see your uniform.

Well, Tidewater said, out of his depth here and in truth not very good at games. My costume is in disguise too. It has a secret identity and the truth is it looks a lot like ordinary clothing.

✦ ✦ ✦

ALONG ABOUT THEIR fifteenth year Lisa began to acquire a new circle of friends. They came and went in the light painter's house, bright as summer flowers, gliding effortlessly on peals of laughter. They seemed more sophisticated than Jenny, they discussed books she had not read, the colleges they were going to, boys Jenny seemed to know by name only. Jenny grew a little bright, a little desperate. She talked too much and said awkward things.

More and more she sought out the light painter. She'd sit hour-long and watch him work. He seemed to be her last refuge, as though he could make her fit, make her part of the gaudy crowd coming and going in shiny cars.

Finally Tidewater mentioned it to Claire.

I can't see how you think it's Lisa's problem, she said. She has her own life to live. It was always you Jenny wanted anyway. And when she's away from here she has her own set of friends, who I don't want Lisa involved with.

When he brought the subject up with Lisa she snapped at him. You need to open your eyes, she told him. You never know what's going on right under your nose. She's changed. She's gross, she lets these awful boys do things to her. She does things to boys.

In Tidewater's view of the ways of the world he suspected that most girls let boys do things to them and perhaps some of them even did things back. He guessed what was at issue here was a question of decorum.

Yet he didn't say this or anything else in his own defense because he was appalled at himself: in a moment of clairvoyance he suddenly saw that he knew Jenny better than he would ever know this smooth, confident young woman, as if Jenny had vouchsafed him a glimpse into the disordered interior of her very soul, a lowering of barriers that all the rest of the world had denied him.

Blood or no blood he had to admit that he was not a very big part of Lisa's life anymore, perhaps no more a part than Jenny herself. It was nothing he could rationalize away, nothing he could make right. It just was.

JENNY WAS IN her sixteenth year when the decision to blackball her was made. Like most of the decisions that mattered in Tidewater's life this one had been made by a committee of Claire and Lisa and passed down to him.

He couldn't argue that things hadn't changed. Jenny's life had the appearance of unraveling. They saw her less now, sometimes it seemed to Tidewater that she came only when she had nowhere else to go. She stayed away longer and longer, like something you have tried to tame reverting to wildness. Lisa brought home rumor after rumor about her. She was suspended from school, she was pregnant, she was on drugs. Lisa watched Tidewater as she told these stories at the dinner table, like a cat laying dead mice at the feet of its master.

Tidewater and Claire were lying in darkness save for the fluorescent face of the clock.

I don't think you can just throw people over the side, Tidewater said to the ceiling. She grew up with us, this is home to her.

That's just the point, Claire said. She is grown up. And she's thrown us over the side as much as we have her. She has other interests, and they're interests I don't want Lisa taking up.

If you mean sex then maybe you ought to talk to her.

Talk to her? Maybe she ought to be talking to me. I expect I could learn from her.

I wonder if her mother talked to her.

For God's sake. Don't put me in this position, Charles. Make me a total bitch while you stand aside and let what happens happen. The way you do. And anyway sex is not what I meant. It's part of it but by no means all. I mean drugs and alcohol and the whole nine yards. What if she and Lisa are out together with a bunch of drunks and drive head-on into another car? What if it came down to her or Lisa? If you were forced into a choice what would you say?

God, Tidewater said, lying still in the darkness, wishing every question had one answer and one answer only, and that he knew them all. Wishing everything was black and white instead of incremental variations of gray.

Besides, she's not even Lisa's friend anymore, no matter how hard you try to pretend they're still ten years old. For the last several years she's been your friend, not Lisa's. You're the only one she cares about.

That's crazy.

And you've always had a soft spot in your heart for her, Claire said, then added: Or a hard one someplace else, which is what I always wondered about.

He lay in silence a long time before he answered. Finally he said, That was a sorry thing to say, Claire.

You're right. It was a sorry thing to say. I guess I meant it to be funny. Hard, soft. It was just something to say.

It wasn't funny, Tidewater said.

No. It wasn't.

Tidewater's position was made more ambiguous by his secret, and he lay there in the dark thinking about it. His mind worrying it the way a tongue worries a sensitive tooth.

A while ago he had fallen asleep watching a football game and sometime in the night Jenny shook him awake.

You fell asleep on the couch.

I guess I did.

They're asleep, everybody's asleep.

What time is it?

Two o'clock in the morning.

I guess I ought to go to bed then.

Charles?

What, Jenny?

I like it here, Charles. I don't want to have to leave.

Hey, kid, nobody's going anywhere.

Okay. Can I kiss you goodnight?

Sure, he said thinking—surely thinking, this was important—she meant a peck on the cheek. When he offered his cheek she laid a palm alongside his jaw and turned his face and covered his mouth with hers. Her robe fell open and he could still see her body all white light and ebony shadows. Her naked breast touched him like a jolt of electricity and her sharp little tongue was alive in his mouth.

When he shoved her away she almost lost her balance and they struggled for an insane moment, him expecting any second Claire or Lisa to materialize in the doorway the way it would happen in a movie and he knew it looked exactly as if he were trying to wrestle a sixteen-year-old girl onto the couch.

She released him and took one graceful step back and calmly adjusted her robe. Goodnight, Charles, she said, her one-cornered smile opaque and enigmatic as always, the smile that said: You think you know what this means, but you're badly mistaken.

If you feel this strongly about it we can wait a few days and see what happens, Claire said. Maybe she'll move in with somebody or something.

I suppose we'll have to do something sooner or later, he said. Do whatever you think best.

✦ ✦ ✦

EVERYTHING WAS ON A PATH that seemed imbued with inevitability, events ran forward like ball bearings on a grooved incline.

A boy let her out in Tidewater's yard. They were arguing. The
boy got out and slammed the door. They struggled for possession
of her purse. Tidewater watched from the porch. The boy slapped
her. The straight fall of her hair swung with the force of the blow.
He seemed not to know that Tidewater was The Lightpainter, not
to care that he was creating a disturbance in The Lightpainter's
yard.

Keep your hands to yourself, Tidewater said, coming down the
doorstep.

How about trying that with your mouth, the boy said. He
looked far older than Jenny, not even a boy, perhaps a man in his
twenties. Tidewater saw that he was drunk. That The Lightpainter might have bitten off more than Tidewater could comfort-
ably chew.

I don't want trouble with you, Tidewater said. But I want you
away from my house.

Or what?

Tidewater hadn't thought that far ahead. Or I'll call the law.

Call the son of a bitches then. But that little thief of a slut's got
my property and she's going with me.

When Tidewater grabbed him the man's feet slid apart in the
gravel. His dishwater blond hair fell lankly across his face. Tidewater was trying to turn him. There was a rank feral smell about
the man, a smell of sweat and whiskey and slow ruin. Tidewater
wrestled him about into a hammerlock and walked him backward
to the open car door and half threw him onto the seat. An audience
had aligned itself on the porch. The man came up off the seat with
a longneck beer bottle out of the floorboard and slammed Tidewa-

ter in the face with it. Tidewater went backward with his hands over his face. The motor cranked, tires slewed sidewise in the pea gravel.

He went up the steps wiping blood out of his eyes. I don't need any of this, he said.

Jenny was hanging on to his arm, trying to touch his face.

Why do I feel I should have been charged admission to see this? Claire asked.

Running water onto a towel The Lightpainter glanced upward at his broken reflection. Blood was seeping out of his hair and into his beard. He looked like a lost and dissolute Jesus, a wild-eyed Jesus illy used and set upon by thugs with longneck beer bottles.

WHEN HE CAME OUT of a place called the Painter's Corner with two sable brushes and a tube of alizarin crimson Jenny was sitting in the passenger side of the van, staring off toward a Dumpster on the parking lot where winter birds foraged for crumbs. He got in and stowed the brushes and paint in the glove box.

I'm glad to see you, he said, and was, feeling obscurely that something had been missing, that his family was complete.

I'm glad to see you too. How is everybody?

Well, we'll ride out and see. Is that what you had in mind, a ride out to the house?

I don't think so, she said. My life is complicated enough with how Claire feels and all. What I need is a favor, and you're the only one I know to ask.

I'll do anything I can, Tidewater said, taking care that the wariness he felt did not creep into his voice: he guessed a favor for Jenny might entail anything from a ride somewhere to bailing a boyfriend out of jail though he expected it was money.

Where are you staying?

She seemed not to be taking care of herself. She had on a sleeve-less T-shirt though the day was chill. There was an air of ruin about her, sweet corruption. There were dark smudges under her eyes and her long brown hair was lank and none too clean. There was a suck mark on her throat like a crescent-shaped birthmark, when she raised a tendril of hair out of her eyes he saw the dark stubble of her armpit and he could smell her, feral and dissolute.

I need forty dollars. I borrowed it off this woman and I've got to pay it back.

It has to be paid back right now?

Well, it's a check I wrote. Postdated. If I don't pick it up she'll turn it in to the cops and they'll get me for a bad check.

Tidewater took out his wallet and gave her two twenties. There was a folded fifty in a side compartment he always thought of as his emergency fund and he withdrew it and laid it on top of the twenties in her palm.

Get a coat. Warm shirts or something. It's turning winter-time. You never did tell me where you were living.

I'm living with this friend of mine in the housing project. I hardly ever stay at home anymore, I can't take the fighting. Her boyfriends hitting on me.

Tidewater didn't know what to say. He felt like counting out more money, as if it was all he had, a down payment on a life someone was going to repossess anyway.

I'm thinking about leaving. Just heading out down the Trace and going all the way to the gulf. Natchez. Is it warm down there?

I don't know. I was never there in the winter. I'd guess warmer than here.

That's where the pirates used to be, Natchez Under-the-Hill. I'd fit right in.

Now the pirates run fancy restaurants and gift boutiques and get their booty off the tourists, Tidewater said.

I'd still fit right in. Bye, Charles, I got to go. Thanks for the money.

She opened the door and got out, clasped her arms and shivered. Gooseflesh crept up the flesh of her upper arms. A wind blew papers across the parking lot like dirty snow.

Get a coat, he said.

I will.

Jenny, he said without knowing he was going to.

What?

Let me help you, he said. You come on back and live with us and we'll work everything out. It'll be hard, but we can do it. If we have to we'll see a counselor. Somebody.

She looked intently into his eyes. Her eyes were pale violet with darker flecks and there were tiny lines in the grainy skin at the corners of them.

I don't need anything like that, Charles. Don't believe everything Claire and Lisa tell you.

Take care, he said. She walked away then turned and raised a hand and waved with just the fingers. Tidewater watched her go wondering where she was off to, half glad he didn't know. He had striven for the simplicity in his life, the linearity. Jenny's life was not linear. It was made up of switchbacks and side roads and mazelike dead ends and to him it seemed chaotic, each day some new crisis, each night some new pleasure. He watched her walk out of his life with a sense of loss and shame for the faint relief he felt.

ALL DAY A CURIOUS band of light lay in the southwest. Weather crawls across the television screen told of winter storm warnings, an early ice storm already rampant to the south in Alabama. Tidewater stood in the backyard watching the heavens. Small nameless birds fluttered in the branches. Dry leaves drifted and tilted on a rising wind that already had winter's edge on it. Above the light the sky took on the color of wet slate. The light swirled toward him like a silver mist rising off some country already locked in the seize of ice.

He drove into town and bought bread and milk and candles. At the hardware a butane camp stove. The supermarkets were full of people pushing overflowing baskets toward the checkout lines as if the countryside lay under siege.

By dusk a cold gray drizzle was falling. Sometime in the night he awoke and went outside. It had turned very cold. The rain was freezing on everything it touched and the brick walk gleamed dully and the trees glittered like they were fashioned from glass.

He woke again when the power went off and the house ground down to silence. All the myriad mechanical sounds of the night-time house vanished and all he could hear was Claire's measured breathing and the soft hiss of ice against the window.

When they arose in the morning the world had been transformed. Tidewater's breath caught in his throat as a child's might. Every leaf, every twig, every blade of grass was caught in its own caul of ice like a purer finer symbol of itself.

The day drew on cold and strange and silent. Everybody seemed to be waiting for something. There was no television, no stereo, no lights. Tidewater had a show coming up in Memphis in less than a week and he sorted through paintings and wrapped them carefully in furniture pads and stacked them in the van. But after a while the cold deepened and the house grew more chill yet and he brought wood from the garage and built an enormous fire in the fireplace and sat before it reading a book.

Everyone had assumed the phone was out of order as well and

when it rang in midmorning Tidewater jumped as if it had broken some physical law.

What? Lisa said, and something in her voice made Tidewater pause in midstep and turn, the coffee cup halfway to his mouth and forgotten.

He could not quite fathom the look on Lisa's face. It said: I know something you don't know, and I can't wait to tell you.

Jenny's dead, Lisa said.

Dead? Claire said. She can't be dead. Dead how?

Lisa's face twisted, grotesquely torn between laughing and crying. She lowered the phone. The hand holding it jerked spasmodically. The phone began to shake uncontrollably and Tidewater crossed the room and took it gently from Lisa's hand. When he held it to his ear there was only a dial tone and he recradled it. She froze to death, Lisa said.

It's another crazy rumor, Claire said. She probably started it herself. No one freezes to death anymore.

Her orderly accountant's mind seemed to have considered these figures and rejected them and Jenny was still somewhere in time, smiling her one-cornered smile and pushing a dark strand of hair out of her eyes the way Tidewater had seen her do a thousand times.

There were other phone calls each with its attendant piece of the puzzle and finally the story told itself.

Her boyfriend, or anyway a man, had let her out at three o'clock in the morning at the foot of the grade that ascended toward her house. Apparently he had taken her to the housing project but for some reason she had been locked out. Ice was already frozen on the hill and continually freezing faster and the man had turned at the foot of the hill and driven back to town. She'd drunk a little vodka and she was taking pills, some kind of medicine the man guessed. She could walk all right though.

✦   ✦   ✦

IN THE MORNING Jenny's mother had gone out to put a letter in the mailbox in case the mailman made it up the hill, and found Jenny frozen to death in a small stream of water that wound through a washed-out gully below Jenny's house.

And seen, Tidewater guessed, Jenny in her shroud of ice, black fringe of lashes frozen to her cheeks and pale face composed like some marvelous archaeological find, some pretty girl flash frozen eons ago and ten thousand years gone in the blinking of an eye.

He felt at some odd remove from things. He sat before the fire not feeling its heat with a book open and unseen upon his lap. He was trying to enter and relive the past, Jenny's past, his own. To replay every word and act of her life and so locate the exact moment when the canker appeared on the rose, when the fairy-tale wood darkened and the trees bore thorns, when a cautionary word could have turned aside fate.

It was impossible. No action was separate to itself but led to its echoes like ripples on water, words were not only words but symbols for things left unsaid.

Just at nightfall he drove Lisa and Claire to the funeral home, hunched over the wheel and sweating out every mile, icy beads of perspiration tracking down his rib cage. The van shifted and veered, the chains skirling on the ice, as if they negotiated some new medium not just unfamiliar but alien.

The funeral home was dimly lit, he supposed by an emergency generator. He thought he was going in the door but abruptly he stepped aside for Claire and Lisa, the room overpowering him, images of crepe and velvet and old polished wood, images that were not in the room but in his mind.

What in the world are you doing? Claire asked.

I'll be back in a little while.

But where are you going?

I don't know. Uptown. I need to see somebody from the power company, if there's anyone around tonight. I'd like to find out when the power's coming back on.

Well, it probably won't be on tonight. If there's any place open you may as well get something for supper that doesn't have to be cooked. Get a pizza or something.

Beyond her he could see the dim sepia room with its air of waiting, a cozy paneled vestibule just one door removed from eternity. Why don't I just have one delivered and you can eat it here, he said.

She gave him a cold cat's look and opened her mouth to speak but he pulled the door gently to and went back up the sidewalk to the van.

The town looked surreal, like some town forsaken and abandoned. After some cataclysmic fall, after the failure of dreams and human will itself. Some of the businesses seemed to have generators but candles flickered room to room in private dwellings and he drove on toward the part of town where he could see that streetlights still burned.

There was a bar called Wild Bill's open but scarcely populated save by its habitual ancient drunkards who sat crouched about the room like troglodytes. The place was poorly lit by gas lanterns and in the hollow yellow light appeared cavernous, the sidewalls curving inward, the dark wall beyond the pool table and hushed jukebox like the entrance to a tunnel moving on into the dark.

Tidewater ordered a bottle of beer and paid for it and sat beside an alcoholic old sign painter named Lee. He had never known Lee's last name.

You painting many signs these days, Lee?

The old man's eyes were rheumy and his toothless mouth loose and wet. He always looked obscurely angry, the world itself seemed to have done him some grievous wrong.

I've quit, the old man said. Nobody wants a regular sign anymore. Last one I done was this little old Swiss maid or somethin. Little Swiss maid totin a milk bucket. Had on this little cloth cap, blue with while dots. I thought, if I ever get this bitch painted, that's it for me. Somebody else can paint the next one.

Life gets more complicated, Tidewater said. Somebody's always raising the ante on you.

Did you notice all that ice?

Well, trees are laying on power lines everywhere and the electricity's off. It's kind of hard to miss it.

I believe this is it. This is the beginning of the end.

The end of what?

Every goddamned thing there is, Lee said. I believe it's comin the end of time. Did you hear about that girl in the Harrikin froze herself to death?

I heard about it. I don't think that means it's the end of time though. I just think it means it's cold.

Maybe anyway it'll do something about these damned mites.

These which?

These mites. They're suckin the blood right out of me, eatin the meat right off the bone. A month from now the wind'll blow me down the street like a paper sack.

As if he'd humor him Tidewater leant to peer closely in the poor light. I don't see anything at all.

You can't see mites with the naked eye and anyhow they're not here now. The old man raised his watch to the glow of the lantern.

They take off ever mornin about seven o'clock like a bunch of blackbirds. Come ten o'clock at night they're back again. I don't know where they go but there's gettin more of them all the time. I believe they're bringin their buddies.

I've got to get on, Tidewater said. I need to find somebody from the power company. Anyway all this talk about the end of time depresses me.

You'd think depressed if you had these mites to contend with, Lee told his back as he went out the door.

It was still raining and the windshield was frozen over with a thin membrane of ice. He waited until the defroster melted it then drove on toward the lights. Full dark had fallen and above the haloed streetlamps the wet sky glowed a deep mauve.

The Pizza Hut was open though almost deserted and while they prepared his pizza he sat in a booth by the window and drank a cup of coffee and watched the freezing rain track on the glass and the sparse traffic accomplish itself on the highway. Little by little a nameless dread had seized him and cold grief lay in him heavy and gray as a stone.

When the pizza was ready he paid and went out. He laid it in the seat across from him. He opened the box and looked at it. As was The Lightpainter's wont he had ordered the top of the line, a supreme deluxe jumbo with everything there was on it, a pizza so garish and begarbed as to serve as a satiric comment on the very nature of pizza.

He cranked the van and drove laboriously out of the parking lot. He could smell the hot pizza and he opened the box as he drove into the empty street and bit the end off a slice and began to chew. The cheese was tasteless and had a quality of elasticity that made it grow enormous in his mouth the more he chewed it. He couldn't swallow it and at last he rolled down the glass and spat and then he took up the pizza and hurled it into the street. The white box went skittering across the ice like a Frisbee. He drove on.

He was not surprised to see that he was driving toward the Harrikin, though the road was perilous and even with the chains on the van spun on the hills and once slid dizzily sideways, so that for a moment the headlights swept the frozen woods in an eerie frieze, the trees tracking palely off the glass in elongated procession.

He drove on into frozen night. Once he had to halt and plot a course around a fallen tree. Once he passed a downed power line where an ice-loaded tree had broken it, the high-voltage wire writhing and dancing and snapping bursts of blue fire.

The house when he arrived at it was lightless the way he had known it would be and it seemed deserted. It set pale and haunted-looking against the dark hills. In the driveway the tractor for an eighteen-wheeler was frozen to the ground, its chrome appurtenances sheathed in ice. He withdrew a flashlight from the glove box and got out with it. He approached the ditch.

It was very cold and the silence was enormous. It was broken only by the sound of trees splitting and branches breaking far off in the woods, like sporadic gunfire from some chaos that had not reached him as yet. Palms on knees he stood on the lip of the gully and peered into it. His breath smoked in the air and froze whitely in his mustache and beard. He wondered what she had thought. If she had thought, if her mind had been put on hold by ninety dollars' worth of medicine. If memories and plans and dreams had already seen the writing on the wall and were fleeing her like rats scuttling over the decks of a burning ship.

He played the light about the rim of the ditch. He found a pink comb layered beneath the ice like an artifact suspended in amber. He studied it at some length. Perhaps it was a clue.

He heard an engine laboring up the hill and he turned. He could hear snow chains spinning on ice, the headlights washed the trees and a pickup truck turned into the driveway, the sealed beams framing him like a searchlight where he stood.

Doors slammed and a man and a woman got out of the truck. The woman incongruous in a knee-length black dress and high-heel pumps. She came teetering across the precarious ice like some grotesque beetle. Jenny's mother. The man stood silhouetted before the headlights. Tidewater wondered was he Jenny's father, brought back under truce by this mutual grief. The man unpocketed a flat half-pint bottle and drank from it then canted it against the inscrutable heavens as if he'd gauge its contents.

You morbid freak. What the hell are you doing here?

For a moment Tidewater stood in silence, trying to think what to say. He made some sort of obscure arms-spread gesture, a mutated shrug. Before he could speak the man pocketed the bottle and approached. You need to move it along somewheres else, he said. There's people in mournin here if you don't but know it.

I know, Tidewater said. I'm Charles Tidewater. I—

I know who you are. Move it along, you're blocking the drive-way.

No, you don't understand, Tidewater said, the words tumbling out in a drunken rush, She was like a daughter to me. I loved her. It all seems impossible, that she's . . . I had to come out here. I drove without knowing where I was going. I thought there might be a reason, a clue.

A clue? There was a trace of amusement in the man's voice. I've got a clue for you. Get back in that van and haul your ass somewheres else before I call the law and have you arrested for trespassin.

I don't want any trouble, Tidewater said.

Trouble wants you, the man told him.

You stole my daughter, the woman said suddenly. Her voice was thin and vicious, hardly more than a hiss. You carried her over there and turned her against her own family. And then when your precious daughter was tired of her you ruined her. You and your hippie ways. Got her on dope and everything else. No telling what else you did to her. Just no telling.

He had raised his hands to protest but she launched herself at him like a harridan. Blood-red fingernails raked his cheek, clawed wildly for his eyes. The Lightpainter stepped backward and his feet slid and kicked the woman over and he fell with her to the earth then rolled into the ditch. Ice cracked the back of his head and he lay on his back staring upward into the freezing rain. He could see the woman's head and shoulders above the lip of the ditch, her glasses gleaming dully like enormous pupilless eyes. Then the man helped her arise and they turned away, out of his line of sight.

Just call the law and let them come get him, the man said. That's what they get paid for.

He knew that he was lying where she had lain. He knew without seeing them that long straight strands of brown hair, like horsehairs, were seized in the ice where they'd snapped when they pried her free. As they'd snapped in the bloody permafrost of the heart.

After a while Tidewater got up. He could feel his clothing peeling away from the ice. He went down the ditch run to where it shallowed and clambered out. He got into the van and cranked it and sat with it idling and his hands cupped over the heater ventilator until he could feel warm air. He knew he had to drive away but he did not know yet to where. He knew that his life had changed, finally and irrevocably, but he did not yet know to what. The light painter felt like one of the rustic agrarians in his own paintings who had thrown aside brush hook and pitchfork and attained an almost undetectable motion, easing from the pastoral landscape that had sheltered him toward the white void of chaos at the picture's edge.

My Hand Is Just Fine Where It Is

WORREL WAS SITTING on the stone steps drinking his third cup of morning coffee when he saw the Blazer turn off into his driveway. The softwood trees were beginning to green out in a pale transparent haze but the hardwoods were bare yet and he could see the red Blazer flickering in and out of sight between their trunks, the bright metal of its roof flashing back the sun like a heliograph. He'd seen it come a hundred times before, but its appearance was still as magical as something he'd conjured by sheer will, and he hoped the magic held through even such a day as this one threatened to be.

He rose from the steps when he heard Angie downshift for the hill and drank the last of the coffee and tossed out the dregs. He set the cup on the edge of the porch. When she parked the Blazer in the yard he was standing with his hands in his pockets. It was March and the wind still had a bite to it around the edges and he leaned slightly into it with his shoulders hunched.

She cut the switch and got out and stood by the car. She wore dark glasses and pushed them up with a forefinger as if she'd have a better view of him. She looked at him with a sort of rueful fondness.

I didn't know if you'd be ready to go or not, she said.

Yes you did.

Well I don't know why. I can't see why you want to come with me.

I don't want to even talk about it, he said. Are you ready?

She smiled. Ready as I'll ever be, she said.

She slid back under the steering wheel and he came around to the passenger door and got in. She had the motor going but was waiting for him to kiss her and he took her into his arms and kissed her mouth hard. When he moved his face back from hers, her green eyes were open. She always looked at him as if he were the only one who had the answer to some question she had been thinking of asking.

Well, she said. I won't even ask if you're glad to see me.

She felt thin in his arms. He could feel the delicate bonework of her shoulder through her flesh, through the silk of the blouse she wore. She'd been thin ever since he'd known her and he always tempered the strength with which he held her but now she seemed thinner. If he held her as tightly as he wanted, he felt he'd crush her. Yet the flesh of the face turned toward him looked new and unused, scarcely touched by the abrasions of the world or its ministrations.

Where's Hollis?

He had to work. They didn't want to let him take off.

The son of a bitch, Worrel said.

Don't say that. He offered to take off anyway and go with me.

The son of a bitch, Worrel said again.

He doesn't know the whole story anyway, Angie said. He just thinks it's tests. I couldn't say the word *malignant.* You're the only one who knows everything.

She said she loved him and he had no cause to doubt it. They were like a drug in each other's veins. A crazy bad-news drug, their hands trembled with the hypo, the needle prodded for an un-collapsed vein. The drug they used was rare and dangerous with unknown and catastrophic side effects—you couldn't buy it, it had to be stolen under cover of darkness when other folks were asleep or their attention had wandered.

If he didn't call or if he made no effort to see her, she came to see about him. She always seemed a little harried, almost dis-traught, glad to see him still there. It was as if she expected to see the house open to the winds and him gone without a trace or a word of farewell, gone to Africa to search for diamond mines or to South America to save souls. But Worrel had given up on prospecting and had come to feel each soul responsible for its own salvation and he was always there. In bed she'd cling to him and call his name as if she were trying to call him back from the edge of something. Warn him.

There had been a time when she was going to leave Hollis for him but the violence of his own recent divorce had sobered her, given her pause. There were other lives to be considered. Hollis had said in no uncertain terms there would be a custody battle. She was not in a good position for one. Hollis was in an excellent position. He was a good provider and a steady worker, and he was also faith-ful, or at least discreet. Angie and Worrel had started out careful and discreet but the power of the drug had surprised them and things had gotten out of hand: at some point, like drunken teenagers trash-ing a house, they had kicked down the doors and smashed the win-dows and sprayed their names on the wails in ten-foot-tall graffiti.

Everything fled from Worrel in the aftermath. Everything: house and car and vindictive wife. Disaffected and disgusted chil-dren fleeing at a dizzying pace like animals scuttling out of the woods from the mother of all forest fires, little scorched and smoking Bambis and Thumpers hell-bent for elsewhere, and Worrel himself seized in the soft grasp of her flesh scarcely noticing.

He studied her profile against the shifting woods of late-winter sunlight, a little stunned at the price he had paid for so tenuous and fragile a portion of her life, though he never doubted she was worth it.

THEY WERE DRIVING out of Ackerman's Field and nearing Nashville when she glanced over at him. Did you find a place yet? she asked.

Since the affair had begun Worrel had become an addict of shading and nuance, decoding her speech as if there were always hidden meanings. What she'd asked could have meant, *Have you found a place for me and the kids?* or it could have meant, *Have you found a place we can be without your ex-wife coming and screaming at us?* But it did not mean either of those things. All it meant was, *Have you found a place?* and he discarded it.

I may move in with you and Hollis, he said.

She glanced from the road to him, half a smile, half a grimace. It's not funny, she said. When are you going to stop treating everything as if it were a joke?

Maybe when everything stops being a goddamned joke, he said.

The last of the traffic lights had fallen away now and she didn't need her right hand for shifting, so she reached and grasped his left, pulling it over to the console between them. Her hand uppermost, her fingers laced with his. She squeezed it hard, then just drove clasping it loosely, her fingers calm and cool against his own. There was something oddly comforting about it, and Angie seemed to feel it as well, for climbing into the hills where perhaps she should have downshifted, she just drove on, the transmission laboring and vibrating until they'd made the grade.

If you need your hand to drive just take it back, he said.

She smiled at him, her face an enigma behind the dark glasses. My hand is just fine where it is, she said.

He turned away and looked at the countryside, aware of the scarcely perceptible weight of her hand, and watched Tennessee roll up—bleak trees, buttercups on the shoulder of the road, the leached funeral silks of winter, the cusp of promised spring the world hung on to.

They had been friends before they had been anything else and they could talk or they could ride in comfortable silence. Mostly they rode in silence, Worrel's mind turning up images of her as you'd turn up pages in an album of photographs and, in the one he looked at most, her eyes looked as they did in the moment before he kissed her the first time. He'd known he was going to and was glad he'd waited until her eyes looked the way they had. As if they'd been simultaneously asking and answering a question. They'd stepped together and Worrel felt as if she'd slammed against his chest, as if they'd stepped onto some narrow ledge of unreckonable height. Looking down made you dizzy and you might plummet later in the next second, though not now; now seemed not only enough but all there was. Later there were other kisses: in hallways, in the moment before a closed door opened, in the moment between the wash of headlights on a wall and the slam of a car door, in the moment when footfalls announced someone was coming but he wasn't here yet. In these tawdry moments are worlds, universes.

The night before they went to the motel for the first time she twisted his mouth down to hers and said against his teeth, I think you're trying to corrupt me. He didn't deny it.

✦ ✦ ✦

IT WAS SEVENTY MILES to Nashville and today it seemed too short a distance. After a while they joined the insectlike moil of traffic and she needed her hand back. She was a good driver, effortless, unpressured, and she didn't even have to look for street signs to find the medical center. She'd been there before.

In the thin watery light, the Athens of the South perched atop its hills like something from a dream. The red Blazer went through the narrow canyons between the buildings with ten thousand other red Blazers negotiating the narrow canyons and everything began to look unreal.

The pale transparent light off the facades of the buildings imbued them with meaning so that they looked to Worrel like monuments erected and fled by some prior race finer than the present folk who milled about like maggots working in flesh.

She parked in front of the medical center and they got out. She looked at her watch. We don't have time for lunch before my appointment, she said. Do you mind waiting until we get through here?

Of course not, he said. I'm not even hungry.

Well, she said, uncertain, looking at the building.

They walked toward it. The marble veneer glittered in the sun. It looked like an enormous mausoleum. The statuary on the lawn looked like relics replevied from a tomb so long hidden from the daylight that the thought of time and its unspooling made Worrel dizzy.

HE SAT IN THE WAITING AREA with a roomful of other people. Nothing looked right. Maybe he was coming down with something. The pictures on the wall were wrong. A Dalí print, a Bosch.

Watches melted, marvelously detailed folk were flared. The pictures seemed part of some surreal scheme to acclimate him to the horror to come.

The people did not seem right either. Everything about them rang false, even their clothing seemed strange, either years out of style or years ahead of its time. When they spoke some of the voices were pitched too high, others dragged endlessly like audiotape moving slower and slower. Their emotions were out of sync, their anxiety too hyper, their stoicism simply cold indifference.

She'd left her purse for him to mind and dangling it by the strap he went outside and smoked a cigarette. He seldom left the country and his eyes were drawn almost against his will to the jumbled skyscrapers and high-rise apartments. Everything seemed leaned toward some common center, the hazy pastel buildings collapsing on themselves. In the sepia light the city looked as strange as some fabled ruin on the continent of Lemuria.

He put the cigarette out in an urn half filled with sand and went back inside the waiting room and took up a copy of *Newsweek*. He tried to read an article on a new survey of sexual habits but the sheer amount of work that had gone into producing the magazine he held in his hands made him tired. Lumberjacks had felled trees that had been shredded and pulped to make paper. Ink had to come from somewhere. Other folks ran presses, stacked the glossy magazines, delivered them; the U.S. Mail shuttled them across the country. Not to mention the people with cameras and word processors, people with curiosity and the knowledge to ask the questions to satisfy it. The magazine grew inordinately heavy, all these labors had freighted it with excess weight. He could hardly hold it. All the information was encoded in bits that swarmed like electronic insects and the words flew off the page like birds. He sat staring at an advertisement for a red Blazer that he was convinced was the very truck that had brought him to Nashville.

When she came through the doorway back into the waiting room, days seemed to have passed. He'd laid the magazine aside and sat clutching her purse. Reaching it to her he pretended not to study her but he did all the same. Having learned nuance and shading he'd become adept as well at interpreting her body language. Her smile was a little bright, her movements a little mannered: she'd put on the restraints and maybe screwed them down a notch too tight.

Ready? she asked.

More than, he said, scanning the room one last time as if he'd mark it as a place to avoid, remember all these miscast faces should he ever encounter them in old movies on late-night TV.

They went out. The cars in the parking lot glared under the sun. He felt hollow and enormous inside.

She was reaching for the door handle of the Blazer when he stopped her with a hand on her arm.

Wait, he said.

Wait? For what?

He was silent a time. Tell me something, he finally said.

I guess there's not much to tell.

Was it bad?

She had her lower lip caught between her teeth. About as bad as it gets, she said.

He thought for a moment her eyes looked frightened then he saw that more than fear they showed confusion. She looked stunned, as if life had blindsided her so hard it left her knees weak and the taste of blood in her mouth. He wanted to cure her, save her, jerk her back from the edge as she'd tried to do for him.

But all he could say was, Do you want me to drive?

I'm fine, she said. I can always drive. I like to drive.

Behind the wheel she searched her purse for the keys. I'm starved, she said. Are you hungry?

Yes, he lied.

Where do you want to eat?

She had the keys, the Blazer caught on the first crank, then sat idling. She studied him intently.

I don't care, he said.

You must care.

I don't care, it's nothing, it's just food. Hell, it's just food. He knew she thought that was a barbaric notion but that was just the way he felt.

Where was that little Italian place we went to? You had the veal, they had these great salads there. Terrific salads. What was the name of that place?

I don't know.

You must know. The salads had the little cherry tomatoes?

Goddamn it, he said, suddenly angry. They all have the little cherry tomatoes.

She knew him, she wasn't fooled, she didn't take offense. She smiled. I can find it, she said. We'll just drive around, I'll know it when I see it.

I still don't see what it matters.

It matters to me, she said. It was the first time we ever went out to eat. You know, in a nice place. You bought me a bottle of wine you couldn't afford.

As she drove back into the street, she kept looking at the buildings, cutting down narrow crooked alleys, taking side streets that seemed to go nowhere you'd want to be—as if the place where they had the cherry tomatoes would materialize before her, between the tacky country music souvenir stores with their ceramic Roy Acuffs and price-tagged Minnie Pearl hats and the interminable pawnshops in whose dust-moted windows guitars hung by their necks like arcane beasts taken as trophies.

The day was waning, the light stingy and oblique. The sun flared behind the buildings and lent them a stark undimensioned quality. After a while they were hopelessly lost. The city looked strange even to her. They didn't speak. It began to seem to Worrel that they had sought and found their own level.

They trickled down sunless corridors and burst capillaries until they were in the city's dark heart. A city within the city where the blood slowed and thickened and clotted in viscous smears of alizarin crimson dried to burnt sienna around the edges. The tires of automobiles bore it away in fading hieroglyphic slashes. Neon flared, the air had grown heavy with the drone of flies. BAR BAR BAR, the neon repeated. 20 NAKED GIRLS 20. Brands of beer seemed to have the significance of the names of prophets on graven tablets.

Finally she pulled the Blazer to the curb and cut the switch and stared uncertainly about her. They had parked next to a vacant lot. Dead weeds tilted askew by the winds, the sun caught in broken wine bottles. The husk of an Eldorado sat so stripped and demolished it seemed to suffer obsolescence on an epidemic scale. A brown dog came out of the weeds and stood staring at them as if it had news of their coming. It was starved to the point of emaciation, just something that stood for a dog, a concentration that might possibly reconstitute a dog, a dog decocted in smoking electric chambers by a mad doctor who'd seen a dog once long ago and conjured one up with only the vagaries of memory as a recipe.

Adjacent to the vacant lot was a row of buildings constructed of umber-colored brick. Between two of them a narrow two-story house was wedged so tightly it seemed to have no sides of its own,

simply its wooden frame front and tin-roofed porch hung parasit-
ically between the brick walls, the rococo gingerbread trim of the
porch paintlorn and rotting. A swing dangled motionless from
rusted chains. The front window had been stoned out and covered
with a metal sign that read CLABBER GIRL BAKING POWDER. A
cracked sidewalk led to the street through packed earth encysted
with bottle caps. Venus flytraps grew in car-tire planters serrated
as if pinked by enormous shears.

The streets were full of drifters who seemed to be looking for
something that they had lost. The homeless by choice and by cir-
cumstance held in common their disconnectedness and the self-
same look of threat in their faces, danger loosely contained like
lightning in a voltaic jar. They looked listless and numb as sleep-
walkers, they moved as if the air itself offered hindrance to their
passage. A man with shoulder-length blond hair stood on the
high concrete steps of the parasite house and had occasional com-
merce with these streetfolk. He wore a quilted vest from whose
cargo pockets he dealt glass vials of some iridescent liquid, smoky
and volatile as nitroglycerin. The drifters paid him with bills that
he folded onto a thick sheaf of like bills and he treated the money
casually as if it were of no moment in itself but simply some hap-
penstantial by-product of the transference of the vials. Occasionally he'd speak into a cellular telephone while watching Worrel
with narrowed blue eyes.

Worrel looked away. He felt the uneasy knowledge that at any
moment everything could alter. The air felt heavy and volatile, the
way it does before a summer storm.

He turned to look at her. Her head was lain back against the
upholstery. Her eyes were closed. Perhaps she slept.

He had no doubt that at some point he'd be confronted; it was
a given, a law of nature. If she did not drive away, if he did not get

under the wheel and take charge himself. Apparently he was not going to. Apparently he was going to sit here and look blankly back into the eyes that locked momentarily with his then slid away, until someone motioned for him to roll down the glass and he did and someone said, in a spray of spit, a reek of splo whiskey, in white-hot crackhead clarity, *What is it with you, motherfucker? And who the fuck do you think you're looking at?*

Until the day waned and the light pooled and drained westward and the streetlamps came on and until the pace of the streets altered and moved in a loose disjointed rhythm and fierce chromatic colors that seared the eye and until the day's possibilities became probabilities and then dead certainties and they were hauled from the Blazer and humiliated, made to plead for their lives, urinating on themselves and soiling their clothing while the last vestiges of human dignity fled. Credit cards gone, money gone, pristine Blazer stripped and burned. Surely they'd slit his throat and rape her fair white body, slit her throat and rape his own fair white body, shoot them full of drugs that would send them at warp speed past any conception of reality the mind was prepared to deal with, snuff them in a bending flash of light that was the very essence of ecstasy. Their bodies would be found in garbage-strewn alleys, septic hypodermic needles dangling from their veins like fey ornaments, or their bodies would drift pale and bloated in the currents of the Cumberland River until they turned up stranded on silt bars like worn-out whores their pimps had no further use for.

Bring it on, Worrel told their sullen faces. Let me have it, you sons of bitches. You goddamned amateurs. There's nothing you can do to me half as bad as this.

He thought of the people waiting for Angie, beginning to wonder where she was. The kids at the grandmother's, the husband probably wondering why there was no supper on the table. He suddenly felt weary and omnipotent, like a troubled god: he knew something they did not yet know, something that was waiting for them like a messenger with a finger on the doorbell and a telegram in his hand. They did not know, any of them, that they were living in the end times of bliss. The last belle epoque. Not the kids at Granny's, whining where is Mama, not the husband bitching about the fallow table.

They did not know that they were going to have their world blown away, walls flung outward and doors ripped from shrieking hinges, trees uprooted and riding the sudden hot wind like autumn leaves, the air full of debris like grainy old 8-millimeter footage of Hiroshima. A cataclysm that would leave the floor of their world charred and smoking, inhospitable for some time to come.

Just for a moment, though, he was touched by a feeling he could not control, that he had not sought and instantly tried to shuttle to some dark cobwebbed corner of his mind. He wanted to forget it, at the very least deal with it later.

He had felt for an instant a bitter and unconsoling satisfaction that terrified him. When she sat eyes closed with her fair head against the seat she seemed to be fading in and out of sight like someone with only a tenuous and uncertain reality, going at times so transparent he could see the leather upholstery through her body, her face in its temporary repose no more than a reflected image, a flicker of light off water.

At these moments, all that was real was the grip of her hand, the intent focused bones he could trace with the ball of his thumb. Nothing was holding her back save the fingers knotted into his own. She was sliding away, fare-thee-well-I'm-gone, vanishing through a fault in the weave of the world itself, but until this moment ended and whatever was supposed to happen next happened, he was holding on to her. Everybody was hanging on to her, all those gasping hands, but for the first time no other hold was stronger than his own.

ACKNOWLEDGMENTS

The author would like to acknowledge the debt he owes to two friends named Amy—his agent, Amy Williams, and editor, Amy Scheibe—and to thank them for their trust and support.

He would also like to express his gratitude to the John Simon Guggenheim Foundation.

About the Author

WILLIAM GAY is the author of the novels *Provinces of Night* and *The Long Home*. His short stories have appeared in *Harper's*, *The Georgia Review*, *The Atlantic Monthly*, *GQ*, *Oxford American*, and *New Stories from the South 1999–2001*. The winner of the 1999 William Peden Award and the 1999 James A. Michener Memorial Prize and the recipient of a 2002 Guggenheim fellowship, he lives in Hohenwald, Tennessee.

I Hate to See That Evening Sun Go Down

1. In the collection's title story, Meecham returns home after a stint in a nursing home. Discuss what appears to be a class rivalry between Meecham and Lonzo Choat. Do you believe Meecham is really a threat or merely a harmless old man? Is Meecham's son, Paul, justified in sending his father to a home?

2. In the story "A Death in the Woods," the body that is discovered on Pettijohn's property disturbs him immensely, while his wife, Carlene, appears quite indifferent. Does her dismissive attitude seem suspicious to you? Do you think Pettijohn suspected something from the start? What do you make of Pettijohn and Carlene's relationship?

3. The narrator in "Bonedaddy, Quincy Nell, and the Fifteen Thousand BTU Electric Chair" says that Bonedaddy "met his comeuppance" when he met Quincy Nell. Did Bonedaddy get what he deserved? Was Quincy Nell justified? Why do you suppose Bonedaddy was allowed to get away with so much?

4. Many of William Gay's characters in this collection have wonderfully colorful names. Why do you suppose "The Paperhanger" is never given a name beyond this moniker?

5. In "The Man Who Knew Dylan," Crosswaithe is a complicated character with a varied past. How have women shaped Crosswaithe's past, present, and future?

6. In "Those Deep Elm Brown's Ferry Blues" Alzheimer's is setting in on Scribner. Discuss the ways in which his mental deterioration is made manifest.

7. In "Crossroads Blues," the main character, Karas, encounters a curious man named Borum who claims that "everything has its price." How does this dictum relate to the story as a whole?

8. In the story "Closure and Roadkill on the Life's Highway," do you think Raymer, the jilted husband, finally gets the "closure" he admits he needs? Do you think old man Mayfield is telling the truth about the money? If not, then what are his motives for creating the tale?

9. In "Sugarbaby," Finis and Doneita Beasley have been happily married for thirty years. Finis shoots his wife's dog and does nothing to stop her when she leaves the next day. Why do you think he is so indifferent? What comment does it make about their marriage? Was Finis really happy or just going along with the routine?

10. Bender, the protagonist in "Standing by Peaceful Waters," has a recurring dream in which there is a ravenous wolf. What does the

wolf represent? Discuss the wolf's symbolic role in the story. How do Bender's dreamworld and reality blur?

11. In "Good 'Til Now," Vangie finally decides to leave her husband on the day her lover, Robert Vandaveer, turns up dead. Do you think Vangie will still have the courage to leave? Robert credits fate with his meeting Vangie. What role does fate ultimately play in the story?

12. In "The Lightpainter," Tidewater gets his name from the ability to capture light in his paintings. In what other ways does this name suit him? Why do you think he takes such a liking to Jenny? Does Tidewater have a superhero complex?

13. When Angie parks the car in a seedy neighborhood in Nashville in the story "My Hand Is Just Fine Where It Is," Worrel worries that "at any moment everything could alter." Discuss how this statement seems to describe the nature of their relationship.

14. Of the collection, what is your favorite story? Who is your favorite character? Why?

15. What themes do you notice appear throughout the collection of stories?